D0815506

THE HOYDENS
AND MR. DICKENS

ALSO BY WILLIAM J. PALMER

The Highwayman and Mr. Dickens
The Detective and Mr. Dickens

THE

HOYDENS

AND

MR. DICKENS

THE STRANGE AFFAIR OF THE
FEMINIST PHANTOM

*A Secret Victorian Journal
Attributed to Wilkie Collins
Discovered and Edited by*

WILLIAM J. PALMER

ST. MARTIN'S PRESS
NEW YORK

Library of Congress Cataloging-in-Publication Data

Palmer, William J., date
    The hoydens and Mr. Dickens / attributed to Wilkie Collins;
discovered and edited by William J. Palmer. —1st ed.
        p.   cm.
    ISBN 0-312-15145-4
    1. Collins, Wilkie, 1824–1889—Fiction.   2. Dickens, Charles,
1812–1870—Fiction.   3. Burdett-Coutts, Angela Georgina Burdett-
Coutts, Baroness, 1814–1906—Fiction.   I. Title.
    PS3566.A547H68   1997
    813'.54—dc20   96–31892

First edition: February 1997

10 9 8 7 6 5 4 3 2 1

This book is dedicated to Jill

EDITOR'S NOTE

This manuscript is the third of six unpublished commonplace books of Wilkie Collins discovered by Mr. Allerdyce Clive, the special collections curator of the library of the University of North Anglia. These manuscripts were bequeathed to the college in the estate of Mr. George Warrington, which contained the papers of his great-grandfather Sir William Warrington, who was Collins's life-long solicitor.

Third in date of composition, this manuscript is also the third which I have had the privilege and profit of shepherding to commercial publication. The first manuscript I titled *The Detective and Mr. Dickens.* To the second, I affixed the title *The Highwayman and Mr. Dickens.* It is with sincere appreciation that I thank Mr. Clive and the University of North Anglia library for the unlimited access they have granted me in aid of the editing and publication of these manuscripts.

Because this is the third of the private Collins journals to take up the Charles Dickens/Inspector William Field friendship and collaboration, its principal characters—Dickens,

Field, Collins himself, Irish Meg, Ellen Ternan, Tally Ho Thompson—have gone through much together prior to the composition of this manuscript. A brief outline of their previous adventures might be of interest to present readers of this third manuscript.

At the time—June 1852—when the events chronicled in this commonplace book begin, Wilkie Collins and Charles Dickens had already participated in two of Inspector William Field's most notorious cases, that of "the Macbeth Murders" and that of "the Medusa Murders," as sensationalized in the true-crime tabloids of their day. Those two cases were described in Collins's first two secret journals.

The Detective and Mr. Dickens dealt with the beginning of the unusual relationship between Dickens and Inspector Field of the newly formed detective rank of the Metropolitan Protectives. Dickens's curiosity about criminals originally led him to Bow Street and Field, and entangled him in the solving of two theatre-district murders. But, in the course of those violent events, Dickens's entanglement became much more personal. He met and fell in love with a young actress twenty-five years his junior, Miss Ellen Ternan. When Miss Ternan was subsequently kidnapped and sexually exploited by Lord Henry Ashbee, the most notorious rake and secret pornographer of his time, it was Dickens, Collins, and Field, aided by a reformed highwayman-turned-actor, Tally Ho Thompson, who came to her rescue. Suffering from the psychological trauma of these violent events, Miss Ternan was placed in Urania Cottage, the Home for Fallen Women established by Dickens's close friend and confidante, Angela Burdett-Coutts, heiress to the largest banking fortune in Victorian England.

The Highwayman and Mr. Dickens brought Dickens and Inspector Field together once again when their friend Tally Ho Thompson was taken up and thrown into Newgate for the poisoning murder of a wealthy London society doctor's wife. Though Thompson was cleared in this case, the suspected murderer, the wealthy Dr. William Palmer, as had Lord Henry Ashbee in Dickens's and Field's first collaboration, went free owing both to a lack of evidence and to the notorious leniency of the English Criminal Court toward wealthy gentlemen of high connection.*

Both of these previous commonplace books are, of course, narrated by Wilkie Collins, Dickens's protégé and closest friend and confidant during these turbulent years in Dickens's life. At the center of both of Collins's previous memoirs lies the development of Collins's own relationship with Irish Meg Sheehey, whom Collins rescued from a life as a street prostitute and police informer in *The Detective and Mr. Dickens* to make his secretary and live-in mistress in *The Highwayman and Mr. Dickens*.

I have similarly titled this third Collins manuscript *The Hoydens and Mr. Dickens*. I use this unusual word "hoyden" in my title because Collins uses it in his prefatory comments, and also because it is such a distinctly Victorian word. I have other motives, however, in choosing such an archaic title. I did not want to title this book *The Women and Mr. Dickens* or *The Feminists and Mr. Dickens* (though that term was already in use at the time of the events which Collins narrates) because I did not want this book mistaken for some dry-as-dust work of academic literary criticism.

By dictionary definition, a "hoyden" is a "high-spirited girl or woman." But in Victorian usage that word carried a more complex sociopolitical meaning. For the Victorians, "hoyden" was a gender-specific word that referred to a woman with a political or social agenda involved with issues such as female emancipation, suffrage, or the English divorce laws. In the oppressively patriarchal Victorian age, equally often the word "hoyden" carried a slightly derogatory connotation of unconventionality, or even sexual looseness. Suffice to say that the ideal Victorian woman, the "angel of the house," would not be referred to as a "hoyden." This more sinister connotation perhaps arose from the fact that "free love" was one of the most actively discussed issues in the feminist circles of that time.

---

*Dr. William Palmer, England's most notorious poisoner, was finally brought to justice and hanged for his crimes in 1856. His effigy now graces the Hall of Murderers at Madame Tussaud's. It is mere coincidence that he bears the same name as the editor of the Collins journals.

Nonetheless, for the Victorians, the word "hoyden" was most often used to denote an animation and intelligence of personality rather than a looseness of morals. However, even if Collins and Dickens use that term "hoyden" in its slightly derogatory tone, we of the late twentieth century in our political correctness must not judge them too harshly. The Victorian was a very chauvinistic age. Even Victoria was uncomfortable with the gender revolution. In a letter to one of her ministers she wrote: "The Queen is most anxious to enlist everyone who can speak or write to join in checking this mad wicked folly of Women's Rights with all its attendant horror."

Finally, because this particular Collins memoir involves so much material set in the midst of the Victorian feminist movement, some of the events are narrated secondhand through the descriptions of Irish Meg. Her lively narrations are particularly helpful for Collins's reporting of those events at which he was not present and those conversations to which he was not privy. Thus, Irish Meg sometimes serves as a conarrator speaking through Wilkie's pen.

But Collins also does something else in this third commonplace book which distinctly sets it off from the two previous and from almost every other novel written in the nineteenth century with the possible exception of Mary Shelley's *Frankenstein* and Emily Brontë's *Wuthering Heights*. In the early stages of this manuscript, Collins actually experiments with a primitive form of narrative flashback which goes beyond the pure exercise of memory which has served as the frame for the narratives of all of his commonplace books.

—William J. Palmer

THE HOYDENS
AND MR. DICKENS

PREFATORIES

༖

(January 4, 1871)

T hat word "Prefatories" is especially appropriate for this
new putting of pen to paper. Another year has fled. It
was the year of Dickens's death, the year that pressed
me to begin filling up these little leather books with my memories of our adventures on duty with Inspector Field. Now it
is a new year, yet it seems strange to have gone through the
ordeal of the holidays without Dickens to buoy me up.

He always loved Christmas so, made such a production of
it that the holiday season came to resemble one of his amateur theatricals. I didn't realize how much I missed Charles
until the Christmas season blazed up and he wasn't there to
prompt me—"Come now, Wilkie, try but a taste of this fine
plum pudding"—or taunt me—"Oh, Wilkie, you're acting
just like old Scrooge"—or tease me about my discomfort in
the presence of children—"If you weren't such a relentless
old bachelor, Wilkie, the little pugs wouldn't terrify you so."
He went to such excess over Christmas!

I missed him terribly this Christmas, his energy, his good
humor, his festive enthusiasm. I have never done well at Christ-
mastide, probably because I have become somewhat of a cynic

1

in my middle age, an attitude that Charles utterly abhorred. Maybe that is why he loved Christmas so. Perhaps he saw it as the yearly rebirth of hope for this fallen world.

Yes, I missed him this holiday season. I missed being ushered as an honored guest into his warm, bright manse so festooned with greens that one expected monkeys to come swinging across the bedecked chandeliers. But I also missed being the only one to accompany him to his other household, more modestly decorated but equally cheery, where he bestowed lavish gifts upon his beloved Ellen. I was the only one of his friends he entrusted with access into his secret life with her. I think Dickens trusted me with his secret Ellen because I had been there at the very beginning, and had remained at their side through all the perils of their—I almost wrote "courtship"—struggle . . . against the criminal powers that she seemed to attract, against the prejudices of an age that could not sanction their love.

Knowing that she would be and feel even more alone than I, I visited Ellen this Christmas season. I was surprised. She seemed at peace, almost relieved that the intensity of their love had burnt out and left her at rest. I guess I was happy for her, that she was taking his death so well, thinking about moving on.

But I was disappointed, too. Perhaps she didn't hold him in the sort of awe that I did. He had been my mentor, the source of what little fame I have managed to grasp. He was, for me, the consummate artist, and the source of all the adventure in my life.

For her, he was just a man that she took into her bed whenever he was free. Perhaps she was relieved to no longer be the invisible woman in his life. When I left her, with a peck on the cheek and a "Merry Christmas," I felt his loss even more intensely. Was I the only one in mourning for "the Inimitable" this Christmas season? It was then that I knew what my Christmas present to myself would be.

I gave myself this new little leather book, and I intend to fill it with more of my private memories of Field and Ellen and Irish Meg and all the rest of the journeyers through Charles's and my shared life.

I never intend to expose to public light what I write here, and I intend this for no reading audience save some far-off posterity which I am sure will have little use for it except as a small curio amidst the larger treasures of Dickens's life and work.

There is some fittingness in my use of the word "Prefatories." So much had happened "prefatory" to the events of this memoir that some space must be allotted for introducing the various and unusual cast of characters before proceeding to the curious and shocking events which drew Field and Dickens back together in their favorite game of detection and pursuit.

This new memoir is set in the rather closed and political world of those embattled hoydens who at the time were intent upon turning Victorian society upon its head. The world of these women was not one which we, Dickens and myself, as gentlemen, had either a great deal of interest in or were even capable of understanding. However, both of us were devoted to our own particular hoydens and actually, in private, encouraged their freedom and unconventionality. Ironically, Victorian gentlemen though we were, we were bound in fealty to our demanding hoydens in ways which mimicked neither the chivalry of the Arthurian epoch nor the domesticity of our own Victorian age. We served them, I my Irish Meg, he his beloved Ellen, as addicts to opium serve the keeper of the pipe.

Finally, I am going to narrate some of the events in this third little leather book in a manner upon which I have not previously relied. In my earlier narratives, I described only those events in which I participated. In this narrative, however, I foresee the necessity of abdicating my voice in favor of another, that of Irish Meg, who was present at events which I would not even have been welcome to attend.

And so, let us begin in a familiar place, with Dickens, closed into a careening coach galloping toward our destiny.

SAINT GEORGE
OR THE DRAGON?

ༀ

(June 3, 1852—Noon)

I t began in a coach, as his *A Tale of Two Cities* would years
later. But this coach collected me on a glistening spring
day and galloped out into the country toward Urania Cottage.*

'Tis difficult to penetrate the world of women, yet the narrative of this newest commonplace book must, for it was those
relentless hoydens who turned the cards in what would be,
perhaps, the most dangerous game of chance that Dickens,
Field, and your most humble servant would ever be drawn
into. It was the women who forced us back on duty with Inspector Field.

"What a brick you are, Wilkie!" Charles broke the silence
which had gathered around us inside that speeding coach.
"You are always ready at my summons, a willing accomplice."

If the truth of the matter be told, his choice of words, "willing accomplice," somewhat put me off. He made it sound as
if we were two criminals setting off on a "crack," as Tally Ho

---

*Urania Cottage was Angela Burdett-Coutts's Home for Fallen Women es-
tablished with Dickens as her closest advisor.

Thompson might have said in his colorful highwayman's argot. But that day Dickens was skittish, and I didn't fully understand why he was so nervous until that ill-considered phrase, "willing accomplice," gave away his guilt.

"You know, Wilkie, success is relative." Charles grinned expansively as the lush green countryside rushed by. "The more successful you are, the more relatives you find you've got." It was a feckless little joke. I smiled at it, but we both knew that it was counterfeit joviality. He went back to contemplating the countryside.

I realized how many reasons there were for him to be nervous. Certainly he was nervous about his Ellen. But why? He had visited her many times in the fourteen months since she had entered Miss Burdett-Coutts's establishment. All seemed quite proper there. Perhaps he was nervous because this was the first time anyone had accompanied him upon one of his visits. As I look back upon it now, I am sure he asked me for propriety's sake. I would not venture to comment upon the dark intent of his interest in this sixteen-year-old actress because I had already preceded him in the execution of such dark intent. My own Meggy was even more deeply sunken into the depravities of the night streets. Meggy, unashamedly, had been a street whore, where Ellen Ternan had been a stage actress, though in the lexicon of many Victorian gentlemen one was no different from the other.

For whatever reason, Charles was exceedingly nervous as we entered the tree-lined drive that led to the front veranda of the sprawling three-storey villa which Miss Burdett-Coutts had purchased for their little experiment in social redemption. That fresh spring day we were come to set his mysterious Ellen free like some princess in a fairy tale. Perhaps that was it. Dickens was a nervous Saint George, fearful of loving this enchanting young woman so many years younger than himself, fearful that he was not the rescuing knight but the ravening beast.

As we stepped out of that coach and entered Urania Cottage, Dickens's agitation, I am now sure, was that of a hitherto good and moral man suddenly forced to question his deepest intentions. Etched deeply into the tension of his face and the hesitance of his step was the clear fact that Dickens didn't know what he was doing, yet was powerless not to do it. He wanted the girl, and he couldn't yet envision, amidst the disparities in their ages and the strict proprieties of the age, how he could possibly have her.

Urania Cottage was a quite pleasant place, and as we disembarked that spring morn all seemed, as Mr. Browning put it, "right with the world."* The porch was festooned with potted flowers and the lacy white curtains billowed out of the open windows like Mr. Pope's mischievous sylphs floating on the air.† Urania Cottage was the brainchild of Angela Burdett-Coutts and Dickens, and that noble lady met us at the threshold.

"Charles, so good to see you, it has been weeks." She took him in tow. "And Mr. Collins. This is the first time you have visited Urania Cottage, is it not?"

"Why yes, uh, no reason, uh, quite pleasant here, I say," I stammered in the face of her knowledge. Miss Burdett-Coutts was a tall, hovering woman with a long neck and a face too small and fair and gentle for her angular presence. She was not unattractive; her dark brown eyes seemed especially lively, quite fervent in their focusing upon one as she spoke. She wore one of the conventional heavy silk dresses of the day, shiny grey with white lace rising high up around her neck as if intent upon twisting off her small head. Her hair was pinned up in the shapeless bread-loaf style (which is still, regrettably, in vogue). "Must be quite exciting, uh, I mean different, uh no, pleasant for those young ladies chosen to reside here." My doddering inanity elicited a bubble of mirth from Miss Burdett-Coutts.

"Oh no, not really," she laughed. "Many try to escape. Some find their former life on the streets much more exciting."

"Ah, but others," Dickens knifed into our conversation, "are utterly changed for the better, learn to respect and consider themselves in a whole new way."

"Oh, Charles," she hurried on as she led us down a long, shining wooden corridor leading to the rear of the house, "I

*See *Pippa Passes.*
†See *The Rape of the Lock.*

6

must talk with you quite briefly before you go to her. She is all packed, one small bag, since she came here with nothing. She is quite enthusiastic about our arrangements."

Dickens nodded attentively, but seemed eager to get to his Ellen, disinclined to tarry to talk trivialities with Miss Burdett-Coutts. From all I could infer, we had come in our coach to liberate Miss Ternan, transport her back to London to begin her new life.

"What is it, Angela? Can it not wait? We can meet to talk at the bank in the city at any time this coming week." Dickens in his nervousness was somewhat short with her.

"Oh yes, Charles, I know, but I've just found it so distressing since it arrived that I wanted you to see it and tell me what to do," she said, and for the first time, she revealed her own agitation.

The anxious tone of her voice brought Dickens up short and he sensed her fear.

"Angela, what is it? I'm sorry. What is wrong?"

"Oh, probably nothing. It is probably some sick prank." Her hands fluttered in the air like startled birds. "But it frightened me when it came, a threat like that."

"What threat?" Dickens had become quite intent upon her distress.

"This letter, it came yesterday." She handed a coarse envelope to him.

The letter was brief and scrawled in a thick and clumsy hand. Dickens held it out in front so that I could read over his shoulder. My very first thought was that it was written by someone attempting to disguise his handwriting, or by a poorly schooled child.

> June 1, 1852
>
> Miss Coutts, of Coutts Bank—You won't get away with this highhand treatment. You rob people at your bank. You keep whores and sodomites in country houses. You turn innocent people out into the street. You encourage women to overthrow law. I know your secrets. I can bring down both your houses.
>
> a private Phantom!

7

"It seems awfully melodramatic." Dickens studied it with the eye of a detective.

"It sounds mad, if you ask me!" I blustered, shocked that a person of Miss Burdett-Coutts's enormous wealth and public stature should have to deal with such impertinent harassment.

"I must say it frightened me, Charles"—she had brought herself quite under control—"at first. I had never received such a thing, and if the family did, my father certainly never mentioned it. It surprised me, but now I feel, with Mr. Collins, that it must be some sort of aberration. But perhaps we should look into it, don't you think?"

As she spoke, Dickens was studying the letter intently. When he spoke, it was as if he were simply thinking aloud, critiquing what the smudged text told him.

"It is purely a threat." He punctuated his certainty by pushing the letter gently at her in the air. "There is no mention of blackmail, no request for money." He paused and read it through once again. "It is written by someone who knows a great deal about you, about your philanthropies, your business." He stopped again to study. "It is written by someone who feels badly treated, perhaps someone you have dismissed, or whose business with your bank turned out unprofitably."

"Yes, I see that now." Angela nodded her head in agreement, her anxiety momentarily forgotten.

"Really, Charles, I say"—I stared intently over his shoulder at the letter—"quite right, yes . . . but couldn't it just be something written in a fit of anger, something the writer will think better of?"

"Let us hope." Dickens turned back to her. "But nonetheless, Angela, this sounds dangerous enough. I shall give it to my friend Field of the Protectives. He will look into it."

"Oh thank you, Charles."

"Do not be alarmed. In fact, forget about this. I'm sure Wilkie is right. It is but an ill-considered outburst. Now, let us go to Miss Ternan." And with that, he seemed to dismiss the whole affair. Only, however, after safely depositing Miss

Burdett-Coutts's distressing letter carefully into the inner pocket of his waistcoat.

As we traversed the cool dark corridor leading out to the garden, Dickens's nervousness reasserted itself.

"You have apprised her of all of our arrangements? She knows where and with whom she shall be living? That her monster of a mother is out of the way? That I shall be her guardian in all things? At her service? She feels comfortable and safe?" He interrogated poor Miss Burdett-Coutts as if she were a servant or some military subaltern.

She hesitated to answer in the face of his earnestness.

He misinterpreted her wariness for discretion.

"You may talk freely," Charles assured her. "Wilkie knows Miss Ternan. He was there when that whole sad affair happened."*

"Quite." Miss Burdett-Coutts nodded her understanding as we emerged from the cool dark tunnel of the house into the bright spring sunshine of the lawn. The green grass stretched back to a thick pine forest, and was dotted in the eighteenth-century style with bushes sculpted in the forms of animals: a large rabbit here, a fat hedgehog there, two proud stags carved out of a privet hedge guarding the back verge of the property. The sunshine made the whole scene glisten in hues of green, an evergreen world peopled with young women in white dresses seated on stone benches.

"Her recovery and progress into womanhood have been quite astounding," Angela assured him with the utmost seriousness. "She has, since your last visit, survived her sixteenth birthday." (Her majority according to English law, and a feat few of her less fortunate colleagues of the London streets can claim— Charles would survive his forty-first that year.) "And it is time for her to return to the world, to the theatre, which is the only life she knows, and for which she expresses a great fondness."

*Obviously Dickens is referring to the Paroissien-Ashbee affair as narrated in *The Detective and Mr. Dickens* (1990). Dickens and Collins, along with Tally Ho Thompson, Inspector Field, and Serjeant Rogers, had rescued Ellen Ternan from the sexual bondage of the Victorian pornographer Lord Henry Ashbee.

"Excellent"—Dickens nodded his satisfaction as we crossed that wide expanse of lawn—"that has been my hope."

As we traversed the greensward, young women in white, virginal I might have thought from appearances if I hadn't known better, glanced up at us from their knitting needles or their reading. Some were probably reading Dickens's own stories and may not have realized that the author was actually walking in their midst.

"There she is." Angela pointed to a bench flanked by those ferocious stags at the farthest boundary of the lawn. As we approached, Ellen Ternan looked up from beneath a wide-brimmed summer hat of white straw, and smiled innocently.

It was the first time I had seen her in fourteen months, since that dangerous night in the roiling Thames. As she rose to meet us, I realized that this was quite a different young woman from that poor confused victim we had saved from suicide. It was how she extended her hand confidently to me and looked directly into my face as we were reintroduced that first intimated the extent to which she had changed.

NELLIE

༡༽

(June 3, 1852—Noon and Later)

One did not have to be overly observant, an inspector of detectives or a hired spy, to perceive the change in Dickens as he took his young ward's hand and basked in the radiance of her smile. Suddenly all his skittishness was gone, and he seemed utterly oblivious of his surroundings and his companions. Since his last birthday, Dickens had culti-vated a rather rakish goatee, but his own smile (for Miss Ter-nan's eyes only) burst out of that sculpted thicket of his face.

"Miss Ternan, ah yes, today is the day, and our English sun-shine favors us."

He was formal yet alive with enthusiasm. He was courtly, even fatherly in his concern, yet he could not hide his ex-citement at seeing her, his attraction to the powerful lode-stone of her smile. I overstate. Perhaps under the influence of later events, the ensuing history of their remarkable rela-tionship, I have romanticized this moment, and that look that passed between them, as enchanted.

"Mr. Dickens," she answered with her proffered hand, which he took in both of his, "there is no way that I can thank you and Miss Burdett-Coutts for all you have done for me."

It was a well-rehearsed speech, the opening sally of an actress who has learned her lines and is taking the stage. If such can be truly said of one of her tender years, she looked wiser, no longer a vulnerable child, more powerful. Her dress could not hide the fullness of her young body. As she extricated her hand from Dickens's possession and turned to Miss Burdett-Coutts and me, her mien showed no trace of the fright and humiliation of those earlier terrible events. Her smile was warm and innocent. Her gaze was open. There was strength lingering about her eyes, the wariness and determination of a survivor, but a hopeful survivor, one who has not despaired of the possibilities of life, not grown cynical from the brutality of experience.

But I think all of this was lost on Charles, or perhaps I am romanticizing again. Nonetheless, I feel with utter certainty that Charles could see nothing but her smile, her white shining presence, as if she were his Guinevere or Dulcinea. Some might misconstrue the fact of such an accomplished and powerful middle-aged man's devotion to a woman so young, especially in the light of her striking dark beauty; but, that day, in that unabashed English sunlight, as I looked at his face, I knew that he was truly in love with her.

Dickens, like some solicitous waiter in a fine European hotel, sat Miss Ternan and Angela down upon that stone bench between those two vigilant stags and opened a formal colloquy upon that young woman's immediate future.

"Miss Ternan, ah, Ellen, if I may . . . ," he began, standing rather stiffly over them as I stood by.

"Nellie," she interrupted him easily. "Nellie is what all my friends call me. Please be easy with that. It is a new name which I enjoy."

A new name which helps to escape the terrible past, slithered across my mind as I stood eavesdropping.

"Nellie, of course." He was still a bit nervous, but he knew what he needed to say. "Miss Burdett-Coutts, ah, Angela, has apprised me of your determination to return to public life in the city, and she has"—bowing respectfully to Miss Burdett-Coutts—"also apprised you of the arrangements we have made together to allow you to do so." He sounded like some pinch-backed countinghouse clerk delivering a bill. "Are you content with those arrangements?"

"Oh, Mr. Dickens . . ."

"Charles please, my friends . . ." And he looked of a sudden to me for help, as if I might throw him some spar to keep him from sinking. I honestly think that in his confusion it was the first moment that he remembered he had brought me along. "This is my friend, Mr. Collins, Wilkie."

"Miss Ternan"—I bowed shallowly, and she smiled ever so slightly—"Charles has told me so much about you."

"Yes, Mr. Collins, I do remember now. You have been a good friend." And again I glimpsed that determined look of the survivor about her eyes.

"Yes, thank you, yes." I really had no idea what I was saying.

"The arrangements," Charles prompted her, regaining somewhat his composure, "have all been completed. You will live, to begin, with Miss Barbara Leigh Smith, with whom you are acquainted, and a Miss Evans.* You will be established in comfortable lodgings in the West End with these two ladies until you are able to make your own living arrangements; or, of course, you may choose to continue in these. The flats are close in upon the theatre district. Since you have expressed a desire to continue in the theatre, I have taken the liberty of making some necessary appointments. Mr. Macready of Covent Garden has requested that you appear for a general audition Thursday next, and, if all goes well, which I am certain it will, you shall, in all probability, be back upon the stage within the month. A lavish new production of *The Taming of the Shrew* is just entering the rehearsal period and that is the play for which you will be auditioning. Until your wages at the theatre begin, you will collect a weekly stipend from Coutts Bank at Trafalgar Square from Mr. Frederick Busch, a minor

*Barbara Leigh Smith Bodichon would go on to become one of the leading voices of British feminism in the second half of the nineteenth century. Author, women's political-group organizer, cofounder of the first women's college at Cambridge, and member of George Eliot's circle, Barbara Smith was one of the leaders of the first groups of British women to undertake concrete political action on behalf of their gender. Marian Evans would become George Eliot, one of the greatest novelists of the Victorian age.

clerk. This modest living allowance will be discontinued as soon as it is ascertained that your earnings are sufficient to meet your living needs." Charles finished this long and quite formal speech with an uncomfortable shrug. "And that, Miss Ternan, uh, Nellie, is it. We, Mr. Collins and I, have come in a coach to deliver you into the city."

Somehow, as he said it, it sounded ominous, as if we were going to deliver her into some lion's den. Unfortunately, the city at that time had the potential to be exactly that, and Dickens was not as innocent in his intentions (though perhaps he thought he was) as he professed to be.

"Oh, Mr. Dickens . . . Charles"—she changed her mode of address to the familiar only at the prompting of Charles's archly raised eyebrows—"it is so exciting for me to begin anew. And Miss Burdett-Coutts, it is you who have made all of this possible. I can never repay you."

Angela Burdett-Coutts raised her hand to stop her: "We do not speak of repayment here at Urania Cottage, Ellen. We speak only of discipline, and self-respect, and the fulfillment of our potential as women. The greatest repayment I can have from anyone who has lived at Urania Cottage is to watch her leave the past behind and start over in a moral, productive life. That is what I hope for you."

"Oh, ma'am, I cannot thank you enough."

Ellen's protestations of gratitude were sincere enough, yet there was a strangeness in the way she delivered them; her words sounded rehearsed.

As for Dickens, his mien also was clothed in a certain strangeness. He looked so eager, yet he was not his usual confident, easy, joking self. It was as if being in her presence had unmanned him. He seemed compelled to observe every possible propriety. I could not help thinking that I was observing a man torn by quite conflicting desires. But who am I to judge from this distance of twenty years? Was my closest friend already struggling between the inclinations of the father and the lover, the knight in shining armor and the dragon?

In the coach back to London Dickens's awkwardness remained. His solicitousness about her meager luggage, the comfort of her seat in the coach, the possibilities of draughts, whether he should order the coachman to slow because she was being unduly jostled, whether she wished to remove her bonnet, whether she desired a blanket, a pillow, a footrest, whether she was tired, or cold, or too warm—his solicitousness, in fact, became quite comical. I watched him make a babbling fool of himself.

She, however, seemed to think nothing of it, and said very little, except once, when she brought Dickens up quite short.

"Will my mother be in London?" Nellie asked, and Dickens recoiled as if he had been tomahawked by one of Mr. Cooper's wild Mohicans.

"No. No, she will not be," Charles recovered. "She is with a traveling company which ranges as far abroad as Scotland and Ireland, and never plays in the city."

Nellie received this news with genuine relief. She clearly wanted no social intercourse with her mother . . . and with good reason. It was that hag who had twice pandered her daughter's virtue, first to their stage manager at Covent Garden, and then to the infamous Lord Henry Ashbee.

As the coach left behind the rural openness of Shepherd's Bush and rumbled closer to the sprawl of the city, the greenery gave way first to the country estates of the northern downs and then to the high houses and wide streets of the northern hamlets. We entered London's own environs through the Notting Hill Gate and struck into the Kensington high road. Finally, I felt compelled to break the awkward silence which had fallen between us.

"Your companions here in the city, Miss Ternan, the women with whom you will live, Miss Smith, Miss Evans, are they friends, acquaintances?" I asked.

"Miss Smith is a truly interesting woman," Dickens began to answer for her.

But before he could continue, Ellen took up the answer herself: "She is my teacher," she slowly intoned, and a radiance came into her face. "She has taught me about myself."

"She is a young woman of astounding intellectual capacity," Dickens interrupted, seemingly unaware of his rudeness, "impressively educated by her father, outspoken in her opinions, yet quite tireless in her efforts to help the young women at

Urania Cottage. She is a close friend of Miss Burdett-Coutts. She is, however, rather . . ."

It was simply Dickens's way of taking control of every situation. I was really quite used to it. He never showed any reticence in interrupting another person. Therefore, you can imagine how delighted I was when Ellen Ternan made it quite clear that she would brook no repetition of such a rude habit of interruption.

"If Mr. Dickens would kindly allow me to finish"—she stared levelly at him—"I think I can give a fuller, more accurate portrait of Barbara Leigh Smith."

"Why of course, excuse me. Please," Dickens yielded.

Nellie went on to describe the prodigious talents of Miss Smith in some detail, not stinting in her praise for the great good intentions of Miss Burdett-Coutts for providing such a tutor and lecturer upon self-esteem to the girls at Urania Cottage.

"And the other young woman? Miss Evans?" I inquired.

"I have never met Miss Evans." Ellen surprised me with her answer (because going to live with someone I had never met seemed unthinkable), but surprised me even more by her next move. "But Mr. Dickens has, I believe, have you not, Charles?" She invited him back into the conversation, to speak for her, to do what she had chastised him for doing before.

Oh, she was good. She knew better than to hurt his feelings for long.

"Yes I have." Charles leapt at this opportunity to redeem himself with the enthusiasm of a young beau. "Just once, briefly, in the company of Angela. She is a highly educated young woman, with an enormous nose, just up from the country."

Ellen covered her mouth and giggled at Dickens's irreverent description of the young lady in question.

"She works for Chapman," Dickens went on, "my publisher, on his *Westminster Review,* the new Liberal magazine. He sings her praises."

Which means she had best beware, I thought; but I did not say it aloud, because though it was a sentiment that Dickens would surely understand, Miss Ternan would not. Suffice to say that our friend John Chapman was one of the most notorious philanderers in London, and no matter how long this young woman's nose might be, it would not protect her from his attentions.

"Yes, she is a writer, I have heard," Ellen corroborated.

"It sounds as if you are in impressive company." I nodded sagely.

"All protégées of Angela Burdett-Coutts," Dickens added enthusiastically. "I truly feel that her goal in life is to support promising young women in working their way in London."

And, from all that I observed in the course of that coach ride into the city, Miss Ellen Ternan certainly displayed the potential to become one of those "promising young women." I must admit that I was utterly taken with her.

She seemed in control of the situation. As we passed through Piccadilly Circus and entered the West End, Dickens leaned out the window and, with a sharp tap of his stick to the topside of the coach, caught the attention of our coachman and directed him to Macklin Street, so named after the famous actor of the previous century.* The stone memorial of Macklin perches on its corner, providing a handy resting seat for crossing sweeps and flower girls. It was, indeed, a quiet, secluded street of high city houses broken up into rooms and lodgings. Number 21 was our destination. It was a nondescript establishment of three sparsely windowed storeys with a single peeling door propped on a narrow stone stoop only two steps up from the street. Our coach pulled up across the way, and Dickens leapt out calling up for the footstool to hand Miss Ternan down.

"I shall carry her bag in and be right back, Wilkie," he called to me.

As they walked to the door, Ellen waved good-bye, smiling. Then she did a curious thing. She stopped him at the threshold of her new life with a hand on his arm just as he was reach-

*Charles Macklin was one of a succession of famous actors, including Edmond Kean, David Garrick, Nell Gwyn, Richard Brinsley Sheridan, Colley Cibber, John Kemble, and Sarah Siddons, who were associated with the Drury Lane Theatre.

ing for the doorknob. With a word which I could not hear, she took her small valise from his hand. He answered her, pleading his case, I imagine, for accompanying her in, meeting the other young ladies with whom she was going to take up residence. But she demurred, banishing him to my less interesting company in the coach.

It was, indeed, an interesting tableau. The bright spring sunshine cast a purity of light upon the scene, so unlike our usual London of fog and mire and grim despair. Dickens and his Nellie stood framed in that doorway. Her radiant smile betrayed her gratitude. Perhaps he was still pleading his case for a glimpse of her rooms. A shake of her head signaled her denial. A brief recoil of his goatee signaled his disappointment. Then, with a formality which seemed surpassingly comical, he stepped back, stiffly extended his hand for a businesslike shake, and bid this object of his morning's attention good day. Not the least bit intimidated by his formality, Miss Ternan, in the spirit of the dancing sunshine, took his hand, pulled on it until he stooped slightly more toward her level, bounced once, sending a shimmer down the length of her long white dress, and placed a playful peck of a kiss upon Dickens's surprised cheek. He stood there, stunned, his hand slowly moving up to his face in the wonder of it, as Nellie made her escape into the house.

Dickens returned to our coach quite flushed. If I was not certain of it before, I was quite certain of it now. He was in love with her, utterly enchanted. I had suspected that he was taken with her, but this confusion in a man of his parts could be nothing less than love at its most defenseless.

Do not, however, misinterpret my interpretation. At that time, all was quite respectable. Their meetings spoke to the letter of propriety. I must admit, however, that I never inquired of Charles whether Katherine, his child-burdened wife, knew of his benevolence toward Miss Ternan. I never inquired as to the public knowledge of this arrangement because I was certainly not the one to comment, considering the questionable nature of my own establishment with Irish Meg in Soho.

When the coach had turned about and rolled off toward Wellington Street and the *Household Words* offices, and Dickens had somewhat regained his composure, he gave not so much as a by-your-leave to the events of that afternoon.

"Well, that's taken care of," was all he said. But I was not deceived. Miss Nellie Ternan had indentured Dickens to her service. It was an afternoon which boxed the compass for the course of the last eighteen years of his life.

THE PHANTOM

⁊ͻ

(July 25, 1852—Late Evening)

A month, and then two, no three, more weeks passed. I remember that time quite well because it was so uncomfortable. An exceptionally heavy English summer had descended like an ancient suit of armor upon London. Like a doomed ship, London lay becalmed in that heavy, thick heat that dries up the very stones, sends the dust and refuse of the barren streets swirling at the slightest whisper of a breeze. You could turn into some narrow mews off Chancery Lane or in the West End, Macklin Street perhaps, or try to make your way down one of the twisting serpentines in Soho near my rooms, and suddenly there would be no air to breathe. The heat would empty your lungs as if with a sharp blow to the chest, and you would find yourself gasping. It was like living in the hold of a ship with the hatch cover battened tight. London's people moved through the city as if tranced, mesmered,* trapped in this stifling pit of heat and ennui.

*Friedrich Anton Mesmer, a German physician working in Vienna, did extensive research in "animal magnetism." He developed an early treatment for what later, in the twentieth century, would be called psychosomatic

20

Almost two months had passed since that bright spring day when I had ridden out with Dickens to liberate Miss Ternan from Urania Cottage. *Bleak House,* by the end of July into its fifth number, was the talk of London.

Angela Burdett-Coutts, in that interval, had received two more threatening letters of the sort she had shown to Dickens and me. Dickens had mentioned passing them on to Inspector Field, but the Protectives were busy that summer with the crowds still flocking to the Crystal Palace,* and with the usual tide of criminality that flowed into the city with the hot oppressive weather. To my knowledge, no progress whatsoever had been made on that case. I should have been suspicious, however, because Field usually moved quite quickly and Dickens rarely passed up an opportunity to head off on one of our evening walks in the direction of Bow Street Station.

As for Miss Ternan, she was employed, through Dickens's intervention with Macready I am certain, at playing two small parts in Covent Garden's rollicking new production of *The Taming of the Shrew.* But that was not the sum of what was happening in Miss Ternan's life. How do I know? Though I had myself seen Miss Ternan only twice in the almost two months that had passed, by coincidence I had been kept well informed concerning her progress. Soon after Miss Ternan had returned to the city, my Irish Meg was invited by Angela Burdett-Coutts (acting on the advice of Dickens and Field I am now certain) to join a ladies' discussion group which met in the evenings at the meeting rooms of Coutts Bank. Those meet-

illnesses. This treatment, which employed a primitive form of hypnotism, came to be called "mesmerism," and, by the time of his death in 1815, had caused him to be ostracized by the medical communities of both Vienna and Paris. By 1852, Mesmer's theories were very much back in vogue. Professional practitioners were numerous both in London and on the Continent. Public shows and carnivals featured charlatan mesmerists. Even curious gentlemen, such as Charles Dickens, dabbled in this strange power and attempted amateur hypnotic experiments.

*The centerpiece of the Great Exhibition of 1851, the Crystal Palace was a huge glass-domed exhibition hall built for the display of the genius of the scientific progress of the Industrial Revolution.

ings of the Women's Emancipation Society were all that Irish Meg could talk about.

In fact, it was, oddly enough, upon the night of her first attendance at a Women's Emancipation Society meeting that the most unsettling event of that period of heat and adjustment occurred. I must turn to Irish Meg for the narration of it, for I was not there to witness it, but it placed all of us upon our guard and it beckoned me into a labyrinth of betrayal and murder that I would never forget.

"He came out of nowhere, Wilkie!" Meg burst in upon me at my desk in our Soho rooms at half ten that evening. "He just came out of nowhere." Her words were tumbling over themselves in her excitement. "We never saw where he came from and then he was upon us."

"Meggy, wait, what is it?" I tried to calm her, but to no avail.

"He must have been waitin' in the shadows for us. He wos like a ghost. Afore we even saw him, he wos upon us, all muffled in a white duster with a rag or scarf tied over his face. He knocked Miss Angela and Eliza down in his first rush."

"Meggy . . . stop . . . please . . . slowly." I had arisen in alarm and, with both hands upon her shoulders, piloted her into a nearby armchair. "What is it? What has happened?"

"We were attacked in the street, that's wot!" She was almost indignant, as if I had something to do with this atrocity.

"Please, start from the beginning. Tell me what has happened. You are not hurt, are you?"

"No. No." Yet I could tell that she was still skittish from the stimulation of it.

"And the others? Miss Burdett-Coutts? She was not injured?"

"No. No. I drove him off. We did, I mean."

"You what!"

"Oh, Wilkie, it wos horrible. He just appeared out of the dark like a ghost, runnin' at us and strikin' out, for no reason."

"Tell me what happened. Tell me. Perhaps we can make some sense of it."

"It wos so dark and hot, not even a star, you know how the nights have been lately, Wilkie, like a bloody dungeon with no air." She took a deep breath, calming herself, then set off in earnest into her story. "He must have been waitin' somewhere

22

in the shadows on our way. It wos St. Martin's Lane, I think."

I took a chair facing her, careful not to interrupt, hopeful of getting at least the bare bones of the story before she became excited again.

"It wos Miss Angela and Liza Lane walkin' in front, and me and Nellie walkin' behind when he came out of nowhere. None of us saw where he come from. He came runnin' real hard out of the dark. Miss Angela and Liza Lane were about five steps in front of us and he knocked them both down. Liza screamed. I remember he kicked out at her."

Meg paused a moment to marshal either her own emotions or the details of her story, or both.

"He wos huge, and all muffled up in white standin' over them. He wos horrible, Wilkie, like a white ghost. He started reachin' down like he wos goin' to hit them or strangle them, and that's when Nellie and I screamed." And she stopped suddenly, as if she had told quite enough of this story.

"And? For God's sake, what happened?" I prompted her. I must admit that I was unable to hide my impatience. But, when she took up her story again, she seemed almost reticent.

"Well, we screamed . . . then we came upon him . . . and, and, and then he ran away and it wos over." She seemed to deflate in her chair as if the strain of the telling had sapped her strength. "Can you make me some tea, Wilkie?" she asked. "It has been a long and difficult night."

I leapt to do her bidding, happy to help in whatever way. However, when I returned short minutes later from the hob with her hot tea, she was already fast asleep in her armchair.

Two days later, I was present when Miss Ternan told Dickens the same story. Her narrative was quite similar to Irish Meg's, with one substantial difference.

In telling her story, Irish Meg had in no way embellished her own role in this strange encounter. Nellie Ternan in her narrative took a somewhat different and fuller view of it.

"Meg drove him off by herself," Miss Ternan declared. "He was kicking and beating Angela and Liza Lane. He had knocked them to the ground. He was this terrible figure, all in white, standing over them. I was terrified. I froze. But Meg ran right at him. I won't tell you the names she was screaming at him. 'Leave them be! Leave them be!' She was cursing him. She jumped on his back from behind and started beating at his head and face with her fists. He turned all around in a circle trying to shake her off, but she kept hitting and scratching at his eyes. Finally, he flung her off and threw her violently along the stones. I saw it all. 'Cursed woman!' he swore at Meg, who was lying on the ground, dazed from her fall. I thought for a moment that phantom figure was going to attack her as he had the other two, but he just ran off into the darkness. Meg saved us all," Miss Ternan concluded forcefully. "If she hadn't run in and jumped on him, we all would have been hurt."

I do not know why Irish Meg decided to play down her part in this violent street encounter. Perhaps her reticence stemmed from the changes in her thinking that seemed to be evidencing themselves on an almost daily basis.

Field was present with Dickens and me when Miss Ternan told her fuller version of the story. The Protectives had been called to the scene of this street attack, but the constable had not been dispatched from Bow Street. Rather, he had come from a newly established station in St. James Fields, so this was the first eyewitness report which Inspector Field had received.

"It is the writer of those threatening letters." Dickens seemed convinced. "Out to frighten Angela. He bears her some grudge. He is angry, or desperate, a madman."

"Perhaps," Field concurred. "But we have no proof of that."

"Then who is this attacker, this white ghost?"

"It could be a simple street robber, a basher. But one of them would never have run away empty-handed."

"Then who?" Dickens persisted.

"I do not know." At least Field answered honestly. "Your letter writer, a robber, a disgruntled bank customer—it could have been anyone."

"But it wasn't just anyone," Miss Ternan broke in. "I was there. I saw him. He wanted to hurt them. He had that scarf tied around his face so that he wouldn't be recognized. Angela would have known him, so he covered his face."

"There. That's it!" Dickens turned triumphantly back to Field.

"Yes, all of that is indeed true." Somehow I sensed that Inspector Field was mildly bored by all of this amateur speculation. "We shall continue lookin' into this affair," he assured us. "Some gin, Charles? Wilkie? It is a hot-weather drink, you know."

We both declined his offer of gin on that hellish day, but before we left, Dickens extracted a promise from him that we would be summoned to share in whatever information became available pertaining to this case.

Outside on Bow Street, Nellie reiterated her gratitude for Irish Meg's courageous action.

"She is a brave girl, Wilkie." Ellen Ternan was quite solemn in her praise. "You should tell her so. She saved all of us from harm."

Back in our rooms in Soho, I confronted my Meg with the facts: "She said you saved them all," I accused her. "Why did you not tell me that part?"

"Because you worry so much, anyway," she laughed it off.

But I knew that was not it. There had to be some other reason. As I remember it now, that was just one of the things that marked a strangeness that was coming over my Meggy's behavior at that time. It seemed as if she were changing before my eyes, and I found it unsettling.

DEATH IN SHEEP'S CLOTHING

(August 11, 1852—Morning)

The one clear and present change in Irish Meg's life at that time was, of course, the Women's Emancipation Society, but, in those days, all of London was changing. The city was like a book that needed to be constantly reread. Dickens and Field read it in quite different ways, and I was just learning to read under their tutelage. It was a book of mysteries, where nothing was ever what it seemed, a book that offered something different with each new reading.

Inspector Field knew how to read this book of the city better than anyone. He read it for its facts, its realities. It was his profession to read it.

Dickens enjoyed reading the book of the city more than Field did. He enjoyed plunging into it on his night walks and turning its pages with delight.

As for me, I found it a puzzling, often disturbing, text in which truth was as insubstantial as the fog and as agile as a cabman's horse. That is why I fill these little leather books, in hopes that if I write down the facts or even the appearances of them, then the whole of it might make some sense.

The Women's Emancipation Society was a most puzzling

chapter within that book of the city. Because both Dickens and I were utterly mesmerized by Irish Meg and Nellie Ternan at that time, and because they were both so dedicated to the Women's Emancipation Society, we had no choice but to try to understand it. What bothered both of us was that violence seemed to be asserting itself as the dominant theme of that particular chapter.

A fortnight had passed since that attack in the streets that had been thwarted by Irish Meg, but it did not take a Gypsy seer with a crystal ball to realize that trouble seemed to be gathering around Angela Burdett-Coutts and the Women's Emancipation Society, which her bank sponsored. Threatening letters, basher attacks in the street—these troubling events had occasioned Field to assign police protection to Angela. And whom had he chosen to serve as her personal bodyguard? None other than Tally Ho Thompson. I personally felt that was tantamount to welcoming the fox into the henhouse, but all the others seemed quite sanguine about the arrangement. But then the worst happened, and raised the stakes in the game beyond what any of us might have imagined.

On the morning in question, it took me a long moment to identify the sound which had awakened me from the deep embrace of both my loving Meg and the sweet oblivion of sleep. At first I thought, whimsically, that a large woodpecker was at persistent work upon the windowsill of our sleeping room, but then I realized that I had been battered out of slumber by an insistent knocking upon my hallway door.

"I'm coming. I'm coming!" I shouted as I padded unsteadily across the outer parlor. Mercifully, those harsh reports ceased at the acknowledgement of my voice. When I opened the door, I confronted Dickens and Angela Burdett-Coutts, each looking as grim as a hangman. "Charles, what is it?" I asked as they charged past me into the room. "What time is it?"

"There has been a murder at Coutts' Bank." Dickens's voice was somewhat shaky, as if under great strain. "You must dress immediately. The Protectives have been notified. Hurry. We have a coach. We must go."

"Wot is it?" Meg, *en deshabille,* rubbing the sleep from her eyes, leaned in the doorway to our sleeping room.

27

I was stunned by her indiscretion. To my great surprise, Dickens and Miss Burdett-Coutts took no notice of her.

"Wilkie, get dressed, we must hurry," Dickens insisted.

Within short minutes we were climbing into Angela Burdett-Coutts's sleek black brougham for the short gallop to Trafalgar Square. As I had left our rooms, still buttoning my clothes, Meg had promised to follow as quickly as she could dress herself.

"A body has been found inside the bank." Dickens apprised me of the facts of the case as the coach carried us toward our destination. "A night guard has disappeared. The day guard, coming on duty at half six, discovered the corpse."

"The security of the bank has never been penetrated before." Miss Burdett-Coutts seemed quite shaken.

"Angela was notified immediately by runner," Dickens took up his narrative. "She came straightaway to me, though she sent the runner on to notify the Protectives."

"To Bow Street?" I asked.

"No, that is part of our problem." Dickens exhibited his nervousness. "It will not be Field and Rogers on the scene. I have sent a messenger to Field, but it may be too late."

Too late for what? I was struck by the agitation in Dickens's voice.

"Who has been murdered, and why in the bank?"

"We do not know." Dickens leapt upon my question, sparing Angela. "But we shall soon see." Dickens pointed to the police post chaise pulling up in front of us at the bank as our coachman, with a jolt and a small skid, brought our horses to a halt.

As we disembarked, two policemen were stepping down from their official post chaise. The Metropolitan Protectives shield and the designation "St. James Station" were painted on its door. Angela Burdett-Coutts, with Dickens and me in tow, cut them off before they reached the bank's wide stone steps.

"Gentlemen, I thank you for coming so quickly. I am Angela Burdett-Coutts, governing officer of the bank. I sent my personal bodyguard to assure that nothing would be disturbed. I am told there is a dead body on our premises."

"Ahem, yes mum." The inspector, a short, pale, balding man with tiny eyes and a tight mouth, stared at her in amazement. He was clearly unprepared to accept this woman as the governor of an establishment as huge and important as Coutts Bank.

"Ahem, yes"—his tiny eyes blinked so rapidly that one almost expected them to give off a ticking sound—"Inspector Collar here, and this is Serjeant Mussbabble." He indicated his black-coated, stovepiped assistant, who seemed of some Thugee descent.

Much to our relief, and Inspector Collar's annoyance, at that very moment the black Bow Street post chaise pulled up, and Field and Rogers stepped down.

"Collar."

"Field."

They exchanged wary businesslike nods.

"There has been a murder in the bank." Dickens stepped forward, ever helpful.

Field ignored him as if he were a total stranger.

"I did not know the Protectives were already on the scene." Field, apologetic and conciliatory, directed his attention toward Inspector Collar. "Rogers and I shall withdraw," he bluffed.

"No. Not at all," Collar buckled. "We have not gone in yet. Come along. We shall both take a look."

As Collar and his man turned to lead us up those broad stone steps, Field sneaked a quick triumphant look at Dickens, accompanying it with a swipe of his crook'd forefinger to the side of his right eye.

We followed Inspector Collar up the steps and through the high oak doors into the bank. Tally Ho Thompson stood alone, on guard, just inside the doors. When we entered, a look of relief accompanied by his ever present grin burst out upon his face.

"Nothin's been touched," he informed us. "Nobody's been let in. The guard's sittin' down over there; he's as shaked as a saltcellar."

"Where is the body?" Inspector Collar rushed to assert his control over the crime scene. Field raised his eyebrows and

29

sent a silent message to Dickens that said we all must tread softly around this other inspector who mistakenly thought it was his case.

"Over there." Thompson pointed to the center of the bank's high atrium.

Inspector Collar led us off in that direction. Tally Ho Thompson formed with me the rear guard of this troop marching resolutely toward the victim. The vast atrium of Coutts Bank was floored completely in marble, which was softened here and there, often under a bank official's desk, by a number of large oriental rugs. The body, however, rested on its stomach in the center of a wide expanse of grey marble directly in front of the long tellers' counter. A heavy woolen cap, unusual for summer, covered its head. A deep green woman's scarf was pulled tight and twisted around its neck. The corpse was a man dressed in a tweed suit, again rather heavy and unusual for the August heat. He also wore walking boots.

"Strangled, eh?" Collar stated the obvious.

"Yes, quite so," Thompson answered from the rear.

"Yes, of course," Dickens and Field politely agreed in the same breath.

"Strangled from behind, I'd say." Collar was an absolute wonder of deduction.

"Yes indeed," Field humoured him.

"With a woman's silk scarf, she looks like." Collar went down to one knee over the body.

"Yes, a woman's scarf," Field agreed, "but it takes great strength to strangle a strugglin' man."

"Not a woman done it then, you think, eh?" Collar was not at all slow in following someone else's line of reasoning.

"Just sayin' it takes great strength to strangle a man, is all. A strong woman could do it."

"Ahh." Collar rose and stood next to Field. The two detectives contemplated the body for long moments. We all—Dickens, Angela Burdett-Coutts, myself, Thompson—waited for one or the other's next pronouncement.

"There is somethin' wrong here," Field finally broke the awkward silence.

Collar started as if awakened suddenly out of a dream.

Field dropped quickly to one knee over the corpse.

"Wot is it?" There was panic in Collar's voice, a fear of being overshadowed.

"Just as I thought." Field sank back away from the body onto both knees with his weight resting upon his heels.

"Wot is it?" Collar repeated himself.

"It is this." Field reached out with his left hand to snatch the hat off the corpse's head while, with a push to the shoulder with his right hand, he rolled the corpse over onto its back.

A collective gasp burst forth from all of us.

"My God!" Dickens exclaimed.

"Oh." Angela Burdett-Coutts covered her mouth with both hands in horror.

Thompson and I stared wide-eyed.

When Inspector Field plucked the hat off the corpse's head, curly tresses of long brown hair cascaded out and formed a pool beneath the corpse's upturned countenance. When Field rolled the body over, it revealed a woman's full form secreted within ill-fitting men's clothes.

We all stood staring down at this unnatural apparition.

"Oh good Gawd!" Irish Meg's voice—she must have arrived when Field was busy with the corpse—turned all of our heads. "It's Eliza Lane!"

THE NIGHT GUARD

(August 11, 1852—Morning)

I t is a woman." Inspector Collar spoke aloud, rather anti-
climactically, what all of us were thinking.

"So it is," Field agreed thoughtfully, his crook'd forefinger working at the corner of his right eye as if at a scab.

"It's Eliza Lane," Meg restated her identification.

"So it is, yes." Angela Burdett-Coutts, who I think had gone
into a temporary state of shock, seconded Irish Meg's identification.

Dickens looked at Field, but Field said not a thing. He was
waiting.

Collar looked briefly at Irish Meg, who was dressed respectfully enough, like a young working woman, but dismissed
her in favor of Miss Burdett-Coutts.

"Who is this Eliza Lane? And wot would she be doin' on
these premises so late at night."

"Oh, she was here last night. She was very angry at all of us,"
Angela Burdett-Coutts spoke in a rush.

"Yes, she wos," Irish Meg seconded Angela Burdett-Coutts.
"She all but cursed us, every one."

"Angela, slow down. Here, sit," Dickens ordered, and with

that solicitous gravity which he assumed whenever his Saint George protectiveness toward a vulnerable woman came upon him, he pulled a wooden desk chair across the marble floor.

After a proper hesitation in respect of the shaken woman's nerves, Inspector Collar pressed on.

"Wot wos that, again, Miss uh, uh . . ." He broke stride on her name.

"Angela Burdett-Coutts," Dickens prompted him rather testily, impatient, perhaps, that Field was just standing in passive attendance while this booby of a policeman blundered about the scene of the crime.

"She, Eliza, poor thing, was angry at all of us." Angela Burdett-Coutts gathered up her voice. "She broke in upon last evening's meeting of the Women's Emancipation Society and accused us all of ugly things."

"And now she's been murdered." Inspector Collar seemed to have a genuine talent for restating the excruciatingly obvious.

Dickens and Field exchanged eyebrow-raising looks which silently commented upon the torpid deductive powers of Inspector Collar.

Said inspector, however, with rather surprising dispatch considering the abundantly evidenced slowness of his intelligence, gathered the crime scene's obvious available information.

From Angela Burdett-Coutts he obtained the names of all the members in attendance at the previous night's meeting of the Women's Emancipation Society.

Next he turned to the day guard, one Mortimer Fix, who had discovered the body upon arriving for duty that morning. "I knew summat was wrong when I arrived an Frenchy wosn't on the doors," the man commenced his narrative. By his speech, he was clearly a refugee from the country who had taken on the aggressive bluster of the city streets. "Nobody wos on the doors. The doors wos wide open an unlocked. That's when I knew summat wos wrong."

Field rolled his eyes at Dickens.

Irish Meg and Angela Burdett-Coutts listened politely. Irish Meg was standing next to Angela's chair with her hand on that lady's shoulder. As I glanced at them, the thought flashed in my mind of how very far my Meggy had come. A mere fourteen months before she had been a foulmouthed, gin-swilling whore of the streets, yet here she stood offering a consoling hand to one of the most powerful women in the land.

"I come right in," Mr. Fix picked up his story, "an there wos no night guard to be found nowhere on the premises. Then I saw the body an I knew summat wos wrong."

A long silence ensued as Inspector Collar slowly ruminated upon the details of the day guard's story.

"The night guard, this Frenchy you called him"—Field stepped in quietly and took over the interrogation—"who is he? Wot do you know about him?"

"He can read, he can," Mr. Fix declared. "He's always got his nose in a book when I comes in the mornin's." The man seemed especially pleased with this revelation, as if it were the capping evidence in the case.

"His name, do you know his name?" Field was displaying a remarkable patience.

"His name?" Mr. Fix's face twisted up quite painfully as if he had been asked to solve the riddle of the Sphinx.

"Yes, his name?" Collar reasserted himself.

"Don' thinks I knows his name"—Mr. Fix's face still writhed in perplexity—"just Frenchy it always wos."

"He is a Frenchman then?" Inspector Collar jumped to his next question, perhaps fearful that Field would once again usurp his interrogation.

"No sir, no sir." Mr. Fix was quite adamant on this point. "Englishman just like me an you, but lived in Paris, come here from Paris he did."

"Aha!" Inspector Collar meaningfully caressed his chin with his right hand.

"You never heard this Frenchy's real name?" This time Dickens intruded upon the interrogation, drawing severe looks from both Collar and Field, and an absolutely murderous stare from Serjeant Rogers.

"I did once, I think, sir." By the painful twisting of his countenance it was clear that Mr. Fix was trying his very hardest to remember. "A *B* it wos, I think. A *B* sir, I'm summat certain."

This declaration threw everyone into confusion. None of the detectives of either the professional or the amateur persuasion had the slightest idea what the man was trying to say. We all stared as he scratched his head and screwed up his face, trying mightily to remember.

"Birchwood it wos, or Barsad, or Bluffnose, or somethin' like." Mr. Fix finally tried a few possibilities. "Began with *B*. Barnbottom. Barbait. Beerbag."

"And wot sort of books wos this Frenchy always readin'?" Field asked the question with a smile toward Collar, as if it were a joke.

"Ol' leather ones, sir, and thick they wos."

Collar seemed stumped for another question, but Field calmly prompted him.

"Perhaps a description?" Field spoke his suggestion in a very low voice as if only addressing Collar.

"Ahem, of course," Collar blustered. "Wot did this Frenchy look like?"

"Oh, tall he is, for an Englishman I mean, nearly six feet I'd bet. An with a bushy brush on his face, so big you can't hardly see nothin' but his eyes."

"Tall with a bushy mustache it is then." Field seemed almost talking to himself.

This ended our interview of the only person who even resembled a witness in this murder case. Collar dismissed the man, made certain that he had overlooked nothing at the scene, and ordered his Serjeant Mussbabble to have the body taken away to the police surgery at St. Bart's.

Inspector Collar was looking around as if trying to find something more to do when Field, who had quietly wandered off, spoke out from near the high entrance door.

"Strange," Field mused, loud enough to turn everyone's head.

"What is it?" Dickens was ever alert to Field's detecting instincts.

"What is strange?" a hint of panic at the prospect of Field having found something that he had overlooked quavered in his voice.

"Here, and here, and here." Field stooped as he made his

35

way across the floor picking up minute particles of something. "Look"—and he held out his cupped hand toward us— "little bits of cork across the floor in a trail from the door."

With that, Field moved quickly to the corpse of the young woman.

"And yes," he exclaimed in quiet triumph, "her boots are corks. See how the backs of the heels are crumbled. She wos murdered out in the street and dragged in, she wos."

"In the street? Dragged in?" Collar's head was swiveling from the doors to the corpse in confusion.

"Yes. See here. As the backs of her heels were dragged across the floor, the edges of the marble slabs crumbled pieces off. She left a trail of little crumbs of cork."

"So she did." Inspector Collar saw it now, and even bent to pick up a little piece of cork that Field had missed.

"Yes, that is interesting." Dickens could not help but enter the colloquy. "But why in the world kill her outside and then drag her in here?"

Field did not answer, perhaps aware that he had already overstepped his jurisdiction in the case. He had clearly surprised Inspector Collar in detecting this trail of evidence.

Everyone looked to Collar for the answer, but none was immediately forthcoming. After a long and awkward pause as Collar contemplated the bit of cork in his hand, he finally answered. "Yes, we must look into this and all the other evidence that I am sure this crime scene holds. We shall study it very carefully. Thank you, Inspector Field."

That seemed our signal to take our leave, and Inspector Field leapt to grease his colleague Collar with the oil of conciliation.

"Inspector Collar," Field began with righteous deference, *"thank you* for lettin' Serjeant Rogers and me observe. This seems a very interesting case, and one I would like to follow along. If there is anything we can do to help in the case, just summon us from Bow Street."

This extraordinary speech (both for its formality and its deference) delivered, Field and Rogers moved, without any farewell to Dickens and me (as if they did not want Collar to suspect that we were acquainted), toward the great doors.

Dickens watched them go.

I watched Dickens, and noted the momentary surprise in his face at this unexpected snub. But he quickly gathered up his bruised dignity. He went first to Angela Burdett-Coutts and, taking her hand, assured her, distinctly within the hearing of Inspector Collar and his man, that he was totally at her service in quest of a resolution of this frightening affair. Turning next to Inspector Collar, Dickens shook that worthy's hand heartily, all the while exclaiming what an interesting case of murder this was, how fascinated by the working of the Metropolitan Protectives he and his magazine *Household Words* were, and how grateful he would be to be kept informed of the turnings and developments of this case.* He was all fulsome smiles as he wrung that startled policeman's hand.

Outside, on the steps of the bank, Serjeant Rogers was waiting.

"He wants you to follow us to Bow Street, sirs." Rogers delivered his master's message and, without formality, scurried off down the stone steps to join Field in the post chaise, the driver of which immediately put whip to his horses and spirited our fellow detectives off in a rush.

*Dickens had, indeed, written four feature articles in *Household Words* two years before detailing the operations of the Metropolitan Protectives. "On Duty with Inspector Field" (August 1850) had been the first of those four essays.

"OUTSIDE OF
MY JURISDICTION!"

(August 11, 1852—Afternoon)

W e did as we were ordered, hailed the next passing growler, and followed Field and Rogers to Bow Street Station. Upon entering, with Irish Meg in tow, we found Field and Rogers reclining in their high-backed chairs before the cold hearth and fanning themselves with blue books in the infernally heavy air.

"Ah, Dickens"—Field rose to greet us—"Sorry I wos so standoffish back there, but I wanted to keep it all very professional with Collar. It is his case, and he is goin' to have to be dealt with."

"Is that why you wanted us here, to apologize?" There was that mischievous twinkle in Dickens's eye. "I can assure you that I fully understood your motives and behavior from the moment you arrived at the scene."

"Indeed." Field jollily tapped the side of his eye with his frolicking forefinger. "In that case, wot did you think of our friend Collar?"

"As detectives go"—a wide grin broke out through the thicket of Dickens's foppish goatee—"and I'm only closely acquainted with one, mind you, and Serjeant Rogers of course," he said as an afterthought, to which Rogers reacted predictably with a sour stare, "the man seemed rather slow and unobservant."

"Collar is a fool!" Field spat. "But he will be thorough, because bein' thorough is all he can be."

"And in his thoroughness," Dickens observed, "Miss Ternan is sure to come under suspicion?"

"Yes, undoubtedly. I presume that's why you were so insistent that I join you at the scene of a murder that is outside of my jurisdiction."

"In the past nothing ever seemed out of your jurisdiction," Dickens taunted him.

An amused grin spread slowly across Field's face.

"That missin' night guard is the key to these goings-on," Field finally broke the silence.

"And we must find him before Collar does." Dickens picked right up on Field's train of thought as if they were Siamese twins.

"Collar could not find his own shirt in his own dresser drawer," Rogers scoffed.

"So how do we go about finding this night guard?" Dickens asked. "This Frenchy."

"You leave that to Rogers and me." Field seemed supremely confident. "But I wants you and Mr. Collins to work t'other side of the street."

We looked quizzically at him.

"We must talk to these women, find out about this Eliza Lane. Meggy will help. I asked her more than a month past to join their group, to observe them, in pursuit of this letter writer who is threatening Miss Coutts."

Catching my rather perturbed look, first in his direction and then in Meggy's, Field proceeded with his explanation.

"I did not inform you, Mr. Collins, because I wanted all to seem natural. Only Mr. Dickens and Miss Coutts knew wot wos afoot. The letters smelled of someone who wos close to her, and I wanted someone on the inside to observe this group of political ladies."

As if by some divine intervention, almost at the very moment that her name was mentioned, Miss Angela Burdett-

Coutts burst in with Tally Ho Thompson in tow. We all turned to her entrance in surprise, but no one said a word because of the taut look of alarm on her face.

"Oh, Charles, Inspector Field." Her voice quavered at the gravity of the message it was her burden to bear. "That terrible murder was not all."

"What is it, Angela?" Dickens moved to her side to try to calm her.

"Coutts Bank! Oh, Charles, this has never happened in all its long history. Coutts Bank has been violated. Ten thousand pounds is missing!"

"ALL A MUDDLE!"

ॐ

(August 11, 1852—Afternoon)

T he whole company was stunned by Miss Burdett-Coutts's announcement. Even Field was struck momentarily dumb.

"How wos it done?" Field finally broke the awkward silence.

Tally Ho Thompson, who had been standing discreetly in the background, took a quick step toward us, all ears, unable to mask his professional curiosity.

"It was taken from the day vault." Angela Burdett-Coutts's voice wavered as she began.

"Wot is the day vault?" Field interrupted.

"It is a barred cabinet about the size of a secretary. The main vault, which is a full iron room with an iron door and multiple locks, is opened only once a day, at two in the afternoon. All currency, receipts, and document transactions which occur in the final hour of business are locked into the day vault for transfer to the main vault the following day."

"Is it customary to have that much in the day vault?" Field interrogated her as if she were the criminal.

"No. Not really. But it varies. Monday is a very busy day at

41

Coutts Bank. All the business transactions of the end of the week find their way to Coutts Bank on Mondays. We also have many rather large depositors, merchants whose ships have come in Saturday or Sunday or that day, and who must make a late deposit. That currency could find its way into the day vault. Ten thousand pounds would not be an unusual amount for a late Monday."

"How did they get into it?" Serjeant Rogers took the liberty of asking a question, and Field nodded his approval.

"They cut the lock out with ripping chisels." She gestured as if she were sketching a picture in the air with her hands. "The day vault has an iron barrel gate that swings closed over its drawers. The lock hangs in a square iron box on this barrel gate. They used ripping chisels to cut off the lock. Each drawer also has a separate lock, but they either picked them or smashed them open."

"And once they wos in, they just emptied the drawers and left," Inspector Field ended Angela Burdett-Coutts's narrative for her.

"Quite so." She nodded.

We had all risen when Angela and Thompson entered, and we still stood in a ragged circle staring at one another.

"It's all a muddle, isn't it?" Dickens broke the silence which had taken custody of the room.

"All a muddle it certainly is." Field slapped the back of his high wing chair, circled around it, and sat down. Dickens ushered Angela Burdett-Coutts to Rogers's chair, much to that worthy's sour and silent frowning. The rest of us stood ranged around them. Dickens actually sat down on the hearth stone and lit a cigar.

"It seems a confusin' muddle of different crimes." Field suddenly vaulted out of his chin-pulling contemplation. "But they are all tangled together if you asks me." With that pronouncement, he was up and pacing, pulling his chin again. "We really have three different crimes here, but they're all part and parcel of each other."

"How do we have three crimes?" Angela Burdett-Coutts asked, puzzled.

"We have a murdered woman and a robbery of bank funds."
Dickens interceded for Field with what seemed like an answer,
but which turned quickly into simply another version of the
question: "But what is the third crime?"

"The threatening letters," Field promptly answered. "Mark
me, they are part of this as well."

"How?"

"How?"

Serjeant Rogers's voice and mine, the only boroughs not yet
heard from, spoke out almost in unison.

"I don't quite know yet," Field confessed. "It's a bloody tangle to be figured out." And with that he sat back down in his
chair and lit his cigar.

He and Dickens sat opposite one another, their minds
swirling around that tangle of crimes like the blue smoke
from their cigars swirling up around their heads. Angela
Burdett-Coutts sat to Field's side and I stood at the back of
her chair. Rogers leaned against the hearth. Meggy had
joined Thompson on a long bench set against the far wall,
and the two of them were engaged in an earnest muffled whispering. For all I could tell, Irish Meg was probably com-
plaining to Tally Ho Thompson that Field had not yet broken out the gin.

"Meggy!" Field commanded her attendance.

She leapt to his call as if she were still one of his familiars
of the night streets. Somehow I resented that. I certainly never
addressed Irish Meg in that way, and, if I did, I suspected that
she would not jump to my call as she did to his.

"Meggy"—Field's voice was more mollifying as she stood before him—"we need to know more about this Eliza Lane who
wos murdered. We need to know wot the other women know
about her. You have become friends with Miss Ternan. You
must go and talk with her and the two other women there
about this murdered woman. Mark all they say about her. The
smallest things can be important."

Meggy's head was nodding up and down faster than the bale
on a spinning jenny. Field paused to think, but he didn't dismiss her. When Meg started to withdraw out of his fearsome

reach, he barked, "Stay!" and stopped her as if she were Bill Sykes's dog.*

"Charles"—Field's attention shifted instantly to his next minion—"I have asked Meg to talk to Miss Ternan because I felt the conversation would be uncomfortable for you and for her and I thought she would speak more frankly to another woman about another woman." He explained this quietly to Dickens, but quickly shifted back into his sharper-edged voice of command. "But I want you to talk to the artsy ladies in that group, the writers, Miss Nightingale, Miss Siddal, Miss Taylor, Mrs. Browning the sickly one. Find out wot they know about the murdered girl. They'll know about her. It'll be all over the prints by mornin'. You and Collins have done this for me before. You knows how to do it. We'll meet here day after tomorrow in the afternoon to see wot we knows."

"Now Meggy"—and he turned back to his spy—"wot happened last night when the murdered woman was so angry?"

*Collins's reference is to that fierce housebreaker's vicious dog in Dickens's *Oliver Twist*.

THE WOMEN'S EMANCIPATION SOCIETY

(Looking Backward to an Evening in July)

My Irish Meg caught her breath and coughed self-consciously at Field's command for her to take center stage, but she knew she couldn't escape. To her credit, however, she saw her chance and decided to make the best of it.

"Fieldsy," she begged, "if I'm to tell it all I've gots to have a drink, a nice gin? That would be good, wouldn't it?"

"Wot a smashing idea!" Tally Ho Thompson chimed in, counterfeiting his best Oxford gentleman's voice.

Even Field had to smile at the audacity of the two of them. With a nod and a wave of his hand, he sent Rogers off to liberate the gin bottle from the cupboard.

In that short interlude while the cups were being washed and the gin bottle was passed around, my mind wandered back to an evening in early July when my Meggy had come home from one of her first meetings of the Women's Emancipation Society. She had come home in such an exhilarated state that I could no longer contain my curiosity, my need to penetrate that society's secrets.

. . .

"Just what goes on at those meetings?" I could not help but ask.

"Oh, Wilkie," she began in a breathless whisper, as if she were telling deep secrets, "they're mostly respectable women and yet they talks about the wildest things."

"Such as?" I inquired, my curiosity piqued.

"Why, wot we're doin' 'tis nothin'," she went right on with great animation.

"What do you mean, 'what we are doing'? You don't talk, in the company of those women, about what we do, do you?"

"No. I haven't . . . yet," she said with a coy grin, and I realized she was teasing me. "But I might," she laughed.

The idea! To think that what we did in the privacy of our Soho rooms might be described aloud to a circle of women in some public meeting at Coutts Bank or at Bedford College!

"Oh, Wilkie, don't look so stricken. I don't talk about us. I listens. They talks of free love, does some of them, the Frenchwoman who dresses like a man in imitation of some other Frenchwoman.† And Miss Siddal who has no meat on her whole body and takes laudanum and poses in the nude for Mr. Rossetti's paintin's, and the midwife to the poor with the bird name, Miss Nightingale, and that housemate of Nellie's."

"Which one?" And I realized that I was eagerly encouraging her gossip.

"Why, the big horsey one, Marian Evans. She's always talkin' about how the laws won't let women either think for themselfs or do any of the things that men do."

"Like what?"

"Like makin' love without bein' proper married," Meg snapped back.

"Oh?"

---

*Bedford College for Women was founded in 1849 by Elizabeth Jesser Reid, and was the second such establishment. Queen's College, founded in 1848 by Christian Socialist Frederick Denison Maurice, was the first such women's educational institution, but it focused almost exclusively on the education of governesses. Many of the meetings of feminist groups in London throughout the second half of the nineteenth century were held at Bedford College.

†The reference to this "other Frenchwoman" is probably to the poet, novelist, and bisexual advocate of free love, George Sand.

"Yes, I mean, think about it," she continued on without so much as a by-your-leave. "Nobody cares that you're keepin' some whore called Irish Meg. Everything's just ducky. But they all knows I'm a whore, so they thinks nothin' of it. Your friends, Mr. Dickens and Fieldsy, they know about us and accepts me as real people, but if most people knew about us, they'd see me as a pox upon your good name."

"But that is exactly why we do not publicly flaunt our domestic arrangement here." I tried to make her see the pure logic of it.

"But I'm not a whore anymore, Wilkie." She wasn't really angry, just frustrated that I wasn't understanding these strange distinctions she was making about the inequity of a double standard for gentlemen's behavior. "You don't still think of me as a whore, do you, Wilkie?"

"But I am in love with you, Meggy," I said, and it was true. I also knew it was my strongest argument with her. "I am addicted to you and I do not care what society says. What do we care, if we have each other?"

"Sometimes I care, Wilkie. Sometimes I sees myself as no better than just a kept whore."

"But you are not a kept whore. We are lovers. I love you. I just said that."

"I knows that, Wilkie. But it's just the fuckin' that binds you to me, and mebbe havin' someone to talk to afterward on a lonely night."

"No, you are wrong." I had to defend myself. "Since the first moment I saw you I have been fascinated by you. I am hopelessly in love with you."

"Oh, Wilkie, it's such a muddle," she said, and snaked her arms around my neck and pulled me to her in a passionate kiss.

I said not a word. This conversation had unsettled me. I wanted things to remain as they were between us.

But Meggy could not leave well enough alone. She was too full of her Women's Emancipation Society and its intellectual delights.

"They's women who writes books and articles, Wilkie, just like you and Mr. Dickens do."

"What books?" My ungovernable curiosity led me right into her trap. She wanted to impress me with the intellectual company into which she had gained entrance.

"Why, Miss Evans has made into English from German a fat book about Jesus, and Mrs. Harriet Taylor, who is really Mrs. John Mill, wrote an essay called 'The Enfranchisement of Women' just last year in one of your magazines, *The Westminster Review*, but they wouldn't put her name on it, and I'll wager none of you men ever read it,* and Miss Nightingale, tonight, at the meetin', she wos readin' from a pile of papers she writ and I writ out wot she said. I keeps a little leather book, too, like that one you writes your ideas in." And with that she sprang to fetch it.

"These women writes in a whole new way, Wilkie. They're strange women, but wot they says strikes home. They writes about wot women are, and how women feel, and wot they ought to do. Here's wot Miss Nightingale read just tonight." She held her commonplace book up before her face and read from it as if it were Holy Scripture.

" 'Why have women passion, intellect, moral activity—all three—and a place in society where no one of the three can be exercised?' That's wot Miss Nightingale asks and that's the main problem, she says—that no one lets women do nothin'."†

She paused just long enough for me to realize that I was in for a long night.

"Barbara Smith—you know, Wilkie, Nellie's other housemate—she is the outspoken one. 'Oh bosh!' she says when some of them starts complainin'. Some of them are really mean and hateful. You wouldn't believe."

"Oh wouldn't I?" I had grown quite sanguine in the face of

*Marian Evans, later George Eliot, translated David Friedrich Strauss's *Das Leben Jesu* from the German to English. Harriet Taylor's "The Enfranchisement of Women," published without attribution, appeared in *The Westminster Review* in July 1851. This article was later credited to Harriet Taylor by her husband, John Stuart Mill, as the basis for his feminist work *The Subjection of Women,* published in 1869.

†Florence Nightingale had to be reading from the manuscript of her fictional story "Cassandra," published soon after in 1852.

her lecture. "Who are these hateful women and just what do they say that is so hateful?"

"We call them 'the witches,' we do. Nellie, Miss Evans, Barbara Smith, Flory Nightingale, and me do. We're the younger ones in the group. There's 'the witches'—the Frenchwoman Marie de Brevecoeur, Sydney Beach, both of them dress like men, mostly in ridin' pants, and Eliza Lane. Then there's 'the riches'—Miss Burdett-Coutts, Miss Harriet Martineau, who started the society, Madame Tussaud, the famous business-woman in wax goods"—and she laughed at her wit with a gay trill like a tiny bell— "and Harriet Taylor, who would not take her husband's name. And we call ourselves 'the wenches.' Those three groups are the ones who are there all the time, but there are others who believe in the society's goals. Like Mrs. Caroline Norton, who has been in court against her husband almost twenty years now, and Mrs. Browning, who is brought up in a wheelchair when she can come."

"The witches, the riches, and the wenches. How poetic." I tried to keep the sarcasm out of my voice.

"We're the wenches because we're younger and we seem the only ones still interested in men."

"Aha." I counterfeited interest to humor her.

"We're really not three separate mobs," she assured me, "except maybe the witches. They *really* are different." She raised her eyebrows to see if I had gotten her drift, and then went right on with her lecture. "But us wenches are mostly there to listen and learn. Some of us sometimes put in our tuppence of truth though, especially Barbara Smith and Flory and Elizabeth Siddal when she is not full of medicine. Nellie and I hardly ever say anythin'. We're really the only ones from the streets, though Flory Nightingale sure talks like she's been there."

"But what do you do at these meetings which makes all of this talk come out? What occasions this talk of free love and dislike of men in general?"

"When we talk, we just talk about ourselves and how we're cheated and enslaved by this society."

" 'Enslaved'? Really, isn't that overstating it a bit?"

"In the mind, Wilkie. In the mind, but sometimes in our

49

bodies, too. Really, it sounds barbaric, but it's true. We read some woman name of Wollstonecraft, or somethin' like, out loud at one meetin'. Most of the women in the society clapped their hands at that one."*

"I have heard of this Wollstonecraft treatise. It is notorious for its hatred of men and its attacks upon the institution of marriage."

"Everybody says that you are tryin' to make us slaves."

"Yet you discuss 'free love' there." I tried to give the argument a lighthearted turn. "Not all of these women must hate men as their enslavers. Is it not hypocritical to denounce men while at the same time plotting new ways to make love to men?"

"Or to women?" Irish Meg said it almost defiantly.

"No! Women? No?" I was stunned at the unthinkable turn this discussion had taken. "You truly discuss such things there, in the presence of respectable women like Angela Burdett-Coutts?"

"Oh, Wilkie," and Irish Meg smiled coyly, "she listens quite intently, she does. And she's not as sheltered as you might think. None of us is. After all, she runs a home for whores."

"Yes, but really . . ."

"We talk about everything."

"And what do *you* talk about?"

"They are very interested in me, they are, about wot my life wos like on the streets, why I sold myself to men."

"They know that you were a . . . a . . . ?"

"Oh, Wilkie, don't be such a Mrs. Grundy, *really*.† They know that you are keepin' me, too."

"They do? Miss Burdett-Coutts does?" Meggy caught the note of alarm that crept into my voice, and she mocked me.

"Everybody in London does. We talk openly at our meetin's. There's some carries it too far though."

*Most probably Mary Wollstonecraft's *A Vindication of the Rights of Woman*, published in 1792. Wollstonecraft was the wife of the philosopher-novelist William Godwin and the mother of Mary Shelley, the author of the novel *Frankenstein*.

†"Mrs. Grundy" and "Mrs. Grundyism" were the slang phrases denoting those Victorians who were intent upon censoring all things sexual.

"What do you mean?"

"After one meetin', when the tea and cakes wos served, two of the witches, the one who scowls all the time and really does hate men I think, Eliza Lane, and the Frenchwoman who dresses like a man, got me aside and wanted to know everything men made me do when they bought me. They asked questions that nobody would ask."

"What questions did they ask?" I could not disguise the curiosity in my own voice.

"Strange questions, like did men make you do them on your knees, or did men make you put on shows, make love to other women."

"And what did you tell them?"

"Oh, Wilkie, stop it, you arc as bad as they are, pressin' a girl. They wanted to know how doin' those things for pay for mcn madc me feel, wot I thought when I wos doin' them."

"And how did you answer that?" For a moment, she seemed to wander off into some quiet, thoughtful place of her own, as if her mind had left her body.

"The truth is that I didn't feel nothin' at all. It wos as if I wos dcad, some kind of ghost wanderin' the streets. I wos there, but I didn't feel a thing, and it wos horrible."

And then she came back from her other world, and her tenderness caught me by surprise. Meg was the most surprising person of all those I knew, even more so than Dickens. For all of the brutality of her past, she could surprise you with her loving gentleness.

"Oh, Wilkie"—she put her arms around me and clasped me tight—"I couldn't feel a thing until you took a fancy to me. You seem to love me, don't you, Wilkie, don't you?"

There was almost a note of desperation in her voice. Like a small miracle, I received a momentary gift of tongues. Memory is a priceless thing and gave me the words to work the miracle.

"Meggy, I have loved you from the first moment I saw you, my fire woman, drinking gin at the Bow Street station. I could not take my eyes off you, and I still can't."

"Oh, I remember that night, by the river." Her voice was happy and she cradled her head in the safe hollow of my shoulder. "You gave me your scarf against the chill. No one had ever done nothin' like that for me. I still have it," she said, and started up to get it to show me, but I pulled her back. I was caught up in the honesty of the moment and wanted to say more . . . and that was my downfall.

"Meggy, I truly love you"—I was entering into uncharted waters, heedless of the hidden reefs— "and you make me happy. I fell in love with you when you were a whore and I love you now that we are lovers, more fully, more comfortably."

"Love me, or love fuckin' me?" Her voice was doleful, as if she had asked a question that she did not really want answered.

"It's not that way at all, Meggy, and you know it. Good God, I love you. What must I do to convince you? You and my writing are my whole life. Except for Dickens and my work, all of my time is spent with you."

"That's it, you have your work. Wot do I have?"

"You help me with my work, we talk."

"About wot? About your work, wot you did all day. I don't have nothin' to talk about, Wilkie."

Meg never cried, but I could feel on my neck the tears that had run down her cheeks. I had never seen her like this before. I held her closer, rocked her in my arms. "I love you, Meggy. Isn't that enough? I love you, and if there is any slavery between us, I am *your* slave."

I was exhausted. This truth telling was more tiresome than trying to keep up with Dickens on one of his night walks.

"I'm sorry, Wilkie." Meg was no longer argumentative. "But these women are makin' me think. Oh, I knows you loves me, and I knows you fell in love with me when I wos nothin' but a street whore, but they're makin' me see myself like I never seen myself before. They make me want you to see me different, see me as somethin' more than just your lover."

It was a strange quiet that had come over the room as she spoke, as if we were suspended in time.

I had expended all my words. *But you are my lover,* I thought, *and I love only you.* But I couldn't say it again.

I have always felt uncomfortable at the confluence of philosophy and the lives of real people. Too many wars have been waged and lovers torn asunder in the name of philosophy and religion and politics. Here was I talking of our love and there was she, feeling all that I was saying, yet captured by philosophy for the first time.

"But we are not only lovers," I finally broke the silence which had closed over us like the sea over two exhausted swimmers, "we are friends, too, aren't we?"

It must have been some divine intervention that had brought those words to my mouth because, for one of the few times in my life, I had said the right thing.

She turned to me and smiled a radiant smile, her dark red hair burning around her face and her bright green eyes flashing. "Oh, I hope so, Wilkie. I hope so. You're the only one I can talk to like this."

The sound of her voice jarred me out of my reverie. We were back at the Bow Street station, and all the cups had been filled with gin, and my Irish Meg was about to begin her story.

WHORES AND SODOMITES

ॐ

(August 11, 1852—Afternoon)

I t wos beezarre, it wos!" Meg began.

"Yes, it was a truly strange outburst," Angela Burdett-Coutts seconded my Meggy's assessment.

"She wos absolutely crazed, she wos," Irish Meg (with the help of the gin) plunged into her narrative. "Her eyes were wide as saucers. Mad, mad she wos, like she didn't know where she wos, but screamin' like a madwoman."

"What was she screaming?" Field broke in.

"Calling us terrible names, accusing us of terrible things." Meg paused to draw deeply upon her mug of gin. "And sayin' we deserved to die for our sins, that we were all whores and saddamites, wotever that is."

At that, Dickens suddenly straightened up like a hunting dog on point. "Whores and sodomites, did you say?" He leapt to her prompt.

"Yes, whores and saddamites, that's wot she said."

Dickens's eyes were alive with his discovery: "Those are the very words."

"Wot words?" Meg's voice made no attempt to conceal

54

her impatience with Dickens's interruption of her narrative.

Field stared for a long moment, then, suddenly, made the connection. "The letters . . . ," he remembered, ". . . the threats to Miss Coutts contained those words."

"Yes," Dickens countered, "those exact words," and he smiled as if he had just solved the case.

"Eliza Lane wos as wild as some Bedlam bitch." Irish Meg pulled back on the narrative as if she and Dickens were involved in some verbal tug-of-war.

As she sat there telling her tale, I could not help but recall that winter night eighteen months before, the fire sending out tongues of flame from her luxuriant red hair. That was when I had first set eyes on my "fire woman." I think I must have fallen in love with her at that first sight. But this was a different woman, no longer the Irish Meg of eighteen months before, no longer a creature of the streets. She was a "new woman" in every sense of that phrase.

"We were all settled at the meetin'—in one of our usual rooms at Coutts Bank," Meg went on. "Most of us wos there, me and Nellie and Miss Burdett-Coutts and Marian Evans and Barbara Smith and poor crippled Elizabeth Browning who arrived late and Flory Nightingale and Marie who dresses like a man. We wos all settled in and ready to listen to some poems of Elizabeth's and a story of Marian's when she just comes bustin' in like she's mad."

"Miss Lane, this is?" Dickens was her questioner.

"Yes, Eliza, Eliza Lynn Lane. She's one of the regular women in the group. I mean, she comes regular to the meetin's."

"And what did she say?" Dickens prompted his star witness as if he were some bewigged and powdered barrister at the Queen's Bench.

Inspector Field just sat there quietly, listening, with a somewhat bemused look on his face.

"She burst in screamin' at all of us, screechin' that we're all a pack of hypocrites. And then she starts in railin' at each one of us, startin' with Angela." Meggy paused for gin.

"What did she say to Miss Burdett-Coutts?" Field closed in

like one of that rapacious pack of lawyers Dickens was at that very time so skillfully skewering in *Bleak House.*

"She called her a pander, one who harbors whores and saddamites."

"There, that is the phrase from the letters," Dickens interrupted, "the exact phrase."

"She said it to all of us," Irish Meg seconded Dickens. " 'All whores and saddamites.' She said it more than once she did, then she started pointin' fingers. 'I knows all your secrets,' she's screechin', circlin' that table like some hungry animal in the zoo."

"Now *that* sounds like blackmail." Field broke his silence in a tone which signaled that finally his interest was fully engaged. "Wot secrets?" Field leaned forward in his chair and took a quick swipe at the side of his eye with his forefinger.

"Like I said, first she cursed Miss Angela, then she turned on Flory Nightingale and called her no more than a common street whore despite all her nursey airs, and next wos Nellie—" Irish Meg stopped dead as if she suddenly realized that she didn't want to tell what that screaming harridan had said.

"Go on," Field prompted her.

"Well"—Meg regrouped—"she called Nellie no more than a rich man's whore, a kept woman, and a guilty murderess."

I glanced surreptitiously at Dickens, who colored perceptibly and bit into his lower lip. I am sure Field also caught Dickens's tick of discomfort because he hastened Irish Meg on with her story.

"Did she attack anyone else?" he ordered Meg to proceed.

"All of us," Meg spat back, "pacin' the room and pointin' her finger. She called me a street whore puttin' on airs, and a kept woman to boot, the bitch. She went absolutely crazy at Marie de Brevecoeur."

"More than at the others?" Field interrupted, noting a quizzical change of intensity in Meg's voice.

"She wos screamin' at all of us. It all happened so fast. She said Marie wos false and a liar and would burn in hell for her unnatural ways. And she turned on Miss Evans and called her

56

a wife stealer and hairytick.* 'You'll burn in hell!' she cursed Miss Evans. The only one she didn't curse individual wos poor Mrs. Browning."

Meg stopped for breath, and we all just stared at her.

"How did it end?" Dickens finally broke the shocked silence.

"It wos like she just ran out of steam," Meg said, more quietly. "She'd gone all around the room, pointin' fingers at all of us. It wos like she'd lost her voice, like she'd been given a speech and she'd said it all by rote. She just stood there like she wos in some kind of trance. Then in a real quiet voice she says, 'You're all a pack of hypocrites.' And she looked right at Angela, who wos sittin' there like she'd been stunned by a blow, and then she pointed right at Miss Angela. 'And you are the worst one of all!' she shrieks, and with that runs out of the room."

"Wot did you do?" Rogers, who had been hanging on her every word, leapt to the question.

"Nothin', we just sat there." Meg shrugged and held out her hands helplessly as if she still didn't understand the story she had just told.

"It was all so strange," Meg said softly after thinking for a moment. "It was as if she wanted to hurt all of us for no reason." Meg stopped again to take a drink of gin and get a firmer hold on her emotions and her narrative.

"Then I lost my temper, Wilkie." Meg turned to me as if apologizing. "I don't know why I did it, but I jumped up and ran out after her. I didn't think it wos right, her yellin' at Miss Angela like that."

*This probably refers to Marian Evans's involvement with John Chapman, who was Dickens's publisher as well as the publisher of *The Westminster Review*, where Marian Evans was employed as an editor without portfolio; that is, she did all of the work and Chapman took all the credit on the masthead. In fact, these charges of sexual license on the parts of John Chapman and Marian Evans were probably accurate. She had become involved with Chapman, one of the most open and notorious philanderers in London, soon after her arrival at *The Westminster Review.* He was her employer, but it also seems that he enticed her into joining, as a frequent visitor and tutor in the French language, the strange *ménage à quatre* of his household, which included his wife, his mistress Elizabeth Tilley, who lived in, and Marian Evans.

"And then?" Dickens spurred her story on.

"And then I ran head-on into Tally Ho outside in the hall-way."

"Thompson?" Field's forefinger flicked familiarly at the side of his eye. "Where wos he while all this wos happening?"

"He wos on the stair outside the meetin' room. When she ran out, she ran right past him, and he ran to the room to see wot wos happenin'. That's when we clapped each other in the doorway. He toppled me but caught me as I wos fallin'. By the time we got untangled, she wos down the stair and run-nin' for the front doors. I chased after her, but she got out into the street. When I got out through the doors, a closed carriage wos pullin' up and she wos gettin' in. I ran up behind her and caught her by the hair, but someone pulled her into the coach and pushed me off, then the horses wos whipped. The guard at the door saw it all."

"Wot did Thompson do?" Field pressed, glancing over his shoulder at that worthy.

"I took Miss Angela home," Thompson answered for him-self.

"And the others?" Field turned back to Irish Meg.

"They just went home, too," Meg answered wearily.

"She, the Lane woman, she wrote those letters," Dickens said slowly, thoughtfully. "But why is she dead?"

"ALL A BLOODY TANGLE"

᠀

(August 11, 1852—Afternoon)

T he murdered woman used the language of the letters in her screamin' fit to the ladies the night before, then she's found murdered where the robbery takes place." Field's crook'd forefinger brushed contemplatively at the side of his eye. "It is all a bloody tangle," he said, and shook his head slowly at the initial opacity of this unholy trinity of mysteries.

Field seemed to want to put an end to our group deliberations, but both Angela Burdett-Coutts and Dickens had other ideas.

"I must report this robbery to Inspector Collar." Miss Burdett-Coutts stated an obvious truth, but it confronted Field as a question.

"Of course you must," he replied, "but there need be no hurry in doin' it. It takes time for a bank to count its money, don't it? Tomorrow you can tell him. For now, you can find out for me everythin' your bank knows about this Frenchy, this night guard who has gone aglimmer."

"I have brought his work papers along. I felt you would

wish to look at them. Unfortunately, there is very little here."
She handed two thin sheets of grey paper over to him. "Because he had just come from Paris, it was somewhat difficult to check his past employment, and, I regret to say, it simply ended up not being done. Inquiries were attempted, but never completed, and his work record was excellent, so it was all just dropped. In fact, I'm rather embarrassed to say, we know little more than his name, John Barsad, and place of residence."

"Will you be going after this night guard?" Dickens asked.

"Yes, Rogers and I will make the inquiries into him. He's at the bottom of some of this I'll wager." And turning back to Miss Burdett-Coutts, Field asked, "Where does he say he lives? He won't be there, but where is it, anyway?"

"The address given is in Lambeth on Lower Marsh Street just off the Waterloo Road across the river," Angela replied.

"Then across the river we must go." Field seemed almost jovial now that the hunt was on.

"May we go with you today? I cannot meet with any of those ladies of the Emancipation Society until the morning, anyway," Dickens eagerly pled his case, "and the heart of this matter lies in Lambeth."

Field's forefinger crook'd and darted to the side of his eye.

Serjeant Rogers frowned.

Dickens waited expectantly.

I wondered why we had to traipse all the way across the river just for Charles's entertainment, but I should have known better. He was like a hound on the scent.

"Why not?" Field acquiesced. "Rogers, bring the coach around. Mr. Dickens is right. We shall waste no time."

Rogers scurried to obey.

Dickens's face broke into a sunny grin of anticipation.

"Thompson, you will stay with Miss Coutts . . . eyes open, yes?" Field barked his order.

"Eyes always open, they is, guv," Tally Ho answered with his typical nonchalance, his trademark grin slinking across his face.

"Meggy, see if you can find Miss Ternan this afternoon, right," Field barked his second order.

The others dismissed, Field turned sharply to Dickens and me: "Gentlemen"—he started toward the door—"let us try to find our Frenchman."

"A STRENGE LOT THEY WOS!"

(August 11, 1852—Late Afternoon)

L ondon's late-afternoon streets were crowded as Inspector Field's black post chaise threaded its way toward
the river. The thick ranks of foot passengers opened before us and closed behind as Rogers on the box coaxed the
horses through the twisted streets. The heat shimmered in the
afternoon air as we crossed the Thames at Waterloo Bridge.
Putrid smells rose off it like steam from an open cesspool. The
streets of Lambeth were hung with a haze of dust unstirred
by any breeze. Lower Marsh Street, which harbored the house
number we were seeking, was dustier than any other area in
London proper that summer due to the huge excavation for
the new train station. Waterloo Station it would be named in
years to come, but, as we rode past, it was simply a gaping hole
overrun with rough men moving dirt.

The number we sought, 49 Lower Marsh, was a high crum-
bling house coated with the dust and soot of a century. It
stood locked in a chain of other such dirty houses. Its windows
were small and narrow, its roof steep and bristling with
stovepipes sticking up at all angles like pins in a cushion.

Up four rickety steps perched a tall, thin common door

wearing five small letter boxes up its front like buttons on a shirt. Each box wore a single number, 1 through 5, signifying, we presumed, the different flats. Field knocked upon the door with his murderously knobbed stick, but no one answered. When he tried the doorknob, it gave amenably to his turn and opened into a common hallway commanded by a narrow stair rising up into the darkness. The only door opening off of this common hall bore no number, yet stood ajar, as if eavesdropping upon the comings and goings by the front door. Field, impatient with the lack of interest in his stern knocking, moved to this door and barked: "Who is in there? Come out for the Protectives!"

A woman of not immediately determinable age in a slatternly dressing gown and smoking industriously from a straight-stemmed corncob pipe slouched into the doorway and stared disinterestedly at Field as if he were some itinerant tinker trying to sell her an old pot. Upon closer inspection, this woman was not old (though her face was lined), but not young, either, in her early forties I would wager, yet with strong marks of hardship etched upon her countenance.

"I am an inspector of the Metropolitan Protectives," Field addressed this staring, smoking woman. "We have been told we could find a Mr. John Barsad livin' here."

"Could've found him livin' here two days ago, guv, but he's gone now, he is." The woman spoke with a blithe unconcern, as if she had seen everything there was to see.

"Gone? What do you mean? When?" Field pursued his dogged questioning, knowing that he was too late.

"Left is wot I means"—the woman, with some impatience, blew smoke toward Field's face—"in the middle of the night two nights ago, lock, stock, and all those books, just disappeared he did, a fortnight's rent in arrears."

"Pardon me, ma'am, but who are you?" Field was asking the questions, but Rogers was writing the answers down with a black pencil in a little paper notebook.

"Smithers, Amanda Smithers." There was no annoyance in her answers, only a world-weariness which seemed to ask, Why would anyone care? "It wos Amanda McMurphy once, but

Smithers changed it to Smithers when he married me. He's in Lambeth churchyard these eight years now."

"Mrs. Smithers—"

"Amanda, sir," she interrupted, and actually gave Field a weak smile, as if perhaps she was considering him a candidate to replace poor dead and buried Smithers.

"Yes, Amanda." Field was being unbearably polite. "Can you tell me all about Mr. Barsad? Wot did he look like? Wot did he do? All you knows about him?"

"Yes I can, sir." And she flashed him that coy smile again through the blue cloud of pipe smoke around her netted hair. "Won't you and your gentleman friends come into my parlor?" With that, she waved for us to follow her through her smoke-webbed doorway.

She sat down on a shiny and frayed couch of pale blue velvet and laid her extinguished pipe on a small deal table at her knee. The four of us ranged ourselves around the tiny parlor room, Field taking a seat next to her on the widow's couch, Rogers filling the small wing chair just beside, Dickens pulling the only other chair in the room, a wooden straight-backed specimen, up to the deal table. I leaned as unobtrusively as possible against the sooty mantelpiece.

"Well," Field reopened our colloquy, "tell us about your Mr. Barsad."

"A quiet one he wos, and a strenge lot they wos who come to visit him reg'lar."

"He had regular visitors, did he?" Field gently prodded her.

"He did, uh strenge lot they made, too, the four of them, him and t'other three. All men. They would come in and go right up. I never seen their faces, but they come reg'lar and they stayed late, sometimes the whole night. I always heard them come and seen them go up, in the evenin's, after dark, but I rarely seen them leave. They'd always sneak out after I'd gone to sleep."

"Four men you say"—Field seemed to be turning her information over slowly in his mind—"meetin' regularly here?"

"Yes sir. Two of 'em would come together most of the time. Then lately another one's been comin' by hisself. Kinda strenge, ain't it?" And then she began to get gossipy with Field, moving closer to him on the couch and placing her hand conspiratorially on his knee. "You'd think a handsome man like that quiet Mr. Barsad would want to invite a woman up for tea and fixin's sometime all by herself, wouldn't you?" She paused to note Field's reaction to this confidence, and when he nodded jovially, she went right on. "But he never did, certainly not me he didn't. Our Mr. Barsad just buried himself in all those books of his, and didn't seem to have no time for nothin' except his strenge night meetin's."

"Meetings?" Dickens interposed, providing a brief surcease in the tender exchange of confidences between the Widow Smithers and this newly discovered object of her affections.

"Wot sort of meetin's?" Field drew her attention back.

"Reg'lar meetin's with the same two men goin' up and stayin'. And strenge noises like they wos Papists doin' scaremoneys, strenge noises and movin' about the flat, him talkin' and them answerin'."

"So you would eavesdrop on Mr. Barsad and the men who went up to visit him?" Field stated it congenially enough, but she took immediate offense.

"Not eavesdroppin' no," she bristled. "Checkin' thc hallways each night. It wos my job as mistress of the house."

"Wot did Mr. Barsad look like?" Field abruptly changed the subject.

"He wos a tall man he wos, and he kept very close. Went out to his work most nights, and held his meetin's the only nights he wos home. Always carried a book with him. I pretended he wos a perfesser. That's sort of the name I give him, though I never said it to his face. 'The perfesser' 'cause he read so much."

"And a mustache, right?" Rogers asked, in the way of all lawyers who already know the answers before they ask the questions.

"No, he wos a clean-shaved cove, he wos."

"Tall is right," Field said levelly, "but he had a quite bushy mustache, didn't he?"

"No sir. No mustache." She was looking at all of us strangely. "He shaved himself clean at least every other day."

"No mustache?" Dickens wasn't really addressing her.

"Good lord, are you all deaf? *He had no mustache!*"

"Yes, well, fine." Field regained his conciliatory voice. "We just thought that the man we were lookin' for had a mustache."

"Well he didn't."

"Can you tell us anything else about him?" Field moved on.

She thought a moment, coyly glancing up once to see if Field was looking at her. "His ring," she finally declared.

Both Dickens and Field spoke at the same time. "His ring?"

"Aye, his ring." It was as if she had gone into a brief trance, musing fondly on this morsel of memory. "He wore the most beautiful blue ring. He always held it up to his face when he talked to you, like he'd put his finger to his lips and all you could see wos that ring flashin'. When he talked to me, I always listened to every word he said."

"Did you ever have any trouble with him?" Field asked. "Any violence?"

"No, no, he wos a good one," she protested, "much better than most of the ones, those workmen on the train yard, who takes my rooms. No, until this last fortnight he mostly paid his rents on time, and never caused no fuss." Then, holding up both her hands in a gesture of assurance, she finished by forcefully asserting: "I don't pry, I don't, but I watches them come and go, and I wonders about the noises and the meetin's. A strenge lot they wos, but I don't pry."

"Could we see the rooms he let now?" Coming from Field it was more a quiet demand, her consent taken for granted, than a request.

"He had the attic room." She submitted without question, trying her washed-out little amorous smile on Inspector Field once again. "I'll show you up."

The merry widow fetched her keys and led us up the steep and creaking steps to the top of the house. The rooms were low and dark. Two greasy little windows graced their ends, tucked back into the steep angle of the roofline like discarded and forgotten letters.

She lit the single gas lamp mounted on the wall inside the door. It sent dim fluttering waves of yellow light out over the weirdly angled space. One thin partition with a low curtained door separated the attic into two rooms. There was little to see. The bigger of the rooms was sparsely furnished with a distressed table which served as a desk, two frayed and torn stuffed chairs, and a dirty rug of coarse material that resembled a horse blanket. As we entered, the scurrying sounds of tiny feet brushed across the floor and disappeared into the sooty walls. Field found a pile of guttered-out candles in one corner.

The back room held a low pallet covered with tattered sacking which must have served as the man's bed. Other than these sparse furnishings, the room offered up little in the way of evidence for Field to ponder, except for one item which seemed to momentarily pique his interest. From beneath the ragged bed, Field extracted a pair of rather petite women's bloomers of fine silk. He studied them carefully before giving them into Rogers's keeping. Their fine smooth fabric seemed out of place amidst the coarseness of all the other furnishings.

Inspector Field thanked the enamored Widow Smithers profusely as we descended from those squalid attic rooms. She, in turn, inquired with transparent curiosity into where he could be reached if any more pertinent information came to her mind.

"St. James Station, it is," Field answered with a backward wink to the rest of us. "Just ask for Inspector Collar."

We left her beaming in the doorway in anticipation of her next rendezvous with her new policeman friend.

A murderous sun, the color of blood, hung over that gloomy black river as we crossed Waterloo Bridge. The bells of St. Paul's tolled seven as we lumbered into Bow Street. I cannot speak for Field, Rogers, and Dickens, and I know it was well past the summer solstice, but for myself I can say that it seemed as if we had just lived out the longest day of the year. I was exhausted.

At Bow Street Station, Inspector Field reminded Dickens of our charge for the following day, attaining interviews with the members of the Women's Emancipation Society. The indefatigable Dickens announced his intention to walk back through Covent Garden to the Wellington Street offices, but

I begged off this time and hailed a hansom to transport me to Soho.

All across the West End in that cab, my feet aching, my neck bristling from the oppressive heat, I envisioned an evening's quiet repose in the cool shelter of my flat, a bottle of sherry uncorked, and Irish Meg by my side offering her delicious companionship. The cab delivered me to my door, and I struggled into the building primed for mindless rest, but there is no rest for the wicked.

Irish Meg and Nellie Ternan were waiting for me in the parlor. Dickens's Nellie was in tears.

THIS OTHER LOVE

(August 11, 1852—Evening)

"M eggy? Miss Ternan? What is it? What is wrong?" I could see in their faces that my hopes for a quiet evening were dashed.

"Oh, Wilkie, you've got to help her." Irish Meg opened her argument like a chancery solicitor. "Nellie is beside herself."

How could I not see that? The annoyed question sparked in my mind. *Why did she bring Nellie here? Why didn't they go to Dickens? He is her guardian.* These questions flooded through me and drowned my enthusiasm for this whole affair.

"Of course, of course, Meggy, I will help. Please, Miss Ternan, do not cry. Tell me what is the matter."

Some hypocrite had taken possession of my tongue and was toadying shamelessly to these two women in utter disregard for my desire to simply recline upon the settee (which they had usurped) and doze off.

"Wilkie, it is very hard for her to tell." Irish Meg spoke as if Miss Ternan had no voice of her own. "She is very—"

"Meggy!" I cut her off, unable to conceal my impatience. "Let her speak. Let *her* tell me what is wrong."

Meg shot one of her withering looks at me, but did not proceed. Instead, she returned to comforting Nellie with an arm around her shoulder and her lips whispering in her ear.

"Miss Ternan," I finally said in a quite even and controlled voice, "I am very sorry if I have been sharp, but it has been such a long and shocking day, and you and Meggy caught me by surprise. Please forgive me. I wish only to be of help. Please, tell me what is wrong and what I can do."

She slowly raised her eyes to mine. They were filled with pain and fear. I was afraid that she was about to burst into tears again. But I was wrong. Somehow, she found her voice, though her words were fragmented and shaken.

"It . . . it . . . it is Eliza Lane . . . who was . . . oh lord . . . who was . . . murdered." That last terrible word drove her to bury her face in her hands once again.

But Meggy, who had her firmly by the shoulders, purred in her ear, "It is all right Nellie, it is all right. You can tell him. He will understand and help us, he will."

Thus bolstered, Miss Ternan raised her frightened eyes and, haltingly, attempted once again to speak.

"I saw her . . . the poor murdered girl . . . I was with her that afternoon. Oh, Mr. Collins . . . I'm so afraid they will think I killed her."

With that frightened admission she again buried her head in Irish Meg's shoulder, which was already wet with her tears.

Meggy's and my eyes met. She must have seen the plea for help in mine because she gave me a quick nod and, in a gentle, almost motherly voice, coaxed Nellie back.

"You must tell him all of it, Nellie," Meg cajoled. "He is the only one who can help us. Trust me, he will help. He is a good man."

What my Meg said about me made me forget all of my fatigue and annoyance.

"Yes, tell me Nellie," I responded to Meg's challenge. "I am totally at your service."

"It's the . . . the scarf I fear," her voice shook.

My eyes darted to Meggy's, questioning.

"Tell him about the scarf," Meggy whispered in her ear.

"Meggy said it was a bright green scarf," Miss Ternan took up her narrative, seeming to steady a bit, "that killed Eliza."

She stopped briefly for breath, but did not break down. "I fear it is my scarf that killed her."

"Yours? But how?" I suddenly felt terribly out of my depth.

"She took it away with her that afternoon." Nellie seemed almost mesmerized by the narrative she felt compelled to spin out. "I gave it to her . . . as a present. She admired it, and she seemed so lost and unhappy, and then Meggy told me she was . . . choked with it."

"But why were you together that afternoon?" I asked.

"That is the hard part to tell," Meggy interceded. "It is sick and not Nellie's fault."

"What is it? You must tell me." I turned my attention back to Miss Ternan. "Did she threaten you? Try to blackmail you?"

"No, no, worse." Miss Ternan seemed once again on the verge of breaking down at the enormity of it.

"She tried to make love to her." Irish Meg usurped Nellie's voice once again. "That is why it's so hard for her to tell it."

Meggy's trying to make it easier seemed to spark her own courage. Immediately Nellie found her voice, and it was stronger and more detached, as if she were telling a story in which she and the murdered woman were mere characters.

"She has been bothering me for weeks," she began. "Touching me, hugging me—once she kissed me on the mouth. She said she saw me onstage in the play dressed as a man. She has asked me to go with her and the others, Marie I think, though Marie has never done any of this to me."

"Done what to you?" I was taken utterly by surprise at the direction in which this conversation had turned.

"Talked of love, this other love, tried to lure me. Eliza only did it when we were alone, but she was always in Marie's company. I had decided they were lovers."

"Who is this Marie?" I turned to my Meggy for help.

"Marie de Brevecoeur, the Frenchwoman who dresses like a man." Meggy taunted my flawed memory. "I've told you about her before."

"What did this Lane woman say to you?" I turned back to Nellie Ternan.

"She was at our rooms that afternoon. That was the first time she threatened me."

"Threatened you!" my voice betrayed my alarm.

"Yes," Nellie went on, "for weeks she had made her perverse advances and I had rebuffed them, but yesterday she threatened me with exposure over the Ashbee affair. She seemed to know all about it."

"Good lord! How?"

"I don't know. She knew everything. She said: 'You were raped by a man. You know what men can do.' "

At that, the tears once again welled up in her eyes and I thought we were going to lose her, but she steadied herself.

"She said: 'You know what men can do, and will. Women are different. Have you ever been with a woman?' And she started touching me again, caressing my arms, moving very close to me, whispering, luring."

She seemed utterly lost in her story, speaking in a low, frightened rasp.

" 'Have you ever been with a woman?' Eliza Lane said. 'We do things men cannot do. If you let me do them to you, you would understand.' "

"You say that she tried to blackmail you into this unnatural love?" I pursued that telltale revelation.

"Yes, she knew all about the Lord Ashbee horror." And the poor thing sank once again into Irish Meg's arms, sobbing.

I waited a moment until her fragile emotions subsided, and then addressed her as tenderly as I could: "How did you reply to her blackmail demands?"

"She told her to go stuff it, she did!" Irish Meg cut in.

I silenced her with a grim scowl. *Let the woman tell her own story,* I glared.

"I told her that I couldn't pay her, that I had no money," Miss Ternan said, and roused herself to continue her narrative. "But that was when she said that it wasn't money she wanted. 'What I want,' she said, 'is to see you naked.' That is when I fled into my bedroom, and locked the door against her. I did not come out until I was sure that she was gone. She took my green scarf away with her. Oh God, and now she is killed with it!"

"It is . . . it is . . . it is monstrous," I finally found the proper word.

Irish Meg's face broke into a scoffing grin. "Not so monstrous," she corrected me, "as some of the things your London gentlemen will pay any street whore to do."

"What did you do?" I changed the subject. "After she had gone?"

"I made myself a cup of tea," Nellie answered, as if it were the most natural thing on earth to do. "Neither Bobbie—that's the name Barbara Smith goes by with us—nor Marian were at home, and I drank my tea and fell asleep, from the shock of it, I suppose. I didn't wake up until Bobbie came in at six and we had to get ready to go to the society meeting." Nellie was speaking very quickly now, in a rush. "Then we went to the meeting. I was terrified that Eliza Lane would be there. I didn't think I could face her, but she wasn't there. Then she came in, and screamed at us. All I wanted was to run away."

I thought a moment. The three of us sat quietly staring at each other, hoping that some solution might arise out of all of our shared confusion. Finally, it came to me.

"But you went home that night, did you not? Surely Miss Smith and Miss Evans were there, can attest to your being in for the evening well before the time of the murder."

"But Wilkie, that is the problem." Irish Meg interceded once again as the tears welled up in Nellie Ternan's eyes.

"What do you mean? I don't understand."

"I was with Charles," Miss Ternan burst out in a voice of utter despair.

"She loves him, Wilkie, can't you see?" The tone of Meg's voice pleaded for understanding.

"What do you mean? I don't see at all." I was talking at Miss Ternan but, again, it was Meg who answered.

"She spent the night with him, Wilkie," Meg insisted, speaking meticulously as one would to a slow-witted child. "Don't you see? When Liza Lane wos murdered, Nellie and Mr. Dickens wos together."

"I did not go home from the meeting," Nellie Ternan whispered. "I was with him that whole night. In the St. George Hotel."

It must have been my face, the pure astonishment, which triggered Irish Meg's impatience.

"Good Gawd, Wilkie, don't you hear wot she's sayin'? Do we have to paint you a pitcher?"

I could hardly believe it. Images of her and Charles in bed at the St. George, Laocoönian images, coiled in my mind. Nellie and Charles in bed together . . . in defiance of all propriety, all class and custom, all of the unwritten laws of the gentleman in Victorian society.

Only now was it all coming clear to me. Unless she could prove her whereabouts, she would be taken up for murder, but the one person who could prove her whereabouts could not afford to do so. If Dickens stood up for her, his reputation as a gentleman, his marriage, his position as a leader in society, his charity work, perhaps even his career as England's favorite writer, would be destroyed. Failing to prove her whereabouts that evening could cost Ellen her life, but proving them honestly would most certainly, in another sense, cost Dickens his.

"We, she, Nellie, was afraid to stay at her flat for fear that the Protectives, that other one, would come and take her away," Irish Meg explained. "So I told her she could stay here for the night."

"Collar?"

"Yes, him."

"When he speaks to Bobbie Smith or Marian Evans, they must tell him that I did not come in that night; then he will suspect me and he will come for me." And, once again, she burst into tears.

"Good lord, Miss Ternan"—I fear my exasperation shone through in the roughness of my voice—"you must stop your uncontrolled tears or they shall make you ill."

Irish Meg shot an angry look in my direction

Her look annoyed me. Had I no voice in any of this? I glared back at Meggy in rebellion, but she was too busy comforting Miss Ternan to notice.

"Wot shall we do, Wilkie?" Meg finally looked up from her ministrations.

I had a quite reasonable answer awaiting her: "We shall all go to bed and get a good night's sleep," I declared. "There is nothing to be done about any of this tonight."

For once Meg agreed. At my direction, she guided Nellie Ternan off to our bedroom, where, I presumed, she would tuck her in and, somehow, lullaby her off to sleep before her body was utterly drained of all liquid.

Alone! I felt great joy and relief in my sudden solitude. Not even bothering to undress, I arranged my greatcoat over my exhausted form reclining on the settee when, to my chagrin, Irish Meg glided like a hectoring ghost from the sleeping room to once again prevent me from enfolding myself in the beckoning arms of Morpheus.

"Oh, Wilkie, thank you, you are a brick. She has been sobbin' ever since I told her of the murder this afternoon. She is sure that she's goin' to Newgate to be hung."

Oh God save me, I thought. I feared that Meg wanted to talk, when all I wanted was to sleep.

"But she is so different now that you've talked to her," Meg babbled on.

I pulled the greatcoat up close around my neck, shifted my body to the most comfortable position on that short velvet settee, and attempted to counterfeit sleep, but Meg continued animatedly like some market-day gossip.

"Oh, Wilkie, I'm so scared of all this. Some of these women are so strange."

"How are they so strange, Meggy?" I said with an obvious lack of enthusiasm.

"They's so different from wot I'm used to."

"How's that?" I turned over and tried to bury my head under a small pillow, but Meggy snatched it away.

"Like that time Liza Lane asked me if men ever hired me to make love to other women, and Miss Evans, Nellie's housemate, she came to one meetin' sportin' a big brown lump on the side of her face, and she moved into Mr. Chapman's house but then came back to live with Nellie and Bobbie Smith at Macklin Street. I got my suspicions about some of these ladies, Wilkie."

"But they are not your problem."

"I know that, but Fieldsy makes them my problem. I'm his spy. I probably always will be. Oh, Wilkie, I don't want everyone I meet to always think me a whore."

"They don't, Meggy. I don't. I love you." It was all I could do to keep my eyes open.

"I wants to be respectable, Wilkie, be educated like them, work for a livin' respectable. Oh, Wilkie, you're the only one I can talk to."

Lucky me! I silently mourned.

"You've been so good with her, Wilkie. This afternoon, all she could do wos bury her head in my shoulder and cry. She is always so quiet, so apart, almost invisible you know, at our meetin's, but tonight with you, she seemed to be findin' her voice."

That is fine, I thought, *but just how can you be so sure that she didn't kill her? She has killed before.* How can you be so sure that she was with Dickens? Simply because she says so?* But I was only whistling in the wind. I knew that it was only too possible that she and Dickens had spent the night together, that Charles was her alibi, God help him. That was the last sinister thought I remembered before I plummeted into sleep.

---

*In the affair of "the Macbeth Murders" as narrated in Collins's first memoir, commercially titled *The Detective and Mr. Dickens,* Ellen Ternan, after being drugged and raped by the stage manager Paroissien, killed her attacker with a pair of household shears.

PHANTOM DREAMS

(Looking Backward to a Night Walk in July)

B ut I could not sleep. Restless dreams haunted my fragile slumber. Perhaps I slept for an hour or two. I was, after all, exhausted. But it was a wakeful sleep, and after some time the torment of my tossing and turning left me wide awake on my back on that lumpy settee staring up at the cciling, plagued by the phantoms of my own mind and my tendency toward visions of impending disaster.

I knew that Dickens loved the girl. He had told me so himself in one of his rare moments of personal revelation. We had been walking his beloved night streets perhaps two weeks earlier, only days after the attack upon Miss Burdett-Coutts in the street which my Meggy had foiled. He was troubled that evening. Over dinner he had shown me a copied text of the latest of the threatening letters that Angela had received. Staring up at the ceiling in my sleeplessness, I remembered it as clearly as if it had happened the day before rather than some weeks earlier.

"They are getting more violent, Wilkie," he had prefaced his concern as he spread the letter out on the desk which also served as our dining table when we ate in at the Wellington Street offices. I had seen the first of these letters that afternoon six weeks before at Urania Cottage, but I had not been made privy to the second in the series. That second letter, Dickens had let drop in conversation, had been much like the first, threatening Miss Burdett-Coutts with violence because of both her business and her Urania Cottage philanthropy. I had to agree, however, that this third letter was more disturbing than what I had seen and heard of the other two.

> *Miss Coutts,*
> *Keeper of Whores and Sodomites!*
> *Judgement Day is at hand!*
> *Your Bank will pay!*
> *Your whores will die!*
> *Your life will be misery and pain!*
> *I am watching you, and my time*
> *is coming soon.*
> *the Phantom!*

This letter actually threatened individuals—Angela herself, the inmates of Urania Cottage—and it was peppered with exclamation marks, the most violent form of punctuation. I could not help but think how much the Grub Street tuppenny dreadfuls would love to get their sensation-mongering little hands on it. "Mysterious Phantom Stalks Whores, Sodomites, and Bankers," they would trumpet in their garish running heads.

"This phantom, whoever he or she is, comes right out and declares that it is stalking her." Dickens broke the grave silence which had fallen between us as I read the note.

It was that unsettling letter that made Bow Street Station our first stop that evening after dinner.

"Angela will be there," Dickens had explained when we set off without even having our usual postprandial coffee. "Something must be done and Field has a plan."

When we arrived at the station house and entered the bullpen, Tally Ho Thompson, ex-highwayman, thief, cracksman, swell mobsman, housebreaker, spy, and, God help us,

78

actor, was the first to come forward like a gentleman to shake our hands. Dressed in a brown tweed suit with a matching vest framing a dark cravat and with a jaunty peaked cap on his head, he looked like a Scotsman going out to play at that silly game of golf. He shook our hands enthusiastically. "Mr. Dickens. Mr. Collins." He pumped my hand so aggressively that he spun me off balance and had to reach out to catch me by the arm to steady me. "Uh, sorry sir, haven't seen you for such a stretch."

Inspector Field, Serjeant Rogers, and Angela Burdett-Coutts were also there but greeted us in a more subdued manner than our friend Thompson. Disdaining either preface or pretension, Field plunged directly into the business at hand.

"This foolishness has gone on too long, it has," Field growled. "We should have paid more attention to it when Mr. Dickens brought that first note. By custom, however, writers of letters like these are makin' empty threats."

"But what do you think this latest, more violent, letter means?" Dickens straightforwardly expressed all of our fears.

"Who knows wot it bloody means?" Field was not one to dwell at length on guesswork. "It could be a disgruntled employee or someone upon whom the bank has foreclosed or someone who has been refused a loan. It could be someone who thinks he knows something or someone who thinks he can scare Miss Coutts into paying. Wot it means is not my main concern."

"What then?" Dickens pressed.

"Whoever this letter writer is, he's out to harass Miss Coutts. The violence of this last makes me think this phantom might really mean her harm. He has already once attempted to attack her in the street."

"Better safe, eh?" Dickens agreed.

"Exactly." Field's forefinger scratched decisively at the side of his eye as Rogers nodded sagely in agreement. "And that is why we've brought friend Thompson along tonight."

We all stared blankly at Field, waiting for some explanation.

"Miss Coutts"—he addressed her (as he always did) as though she were a bank rather than a person—"I would like you, just temporary to be sure, to take on Mr. Thompson here as your personal bodyguard, just till we clear up this puzzle of the letters."

"Of course, Inspector, as long as he does not interfere with my movements in the course of business or intrude upon my privacy," she answered.

"Oh, Mr. Thompson knows better than to do that, don't Mr. Thompson?" Field snapped at his familiar.

"Aye guv. 'Course not. Miss won't hardly know I'm here, she won't." He accompanied this declaration with that same mocking grin which called into question the sincerity of any word that maddening Harlequin ever uttered.

Field was not amused by Thompson's facetiousness. He chose, however, not to strike out at it with remonstrance. Instead, he did what initially seemed like a rather strange thing.

"Mr. Collins"—he turned to me—"do you have the time?"

Though it was a quite common, harmless request, it mildly surprised everyone because it had no relevance whatsoever to the discussion of this phantom which had hitherto formed the context of our conversation. Nonetheless, in politeness, I immediately moved to accommodate Inspector Field's request. I reached for my gold repeater, which I wore on a gold fob that led into my right-side vest pocket.

It was gone!

My eyes leapt to Field's face. A tiny grin pursed his lips, and I realized that he had known all along.

Of course it was gone. Whenever I entered Field and Thompson's company my watch tended to disappear like a handkerchief loaned at a funeral.

"Thompson, wot time is it?" And all heads swiveled toward that rogue, who was at that very moment extracting my gold repeater from his coat pocket.

"Half eight by this piece here." He consulted my repeater as if he had no clue as to how it had made its way into his pocket.

It was only a handshake and a slight jostling when I entered the room, I remembered. *That is when he lifted it.*

I found Tally Ho Thompson maddening. He seemed to have reserved me as the butt of his favourite joke. This was no less than the third time he had stolen my watch, and although Field always made him return it, it was all turning into a familiar game which I no longer enjoyed playing.

"I am sorry, Wilkie," Field moved quickly to smooth my ruffled feathers, "but I told Thompson to do it. Just a little demonstration for Miss Coutts." And he turned to that lady. "Your bodyguard is a very talented cove, Miss Coutts. He knows all the ins and outs of how the world works. He'll take good care of you, he will, or he'll have to answer to me." And he shot a grim look at Thompson, accompanied by a punctuating swipe of his forefinger at the side of his eye.

"I'm sure he will, Inspector," Miss Burdett-Coutts laughed, a bit nervously, in agreement.

"Now Thompson"—he addressed him as one would an erring child—"give Mr. Collins back his watch like a good bloke."

Thompson passed it over with yet another flash of that maddening grin.

I took it back, vowing never again to wear it in his presence.

"Thompson as Angela's bodyguard is fine," Dickens returned us all to the subject, "but what must we do to find the writer of these letters?"

"That is exactly wot I intend to do," Field said slowly and evenly, "but unfortunately this particular individual has not yet made a mistake, and, to my discredit, I have not been ready to catch this individual if this individual did make that mistake. That state of affairs, I assure you Miss Coutts, is about to end."

Not a soul in that room could fail to note the determination in his eye and the steel in his voice.

"But I am not the only one who has been threatened." Angela surprised us all with this bit of intelligence. "Miss Smith was accosted and cursed in the street last evening by a figure all wrapped and muffled in a greatcoat despite the heat."

Dickens and I looked quickly at each other. *Could it be?* Was it the same ghostly figure who had attacked Angela and whom Irish Meg had driven off?

"And wot did this, ah, *figure,* say, do?" Field's curiosity was piqued.

"He called her a"—Angela's voice caught for but the briefest instant—"a whore, and he said she would die like all the other whores."

"Duly noted," Field answered. "Perhaps it means something in this affair, but men call after women in the streets of London every night, chase after them, strike out at them."

"But why wearing a greatcoat in the middle of summer?" Angela protested.

"It is curious," Field conceded.

I could not help but think that he was merely humouring her.

"We shall look into this as well," Field hastened to assure her.

"So how are we to proceed, Inspector Field?" Angela asked in her soft, composed voice.

"Thompson will be always nearby. He knows wot to do. As for these letters, they have been delivered to your house and to the bank. We will be ready when the next one arrives. Your bank guards and all of your clerks on the bankin' floor will be told wot to do to catch the messenger. Your house will be watched. We will be ready if this person makes a slip."

Field completed this business with assurances to Angela that he would concentrate all of his energies toward finding this phantom.

She left with Thompson in tow.

At that, Dickens and I bid Field and Rogers good evening.

Out in the street, however, Dickens exhibited an agitation which I knew had only one cure.

"We must walk, Wilkie," he declared. "This is all too disturbing and I fear there is even more to it."

"Charles, what is it?" I asked as we turned out of Bow Street and entered the teeming streets of the West End. He waited to answer until we had passed through the Strand and were well on toward the river.

"Who could be sending these letters?" I prompted him as his long legs drove us along.

"Oh, Wilkie, there are so many possibilities." And with that cryptic remark he actually quickened our pace, lost in thought, as if trying to decide whether to go on, to divulge even more disturbing information.

I always find it amazing how, in looking backward, one remembers things that only prove relevant in the context of future events. That night after the murder and the robbery at Coutts Bank, as I lay plagued by my waking dreams, what Dickens had told to me weeks earlier suddenly made sense. I realized that I had taken an unsuspecting hand in his undoing.

"What is it, Charles?" I finally asked, rapidly losing my breath as I tried to keep up with his breakneck pace on our forced march toward the river. "Stop, and tell me what has gotten you so upset."

He pulled up short and turned to me, a look of pain crossing his face like a dark cloud.

"It's Nellie, Wilkie. I fear she may be involved in all of this."

"But how?"

"I have learned from actor friends that her mother has returned to the city."

"My God!" I gasped. "Has she approached Miss Ternan?"

"No. No." He waved me off. "And I do not think that she will. She knows that Nellie is well protected, and who her protectors are."

"Do you think that she is the author of these threatening notes?" I felt that I had almost caught up with Dickens's headlong flight either toward or away from the truth. Of course, as usual, I was still lagging quite far behind.

"Who knows?" He shrugged his arms in exasperation. "That hag is capable of anything. But no, that is not the worst of it."

By now we were stopped dead beneath a lone streetlamp on some dark cavernous street of Thames-side tenements somewhere between Blackfriars Bridge and the Strand.

"And what could be worse?" I pressed him.

He started back as if I had struck him a blow to the face.

"Oh, Wilkie, she has done so well, become whole again after the horrors of that nightmare. I must protect her, can you not see?"

"Of course, yes, protect, yes, I see," I stammered.

"Certainly you have noticed my feelings for her. I cannot drive her out of my mind, Wilkie. She haunts me."

None of us then were ever comfortable in the presence of such personal emotion. We were such a close and careful lot, and none was ever more guarded than Dickens. Yet here he was confessing to me his most private feelings.

"Good God, Wilkie, I think I am falling in love with this girl." He was almost pleading with me now in a pitiful and helpless way as if he wanted *me* to rescue *him* from this torment. "Do you see what I have gotten myself into? I am cursed. I love her. There, I have said it. Oh, Wilkie, she is all that I can think about."

"But Charles, I—" But he would not let me intrude upon the intensity of his feelings.

"My only comfort is in motion, Wilkie, you know that." His fervent argument raced in like the night mail. "Yet on this, I have been standing still, untracked, for more than a year. It is maddening, Wilkie, can you not see?"

"Yes, Charles, I do see. I think I see." But again he ignored my stammer of incomprehension and plunged forward desperately. He strode like the writer he was, desperate to get the words down on paper before his inspiration fled. I realized that for the last year he had been working on two complicated—good lord, labyrinthine!—works of fiction. *Bleak House* had become the toast of London. His impossible love for Ellen had become the torture of his soul.

"Nemo was the lucky one, Wilkie. He died and no one ever knew he was gone.* Me, I don't know what to do. I love her and I cannot have her. If I could have her, what would I do with her? If anyone knew that I loved her I would be hooted about town like a madman. Yet I love her, God help me, and there is nothing I can do about it. Oh, Wilkie, what under heaven am I to do?"

It was only then that my head cleared and I realized why he had chosen me to tell. It was only then that I realized the terrible torment he was in. His love for Ellen, his concern for, yet aversion to, his wife Kate, his worry for the children, the oppression of his public image, the censure of his age, all of those persistent furies dashed about his mind, tearing at his sanity. What Dickens knew, and I realized, was that he was one of the most visible men of his time and thus could never af-

*Nemo is a mysterious character who dies early in *Bleak House*.

ford the luxury of being himself. Nonetheless, at that moment, he had chosen to be himself to me, and I knew, instinctively, that if I was ever to be truly his friend I must help him.

"If you love her, Charles"—I felt as if I were speaking in a dream—"then you must have her."

"I know, and it terrifies me."

These weeks later, lying there staring up at the ceiling in the darkness of that long night of the day the murder was discovered, I wondered if my well-meant advice had played a major part in causing the predicament that he and his beloved Ellen now found themselves in.

ON THE RUN

༄

(August 12, 1852—Morning)

I lay awake thinking back upon all these things until day broke. Irish Meg and I were awake long before Ellen Ternan. We were both ravenous and soon found ourselves facing each other across our dining table with all the fragments of our meagre pantry spread in disarray between us. The remains of a loaf of bread, a small rotting parcel of cheese, some broken bits of roast, a pitcher of water, a pot of mustard, and a small cabbage had been hurriedly assembled. A pot of hot tea was brewing at the hearth.

"I tell you, Wilkie, I wanted to scratch her eyes out last night," Irish Meg opened our colloquy, "and now she's dead. I don't hardly believe it. She threatened every woman in that room. Any one of them could have killed her. I didn't really care wot Liza Lane said about me, but she wos so hateful to the others. Miss Angela wouldn't hurt a flea and just wants to help other women, and Nellie hasn't done anything wrong."

"This Eliza Lane, she said terrible things about everyone. How did she know all those things?" My curiosity drove our conversation. "Did people talk about their private lives that openly in your meetings?"

"No. Not really. But people can know things about all of us just by watchin' close. But she seemed to know everything. It makes me so angry. Wot I wos in the past seems to haunt me like some phantom."

"What do you mean, things can be watched?" I asked in all innocence.

"All you has to do is listen to me talk and you knows I ain't from the same company as Miss Angela or Barbara Smith. I give myself away, Wilkie. But we're not the things Liza Lane said we are. Women shouldn't say such things about other women. Her truth's all twisted, it is."

"Twisted?"

"I don't know. She wosn't like that in other meetin's, all violent and agitated. But the look on her face this time . . . like she wos under some spell, her eyes all blank. Strange!"

A long pause ensued as we picked over our morsels of food and digested our thoughts.

"Wot are we to do, Wilkie?" Meg demanded, as poor Nellie wandered into the pantry rubbing her eyes and looking as forlorn as if already condemned to the gallows. We both turned to stare at her, somewhat embarrassed that she had caught us talking about her in her absence. But Nellie seemed unaware of what we had been discussing and joined us at the table.

I tried to think of something to say, some solution to Nellie's (and our) predicament. Her scarf, her whereabouts the night of the murder unaccounted for, her past—sooner or later all of those facts must surface in this case and demand explanation. I knew that she could not remain with Irish Meg and me in our rooms hiding out. She must return to her normal pattern of life, or else the appearance of guilt and flight would surely condemn her.

"Nellie, you must go home." I finally broke the awkward silence. "You must not allow the Protectives, this Inspector Collar, to suspect that you are trying to avoid him. We must not invite unwholesome speculation. We must gain some time until Field and Dickens can find the real murderer." It all seemed perfectly reasonable to me. Collar appeared a rather slow-witted policeman, certainly not a match for the redoubtable Field.

That seemed to settle it. For once Irish Meg seemed willing to abide by my advice. Poor Nellie was so confused that I am convinced she would have done anything that anyone suggested. The women combed and dressed themselves for going out. I performed a rudimentary toilette in the pantry and changed out of the shirt I had slept in. Sleepy Rob,* who had become a morning fixture on our street, almost my (and Dickens's) private driver, was dozing on the box of his double hansom at our very doorstep. I roused him with a sharp tap of my stick to his wheel and directed him to Miss Ternan's lodgings.

I certainly could not have foreseen what awaited us in Macklin Street. As we turned the corner into that thoroughfare, I noticed a black Protectives post chaise occupied by two men, one, the driver, on the box, the other sitting waiting in the carriage, pulled up directly in front of Miss Ternan's doorstep.

By sheer reflex, whether out of guilt or fear or some unaccountable protective instinct, I swiftly stuck my head out of the opposite window of our cab and ordered Sleepy Rob to "Drive on" while simultaneously pushing, rather roughly I fear, Miss Ternan to the floor out of sight.

It was Inspector Collar and his man sitting in wait upon Miss Ternan's return. As we drove by on the opposite side of the street, a bright green scarf of fabric being pulled and knotted in Collar's hand caught my eye like sunlight glistening off the barrel of a pistol.

I was horrified at what I had done. Meggy and I were now officially harboring a suspected murderess. My immediate sentiment was to turn back, to give her up, but I knew that Irish Meg would never allow it.

"Oh, Wilkie, that wos close," Meg exclaimed.

"Oh God, they know." A dark cloud of despair passed over

---

*In the affair of "the Medusa Murders" recounted in *The Highwayman and Mr. Dickens,* Sleepy Rob the cabman had played a pivotal role in saving Dickens from harm.

Miss Ternan's face, and I was sure she would once again burst into tears, but she did not.

At the end of the street, I leaned out the window and directed Sleepy Rob to drive us to Wellington Street and Dickens.

TWO GENTLEMEN
AND THEIR CONCUBINES

(August 12, 1852—Morning)

B y not so striking a coincidence, at the very moment that we pulled up in Sleepy Rob's cab at the *Household Words* offices in Wellington Street, who else but Dickens should be disembarking from another cab in front of the building. Before we had even extracted ourselves from our cab, Dickens was charging toward us.

"Where have you been?" he scolded, as if we were errant children late arriving home from school. "I have been searching for you what seems the whole morning. I have been to both Macklin Street and Soho."

"We were at my flat in Soho," I attempted to pacify him.

"I was there but a short time ago."

"You must have just missed us," I assured him. "And Collar is—"

"Waiting for Nellie in Macklin Street. Yes, I know," he finished my sentence for me. "That is why, to warn you, I have been tearing across the city this morning."

"Oh!" My mouth, a moment previous so full of news, dropped.

"Oh?" Irish Meg echoed.

"Oh, Charles." Miss Ternan ran straight into his arms, buried her face in his chest, and clasped him tight right there in the public roadway in the bright sunlight for all of London to see.

He held her close for a long moment, like a father comforting his frightened child, but then pushed her away.

"We must not linger over this turn of events." Dickens spoke quickly in the desperation of the moment. "Inspector Collar is perched like a vulture waiting to carry Nellie off. We must hide her, then we must go to Field."

"But where, how?" I stared dumbfounded at Dickens with my hands stretched out in a shrug of helplessness.

He pondered our dilemma a long moment.

I became acutely conscious of our vulnerability to prying or suspicious eyes, the four of us, standing there in bright daylight, in the public way, discussing murder.

Irish Meg was waiting, impatiently I am sure, with a look that fell somewhere between fear and frustration, for us men to decide.

Nellie stood tearful by her side.

It came to us both in the same breath of time.

"The shooting gallery," I blurted out.

"Yes, the shooting gallery," Dickens agreed.

We, all four, crowded into Sleepy Rob's cab and proceeded to Leicester Square and Mince Lane at that worthy's usual plodding pace.

Trotting across the West End, I had a moment to actually stop and think about what we were doing. I remember it as one of those junctures in time when the reality of events tends to overwhelm one. I realized the enormity of the rash decision we had made. We were harboring a suspected murderess, a fugitive from the Protectives. I was terrified at our prospects, but could not help but thrill to the danger, the risk, that Dickens was relentlessly teaching me to court. Writing about these feelings from a distance of twenty years is like trying to write a dream.

Sleepy Rob's cab clattered up Mince Lane and thumped to a bumpy stop on the dingy doorstep of Captain Hawkins's Shooting Gallery. In bright daylight this establishment presented an even more squalid face to the world than it did in the gaslit evening when all of the other disreputable establishments of the gaudy Leicester Square vicinity—the gaming parlors, pawnshops, drinking rooms, and low houses—were open and huckstering.

Dickens stepped out and banged hard three times on the shooting gallery door. He had ordered us to stay within until it was opened, and we did so. What seemed an eternity passed as Dickens waited at that smudged and bolted portal. Finally, it opened a crack, then a dark crevice.

"Who's there?" a raspy voice from within challenged.

"We are friends of Inspector Field," Dickens reassured that suspicious gatekeeper.

The door crept open warily to reveal Broken Bert Moody, that twisted conglomeration of spare parts. He stepped out onto the curbstone perched on his wooden leg, leaning on his wooden crutch, and squinting at us with his one good eye in the bright sunlight. His dirty green parrot sat like a ship's figurehead on his crooked shoulder and stared balefully at Dickens.

"You're the writer fella wot broke Tally Ho out of keep, arn'tcha?" Broken Bert recognized Dickens.*

"Yes, I am," Dickens confessed.

"Come aboard then, mate," Bert welcomed him.

"Cart yer bloody arse on board, mateys," the profane parrot chirped distinctly.

Dickens motioned for us to descend and ordered Sleepy Rob to wait, and the four of us, the two gentlemen and their concubines, followed that lurching apparition and his foulmouthed parrot into the dark interior of the shooting gallery.

Within, in the dim yellow light of two gas lamps set at either end of a high counter strewn with an odd collection of dueling pistols and fowling pieces, we were greeted cordially by Captain Hawkins himself, the proprietor of this sorry excuse for a place of violent entertainment. Over six feet tall, with the broad shoulders of a wrestler and the shorn bullet-head of a

*In *The Highwaymen and Mr. Dickens*, Dickens was instrumental in helping Tally Ho Thompson escape from Newgate Prison.

convict, Captain Hawkins presented a fearful, intimidating presence which was immediately belied by his cordial welcoming voice and his outstretched hand.

"Mr. Dickens, sir, it is an honor, it is, to see you again. Any friend of Fieldsy's is always welcome here at George and Bert's humble house."

"Flog the focking fops," Serjeant Moody's filthy parrot chimed in quite jovially.

Dickens took Captain Hawkins's hand even as that worthy was apologizing for his shipmate's profane parrot.

"We have a problem, Captain, that only Field can solve." Dickens waved off his apologies and started right in. "These ladies need a safe harbor where they will not be bothered until Inspector Field can be found and put on the case."

"Serjeant Moody, fix tea for the ladies." Hawkins hesitated not a moment in deciding.

"Whores an tarts! Whores an tarts!" Serjeant Moody's familiar screeched as his master on his wooden leg and wooden crutch lurched toward their modest galley on the hearth.

It was all I could do to keep from laughing at that perverse bird's wild pronouncement. It had no idea how close to the truth it had come.

Hawkins again burst out in a broadside of apologies for the bird's foul language, but Dickens waved him off and drew him aside into the dim light by the paper targets for a private colloquy. Money changed hands, I am sure. Hawkins tried to refuse, but Dickens would have none of it. I remained with the women, but could not protect their ears from the continuing epithets of Serjeant Moody's obscene appendage.

"Fock theer beards an boff theer bottoms," the bird chirped merrily from his perch on poor Broken Bert's higher shoulder. "Meat for the cocks o' the crew, they be! Meat for the cocks o' the crew," it trilled gleefully like a ship's boatswain piping aboard a fresh cargo of provisions.

Dickens and Captain Hawkins returned from their private consultation. The hulking captain was all courtliness and concern for the ladies' comfort. He produced out of the gaslit shadows two wooden kitchen chairs for them to sit upon and bustled off to help Serjeant Moody and the parrot with the tea.

"You must stay here, Nellie, until we can find Field and decide what to do. Somehow, Collar must be kept off. Field will find a way." Dickens spoke softly, like a father to a child. "Meggy will stay with you. We will return as soon as we can."

With those swift words we left them with those two old soldiers at the shooting gallery. It was almost noon when we climbed back into Sleepy Rob's hansom cab and set off for Bow Street Station.

What better experience could I ever get for the writing of novels? We were moving ourselves and other characters around the city, designing plots. My sole complaint was that I had always envisioned writing novels, not living them.

MOTHERLY LOVE

(August 12, 1852—Noon)

Neither Dickens nor I was prepared for the surprise witness lying in wait at Bow Street Station. We burst into the bullpen full of our dilemma and were brought up as short as two taunted guard dogs snapped back at the end of their tethers. Sitting uncomfortably in a straight-backed wooden chair before the cold hearth under the obvious interrogation of Inspector Field and Serjeant Rogers was Mrs. Peggy Ternan, the despicable mother of Dickens's tender fugitive. We gaped at her in astonishment. Peggy Ternan was tall and wide-shouldered, even when sitting down. This stature best explained the power she was capable of exerting as an actress on the stage. Even though she was a woman of almost fifty years, and rather heavily rouged, you could still see her daughter Ellen's beauty in her face. They shared the same wide forehead and intelligent expanse between the eyes culminating in those clean high cheekbones. Yet this older woman, the mother, was hardened and marked by years of corruption and a life of deceit. From the tight sour look she shot at us, it was clear that she was not voluntarily enjoying the company of our detective colleagues.

"Aha! Charles and Wilkie"—Field mimicked politeness and formality—"you both remember Miss Ternan's bawd of a mother."

"I'm an actress," the witch shot back in her haughtiest stage elocution, "and have been all of my life."

"You are an old whore, and a bawd who sold her own daughter,* and I'm goin' to make you for a blackmailer if you don't tell me the honest truth right now!"

Field, standing right over her, was screaming down into her painted face in the throes of his most dramatic wrath. That noxious woman was not the only stage actor in the room.

"You have been writin' threatenin' letters to Miss Angela Burdett-Coutts, haven't you?" Field pressed on. "We knows it wos you who wos harassin' her because you're the only one who knew wot to write. We can hang you for threatenin' respectable people, we can. Just like we hang thieves and housebreakers, we can," Field finished his harangue in a voice full of hard, quiet menace.

"I . . . I . . . I did not write the notes," the hag, visibly shaken by Field's angry assault, stammered. "He made me tell him what to write. They knew that the Coutts woman . . . of the bank . . . had bags of money."

Serjeant Rogers was busily noting everything down.

"Who is 'he'? How did he, whoever he is, force you? Did he say he knew Miss Coutts? Did he say he knew your daughter? Where did you meet him?" Field battered her unmercifully with questions until she buried her face in her handkerchief, her chest heaving, in the finest of stage hysterics.

Utterly undaunted by her theatrics, Field clamped down upon a fistful of her hair and roughly pulled her head up out of her hands. Her eyes were perfectly clear, and her cheeks were dry.

"Don't play your false lying games with me, you old whore," Field spat into her face, still holding tightly his handful of her hair. "Answer me. Who forced you, and where?"

---

*As recounted in *The Detective and Mr. Dickens,* it was Field's speculation that Peggy Ternan the mother was intent upon selling her fifteen-year-old daughter Ellen's virginity to the highest bidder.

"They came to my rooms, more than a fortnight, two fortnights, ago, in the spring."

"They? Who is they?"

"There were three of them, two men and a woman."

"Who were they?"

"That is it. I do not know."

"Wot! If you lie to me, woman . . ." Field's voice was heavy with threat.

"I had only been back in London a short time. I had gotten a small part in Drury Lane's *School for Scandal*, not what I was used to at all, but I had not worked in the city for more than a year and they forget you very quickly in London. Honestly, I had not gone near Nellie. I stayed away from her as you told me."

"We don't care about any of that!" Field rudely interrupted her. "Tell us about the threatening letters."

"I did not write any letters. I did not even know about any letters until you started waving them in my face when I came out of the theatre this evening."

"Get on with it, woman," Field barked, his patience rapidly ebbing.

Dickens and I looked on with a kind of mesmerized horror.

Rogers, seemingly oblivious of the heightening violence in the exchanges between his master and the woman, simply kept scribbling every word on his notepad.

"It was a warm night. They must have followed me up from the street because when I got out my key to let myself into my rooms, they were on me right away."

She paused to take breath, but Field stared down at her as if looking for an excuse to strike her. Instead, he gave one sharp tap to the back of her wooden chair with his forefinger.

"There was a regular gang of them. Two men and a woman. The man with the mustache did all the talking, the others hung back. 'Here, let us help you in, missus,' he said, and he plucked my keys right out of my hand."

"He had a mustache, you are sure," Field interrupted.

"Bushy handlebar mustache," she confirmed. "Oh, he was a charmer, he was, a tall man with deep blue eyes and the most beautiful bright blue ring I have ever seen. He held it right up to my face while he talked to me. I couldn't take my eyes off of it."

"Go on, wot did he say?" Field had calmed.

"He opened the door and they all came right in. It was dark, so he told me to light the lamps. 'You're Mrs. Ternan,' he said, 'the murderer's mother.' The others stayed back, by the door, but he stood right up close, and that is when I noticed his blue ring. He held it right up next to his face when he talked."

"Wot did he ask?" Field's voice was cajoling, almost soothing, as he coaxed her story out.

"He asked me all about my Ellen, and where she was, and what she had done, and how she had gotten there, and I think I told him everything. It was very strange, as if I was in some sort of trance, but I remember everything, his ring, his questions about Ellen, the women by the door."

"Women?" Field leapt at this slip of her tongue.

"There was a woman, a large woman with broad shoulders. She stood by the door."

"But you said *women?*" Field pressed.

"I did?" the old wench seemed genuinely puzzled. "I did not mean to. There was a woman with the men, I think. I'm sure that was a woman, but I did not get a very good look at all of them. The man with the ring was standing between us."

"And then wot?" Field's voice was seductive.

It was obvious to Dickens and me that Field's witness was wearing down.

"The last thing he asked me was how she got into Miss Coutts's house for whores and why she wasn't brought to the bar for murder, and I told him I did not know, but thought it was all done by Mr. Dickens and you, sir, who warned me to stay clear of her and move on."

"And that wos it!" Field shouted again, so startling her with his suddenness that she raised her hands in front of her face in fear that he might strike her. "You used my name to this stranger in this business. I ought to throw you into Newgate for that alone and let you rot out the rest of your wretched life."

"I'm sorry. I'm sorry." The old hag seemed visibly shaken. "But I did not know what I was doing, as if I had no choice and had to tell him everything he asked."

All the while Dickens had been listening intently, but at this the forefinger of his right hand leapt to his lips in a sharp instinctive gesture of recognition. From the look on his face, I was sure that he was about to intrude upon Field's interrogation of the hag, but he didn't. He waited, listening, as Field continued badgering the woman.

"So wot did he do then, woman? After you told him that I wos on the case?"

"He looked at me hard and told me not to say a word to either you or Mr. Dickens. Then he gave me two half crowns, and the whole lot of them left. That was it, all of it. I haven't seen them since."

Field glared silently down at her.

She looked up for a moment, waiting for him to scream at her again, but he did not, and she could not hold his murderous gaze. She turned her eyes like a trapped animal first to Dickens and then to me. Finding no sympathy in our faces, however, she ducked her head and became intent upon her nervous fingers working the folds of her handkerchief in her lap.

"Rogers, get her out of here." Field finally turned away in disgust, as if she were one of those foul river smells that wafted through the window whenever a whisper of a breeze taunted the stagnant air. "Make her sign the statement you have taken, then turn her out," he ordered.

Rogers leapt to do his bidding.

No sooner had the door closed upon her than Dickens was crossing the room to Inspector Field.

"The blue ring," Dickens said, talking almost to himself as if thinking aloud. "She kept mentioning it, as if it was fixed in her mind's eye."

"So?" Field stared quizzically. "All women likes baubles."

"No." Dickens was still musing on it, caught in a deductive

dialogue with himself. "No, I have studied this. He was using the ring upon her. I think this man is a mesmerist."*

*According to Dickens's most recent biographer, Peter Ackroyd in *Dickens* (1990), Dickens was somewhat of an authority on "mesmerism." As early as 1838, he had attended mesmeric sessions conducted by John Elliotson, a professor of clinical medicine at University College Hospital in London. After attending four such sessions, Dickens wrote: "I am a believer. I became so against all my preconceived opinions and impressions." Later, when Elliotson lost his position at the hospital due to the "sensational" aspects of his researches, Dickens supported him financially and made him the Dickens family doctor. Elliotson's particular technique was to cast his subjects into a deep trance and then provoke them to acts of extraordinary behavior by means of what he called "animal magnetism." It is also documented that Elliotson actually taught Dickens the art of mesmerism, at which Dickens became rather adept. Ackroyd's commentary on this is especially telling in the context of Collins's memoir of events fourteen years later: "Of course all this was connected, too, with nineteenth century ideas of power and dominance—particularly the male over the female . . ." (244).

"YOU MUST GIVE HER UP!"

(August 12, 1852—Early Afternoon)

A wot?" Field exclaimed.

"A mesmerist?" I lamely echoed Dickens's strange pronouncement.

We both stared in astonishment at Dickens.

Not only was he serious, but he fancied himself an authority upon the subject. Hesitating not a whit, he charged into his explanation: "Don't you see? He uses the ring to capture his subject's attention, to lure him into the mesmeric trance. Once he draws him or her into his power with the subtle movement of the ring, he can control him, make him do anything he tells him, or, in this case, make the subject tell him anything he wants to know. Remember his landlady in Lambeth? She, too, remarked the ring."

"You *are* serious." I was still mired in my customary skepticism.

"He can do that?" Field's curiosity had bested his skepticism.

"I can do it," Dickens answered brightly. I actually think that Field was about to challenge him to cast a spell, but he never got the chance.

At that very moment, Inspector Collar and his man barged into the bullpen.

"Now see here, Field"—Collar dispensed with all of the amenities—"the girl has disappeared and I suspects you and Mr. Dickens here knows more about it than I do."

Luckily, Field truly knew nothing about Ellen Ternan's disappearance, and, therefore, his reaction to Collar's wild accusation was genuine. Having arrived at Bow Street when the interrogation of old Peggy Ternan was already under way, we had not yet had the opportunity to apprise Field of the facts of Miss Ternan's involvement and sequestered state. Thus, when Field's mouth dropped open in a look of utter incomprehension, and when his shoulders and hands shrugged outward in a gesture of surprised ignorance, he was in no way acting.

Dickens and I said not a word.

I risked a guilty glance in his direction, but he silenced me with a tight-lipped glare.

"I'm sorry, Inspector Collar." Field was all politeness. "But you have me at a disadvantage. Wot girl has disappeared, and wot are Mr. Dickens and me supposed to know about it?"

"Miss Ternan. She's gone. And I knows all about her, and you and Mr. Dickens's connections with her. There's a private file at Central Station."

I could not help glancing at Charles. His face was a total cipher. He was waiting, I am sure, counting upon Field to handle this crisis of credibility.

"Ah yes, Central Station, where the clerks buzz like worker bees." Field sighed in resignation. "Yes, you are quite right," Field confessed, glancing quickly at Dickens. "I know of Miss Ternan."

"You know she is a murderess—"

"But I know no such thing." Field stopped him right there. "She wos, indeed, a witness to a murder case some eighteen months past, and Mr. Dickens is, indeed, her guardian, and she is of the acquaintance of this murdered woman, but that is the all of it as I knows it." Field delivered this speech with a calm equanimity that utterly disarmed Inspector Collar.

"Then you do not know where Miss Ternan has gone"—

Collar's voice was in full retreat from its accusatory belligerence upon entering—"and you have not interviewed her in reference to this particular case?"

"No sir, I have not." Field looked him full in the face while delivering this denial. His whole mien bespoke that it would be unthinkable for one officer of the law to lie to another.

It was nothing less than a miracle that we had not yet had the opportunity to tell Ellen's story to Field, whose straightforward denial had the immediate effect of reducing Inspector Collar to a succession of "hems" and assorted "haws" as he groped for a way to smooth over his unconsidered accusation of Field's collusion in the case.

"Ahem, uh, considering the girl's past record, and your, well, her, ahum, what I mean is . . ." A strained cough strangled in his throat. "Um, Miss Ternan has not been home for two days, ahem, and she happens to be a suspect in this murder at Coutts Bank. We have certain evidences that ties her to the case."

"That *is* interesting." Field feigned fascination. "Please, I am curious. Wot makes you think she is the one."

"Yes, Inspector." Dickens suddenly found his voice. "Please tell us. This is absurd. Miss Ternan could never commit such a horrible crime."

"She wos suspected of doin' one just as horrible once before," Collar answered.

"Yes," Field agreed solemnly, "but there wos no proof in that case. Wot makes you think she is guilty of murder now?"

"It wos her green scarf that strangled Miss Eliza Lane." Collar showed Field his hand, extracting his winning card, that bright green scarf, from the pocket of his jacket.

Field flinched as if he had been dealt a blow to the chin.

"But she is neither tall enough nor strong enough to strangle a woman of such stature." Dickens, speaking rapidly, in a passion, argued her case as if he were before a magistrate. His vehemence proved valuable as it temporarily distracted attention from Field's momentary confusion and gave that worthy a chance to collect himself.

But before Collar could answer, we were all further distracted by the sudden entrance of Serjeant Rogers.

"The witness has signed, sir," Rogers began, "and Mrs.—"

"Ah! Yes. Thank you, Rogers," Field cut him off. "Release her. We knows where she bides. She'll not get away from us."

Rogers was caught up short by Field's abruptness, but, without questioning, turned on his heel to do his master's bidding.

Dickens exchanged a quick glance of relief with me. It signaled what was slowly registering in my own comprehension of the situation. Even though Field knew nothing yet of Nellie's involvement in Eliza Lane's murder or of Nellie's whereabouts, he was already instinctively protecting her from the eager suspicions of Collar, intuitively colluding with Dickens and me in the harboring of our fugitive. I have never ceased to marvel at the acute perception of Field. He could read a situation faster than any man I have ever met. Without the slightest prompting, he seemed able to choose by instinct the right course of action.

"Wot wos that?" Collar asked offhandedly as Rogers disappeared out through the door.

"Oh nothing," Field covered up the intrusion, "just a witness in another case. But Miss Ternan? I have heard nothin' of any of this. Her scarf? Is she really gone, fled? It does not sound like her."

"No," Dickens broke in before Collar could answer, "it most certainly does not. It is not like her at all."

He is protesting too much, I thought, but Collar, locked in his territorial battle with Field, did not seem to note Dickens's vehemence.

"It is her scarf, quite so," Collar hastened to answer. "Her name, 'Nellie Ternan,' and the words 'Urania Cottage' are sewn with white thread right here in the corner." He handed the scarf over to Field. "And she never came home the night of the murder, nor last night, neither. Her housemates do not know where she's gone. We waited all mornin' at her house, but she never arrived." His silent serjeant nodded violently in support of that fact.

"Perhaps she is just off visitin' relatives in the country," Field said, and then, as if some mischievous devil made him say it, with a quick flick of his crook'd forefinger to the side of his eye, he added, "her mother, perhaps."

Dickens darted a look in my direction. It was all that either of us could do to keep from bursting out with laughter at Field's cruel wit.

"In the middle of the night leavin' for the country?" Collar countered. "I do not think so."

"Ah, but she did not leave in the middle of the night." To my horror, it was my own voice I heard.

"How do *you* know?" Collar snapped, as the company, including Rogers, who had just come back into the room, turned to stare at me.

"Because I know that she spent last evening, and quite possibly the whole night—she frequently does—with my private secretary, Miss Margaret Sheehey, whose rooms adjoin mine in Soho."

"You saw her?"

"Yes, I did."

It was not wholly a lie, but what horrified me was that I told it almost involuntarily. When I heard my own voice divulging information there was no need to divulge, I was sure it was someone else.

"She departed this morning with Miss Sheehey," I added.

I glanced quickly at Dickens, and he was staring wide-eyed at me, whether in horror, or simply in surprise, I cannot say.

Field looked at me as if I were an idiot he would like to strangle, but that was often the way he looked at me.

"Do you know where she has gone?" Collar pressed me.

"No, I don't." With that, I was fully committed to lying. Swift images of being hung on the gallows in Newgate yard flashed in my mind's eye. "They went out before I awoke this morning."

Then Inspector Collar did a curious thing. He turned suddenly upon Dickens as if, perhaps, Charles had been his prey all the while.

"And Mr. Dickens, have you seen your young ward the last two nights?"

Dickens was startled, yet he did not hesitate. He, too, chose to lie.

"Why no, I have not. I have been with Mr. Collins both nights before retiring to my offices in Wellington Street, where

I make my abode during the workweek in the city. My family, presently, is in Dover."

"Ah yes, well, no help here it seems," Collar said sourly as he wedged with both hands his square brown hat down upon his square bald head and turned to go. His man pivoted like one of the palace guards to follow him.

"We still wish to follow this case," Field petitioned cheerily as they made their way to the door, "and be of any assistance that we can. If you could keep us informed . . ."

Dickens and I stayed back in the bullpen as Field showed them out. When our eyes met, the guilt we shared seemed almost palpable.

"Well now, that wos a close one, were it not, now gents?" Field was deceptively jovial when he returned with a puzzled Serjeant Rogers in tow. "Does you two swells feel like tellin' me just wot the devil is goin' on here?"

We quickly told him almost all of it, if not the whole truth of it. We told him of Eliza Lane's unnatural advances toward Nellie, of her taking Nellie's scarf away with her that afternoon before the murder, of Nellie spending the night with Irish Meg, of our hiding her in Captain Hawkins's Shooting Gallery. But the one thing we still held back was the most important thing of all, where Dickens and Ellen Ternan had spent the night of the murder.

He pondered the whole story for a long moment, then asked the inevitable question: "But that fool Collar says Miss Ternan did not come home the night of the murder in Coutts Bank. Where wos she that night?"

An oppressive silence closed over us like a thick fog. We seemed suspended there in time, as if the whole world were holding its breath.

"Why, she, she came home with Meggy and me that night, too." Even as I spoke I felt the noose tightening as I mounted lie upon lie up to my own private gallows.

To this day, I do not know why I felt compelled to lie for Charles. Of course, I wished to protect him. For a Victorian gentleman of the stature of a Charles Dickens, the worst threat was to his reputation, the public image that his vast reading audience held of their great man. Married, a public figure, the moral voice of his age, it would be death to be caught in a hotel room with such a young woman, and an actress to boot. But there was more to it than that. He had given me my life. I had freely chosen to follow him everywhere, so it seemed only natural that I should lie for him as well. But the worst part of this was that in lying for Dickens I was betraying Field, and that was a dangerous thing to do.

Field seemed to accept my lie without further thought, and gratitude for it fairly beamed out of Dickens's eyes.

" 'Tis a gang of ruffians have done this," Field declared, "all led by this French cove. First their aim wos at blackmailin' Miss Burdett-Coutts, but then their aim turned to the robbin' of her bank."

"But then why was the Lane woman murdered in the bank?" It was Dickens's turn to press.

"And why wos she dressed in men's clothes?" Serjeant Rogers, who thus far had not participated at all in our deliberations, piped in.

"That's it!" Field sharply rapped the back of his thick rocker with his forefinger. "That's it, Serjeant. It's not a gang of ruffians at all. They're all women they are, all women in men's clothes, except for our friend Frenchy with his magic ring and his disappearin' mustache. He is the leader of the gang, I'll wager me walkin' stick."

We looked at one another, each of us mulling the strangeness (and the logic) of Field's scenario.

"We must talk to all of the women in that group." Field was not dwelling upon the strangeness of this revelation, but rather planning our next step. "Meggy can help you. You two approach as many of the literary ladies as you can this afternoon. We must make quick work of it. Rogers and I will try to find the two who dress like men. It is these women will lead us to that night guard, Frenchy, I am convinced of it."

"But what of Miss Ternan?" Dickens asked. She was never out of his mind.

There was an uncharacteristic tenderness in Field's voice that rarely raised its head above his exceedingly rough exterior as he faced Charles: "You know, Charles, do you not, that you must give her up."

For a moment my mind raced and I didn't know quite what Field meant. *Does Field know that Nellie is his mistress?* I thought. *Does Field mean that he must give her up? Or that he must surrender her to Collar?* Of course, he meant the latter.

Dickens was speechless, staring sightlessly at Field.

"You know that the longer you keep her hidden, the more she looks like a murderess."

Both Dickens and I breathed a collective sigh of relief. Of course Field was right, but the important thing was that he did not yet know the real facts of the case of Dickens and his Ellen. More surprising was the gentle tone of kindness with which Field spoke. For all of his murderous intimidation of the denizens of his world, at that moment Field was a friend. What I had come to realize was that their relation was not based solely upon utility, the using of one another for their own purposes, as it had been at the beginning.*

"I would like to find this murderer before Collar finds Miss Ternan," Field continued, "but I don't think it can be done. Really, the best thing is to give her up."

"But . . . but they shall take her off to Newgate." The strain and worry made Dickens's voice waver. "They will charge her with murder!"

"Perhaps, but the scarf alone is not enough." Field was trying to be reasonable with a man in love, which was akin to asking a gorilla to light your cigar. "I am certain you and Mr. Collins can concoct some story of her whereabouts. Tell Collar she wos off in the country visitin' her mother," he chuckled.

Even Dickens, who was listening to Field like a man staring straight up at the blade of the guillotine, had to laugh, but his mind was working at high speed.

"We shall get Jaggers of the Middle Temple," Dickens said. "He will shield her from Collar."

---

*In their first case together, recounted in *The Detective and Mr. Dickens,* this unusual friendship had begun because Field realized that Dickens and Collins could gain access to places, such as the private gentlemen's clubs and the private homes of lords of the realm, and gather information which he or his men could not. Dickens, of course, with his adventurous spirit, was more than happy to become Field's agent in these investigations.

"Perhaps," Field speculated, "or perhaps his presence right off will just make Collar more suspicious, inflame him to press harder."

"But she is innocent." Dickens's voice was almost a wail of frustration. "She must be protected!"

Aha, Saint George to the rescue once again, I thought.

"Of course she is." Field's voice was all pacification. "I knows that, and you knows that, but Collar thinks she is his murderer. . . ." Field paused for effect like an actor delivering a climactic line. "And until I can prove she is not, we need to keep Collar in hand. Do you not see, all we are doin' is stealin' a little time while I try to figure this whole affair out."

"What do you mean?" It was all moving too fast for Charles to comprehend.

"Do you not see?" Field had turned up the heat of his persuasion. "If Collar has your Miss Ternan in hand, it will distract him from this case. With all the attention on the suspected murderess, it will keep the robbery and Coutts Bank out of the public eye."

Dickens was not happy. Again he started to protest, but Field cut him off.

"Do you not see? Our investigation is well under way. If Collar thinks he has got his murderer, he will not be underfoot."

Dickens seemed to collapse inward upon himself, to deflate like one of those huge festive hot-air balloons that we once observed floating over the park in Paris. He surrendered with a silent shrug of his hands. He was already dreading having to break the news to his Ellen.

Field never gave Dickens a chance to reconsider. He leapt instantly to logistics and timing. "Give her up to Collar at St. James Station tomorrow morning," he advised. "That will give us at least a one-day lead on findin' the real gang who did this. Tell him any story you want about her whereabouts. Then, later, go get your precious Jaggers to speak for her. Maybe he can keep her out of Newgate, but I doubts it."

Dickens acquiesced with yet another silent shrug.

"Leave her at Hawkins's place for today"—Field had subtly shifted into the giving of orders—"and go speak to those other women for me. We must find out all we can about this gang of women dressed as men or wotever they are. Meanwhile, I'll make sure they cannot leave the city."

With that, our discussion came to an abrupt end. Field nodded silently to Serjeant Rogers, who opened the bullpen door and stood aside for us to pass. In a mere moment we were outside in the heat of Bow Street.

"Oh, I don't like this, Wilkie," Dickens said helplessly. "We must find the real murderer or both Ellen and I are doomed. She at Collar's mercy, I at the mercy of the Grub Street sensation-mongers."

"Field will find them," I tried to comfort him.

"I don't like this, Wilkie," he repeated, like a man in a trance. "Don't you see? I love her and he wants me to put her in prison."

A BURIED SECRET

(August 12, 1852—Early Afternoon)

As we stood in front of Bow Street Station, Dickens fought to compose himself. He won out by shifting his concern to the business at hand, the tasks that Field had assigned to us.

"Wilkie, we shall seek out these women and interview them about this Eliza Lane, but our first stop must be Coutts Bank."

Charles set our afternoon's schedule without ever considering that I might be otherwise engaged. Without any thought to my preferences, he simply informed me of this as we were stepping into Sleepy Rob's ever loyal cab, which had been waiting for us all the while.

"I promised Angela that I would keep her informed. She must be told of Ellen's predicament, be warned of that hag Peggy Ternan's presence back in the city."

I, of course, offered no objection. In a sense, I was much like Sleepy Rob's horse. Without any question, I went where I was directed. What rankled is that Dickens assumed no less of me, tugged at the reins with the easy assurance that I would follow his lead no matter where we went or at what risk.

Coutts Bank guards the Strand entrance to Trafalgar

Square, looms darkly like Gibraltar over her straits. It is the royal family's bank, a symbol of the stability of Queen Victoria's rule and the power of England's empire. It is a fortress of money, its stone pillars rising from the top of its wide stone steps to the base of its Corinthian roofline. And it is all governed by a woman, Angela Burdett-Coutts.

As we climbed those grey stone steps, the heat so beat upon us that entering that cavernous building of marble floors and mahogany desks provided a relief, an escape from the heat and the airless, stifling torpor of the London streets. We found Miss Burdett-Coutts in her private offices on the second floor and were ushered in immediately by her clerk.

"Oh, Charles, I am so glad to see you." She rose fervently from her desk upon our entry and seated us on the purple plush couches around a low deal table that also inhabited her office rooms.

"Angela, has that man Collar been here this morning?" Dickens plunged right in as soon as we were seated.

"No, but—" she began to answer.

"Good," Dickens did not let her finish, "there have been some new developments that you should know."

"Oh no, I have been afraid of this." Miss Burdett-Coutts startled both of us with the tremor of anxiety in her voice, as if she already knew the bad news that Dickens was about to deliver.

"Angela, there is no need for great concern," Dickens tried to calm her. "It is about Ellen. Collar suspects that she is involved in this murder."

"Oh my God!" It was Miss Burdett-Coutts's turn to be startled, but as she sank back into the cushions of the couch there was also a quite palpable exhalation of relief in her voice, as if she had just been spared a painful revelation. "What is it? What has happened?"

With dispatch Dickens related all the happenings of the morning. Miss Burdett-Coutts listened intently, absorbing each new revelation, from the scarf to the sequestering of the fair fugitive to the reappearance of the mother, with ascending expressions of alarum and sympathy registering on her face. When Dickens had finished, she gathered herself for a long moment and then leaned ominously toward us, her face still clouded with that anxiety she had exhibited upon our first entering her office.

"Oh, Charles, this is all getting so out of hand," she began. "I fear there is more."

This conversation was developing like a lawn-tennis match. It was our turn to be startled once again.

"Angela, what is it?" I could not tell which of them was more fluttered by the revelations that were flying like a shuttlecock back and forth across the table.

"I fear there is something that you and Inspector Field ought to know. I had not thought of him until this horrible murder and robbery at the bank, but his memory has hung heavy in the back of my mind for oh these many years. I did not want anyone to know about him. I honestly do not even know if he still exists or where he is. But he could be involved in this."

"For God's sake, Angela, who are you talking about?" There was exasperation in Dickens's voice, a frustration that this was all so complicated already that no more complication was really welcome.

"My husband."

"Your what!" It was not difficult to understand Dickens's consternation since everyone believed Angela Burdett-Coutts to be unmarried.

"Well, not, not really my husband," she stammered, "my once husband. He deceived me, ran off, jilted me after demanding money from my father. It was annulled."

Dickens just stared, wide-eyed, at her.

Thus Angela Burdett-Coutts began her strange narrative. I cannot reproduce all of her exact words, but here, in summary form, are the startling facts of the history she unfolded for us.

"His name was James Barton and he seemed the perfect gentleman," Angela began. "He was such a talented man in so many ways, but it seems his greatest talent was for seducing women, rich women, widows mostly, and making off with as much of their money as he could. I guess I was different, much younger, only twenty-three. I think he planned from the beginning to marry me, actually did marry me. My father

113

saved me from a life with James Barton, but I don't think James Barton ever intended to have a life with me in the first place."

One could clearly perceive that this revelation was quite painful for Angela to tell. Sadness and regret were palpable in both her voice and her countenance. She told us how she met this cad, Barton, at the stables off Rotten Row in Hyde Park. At that time, almost twelve years before, she was in the habit of riding almost every day, which she still did, though on a less frequent and strenuous schedule. Barton also kept a horse there and got into the habit of riding with her a number of times a week. Soon he was always there waiting for her when she arrived for her ride. He was older (about seven years, in his early thirties), handsome, unutterably charming, and such a joy to be with that the young Angela fell hopelessly in love in the shortest possible time. It was just she and her father living in the family mansion in Kensington, her mother having died some years before. She told how her father was utterly devoted to her.

"It killed my father to have to do what he did," Angela said, reflecting upon this pivotal event in her history. "All he wanted was for me to be happy."

"What did your father do?" Dickens asked, rather unimaginatively I thought.

"He paid him to leave me alone." And at that revelation Angela began to weep as if the unearthing of this buried secret was something that still, all these years later, caused her great sorrow.

It seems that this Barton convinced her, on the pretense of a holiday at the seashore, to run off to Bournemouth Sands to get married.

"Now, I cannot believe that I was so gullible, so stupid"— Angela was actually laughing at herself through her tears— "but I was madly in love and he was so handsome and charming."

But her father, Martin Burdett-Coutts, had been suspicious of this Barton chap all along and had hired a solicitor to make inquiries into Barton's past. By the time that the solicitor reported to her father, however, it was too late. She and Barton were off and the sham marriage was done. But Barton never attended their honeymoon. As soon as the marriage ceremony was ended, he abandoned his new bride in their seaside hotel in Bournemouth and rode straight to London to break the bad news to her father and extract his pound of flesh; several thousand pounds of cash might be a more accurate representation of it. In return for the money, husband Barton disappeared into the Continent without even so much as a farewell note to his unblushed bride.

"Oh, he was so smart about it," Angela remembered. "He married me, but he made certain that the marriage could be annulled if the right terms were met. The merchandise was as yet undamaged." Angela tried to make a weak little joke out of it. "Father bought him off so that he would not hurt me any more."

An awkward silence hung over the three of us for a long moment when Angela had finished her story.

"Why are you telling us this now, Angela?" Dickens gently coaxed her back to the present.

"Because, because . . . it could be him," she stammered. "Perhaps he is back. Perhaps he is writing these letters. Oh, Charles, I have never talked of him to anyone. When Father died six years ago that part of my life ended forever and I became the chief officer of Coutts Bank. Now the past is coming back to haunt me. I cannot allow it."

"Just what makes you think that it is him?" Charles was leaving his role of understanding confidant and gratefully reassuming his more familiar role as inquisitive detective, collector of people's stories and the motives of their hearts.

"I cannot say for certain," she said, then thought on it for a long moment. "It is just his style. This is a bad man, Charles, a very intelligent and resourceful man. Everything that Inspector Field has conveyed to me by way of Mr. Thompson reminds me of him. He can play any role he wants. He can be one person one moment and another person the next. That was how he was so successful with all of those women before me. That was what my father found out about him."

The poor woman looked exhausted as she sat there on that regal couch. It was as if this outpouring of the secret past had drained her of all her strength. Dickens moved next to her on the couch and took her hand. Reassurance was the only thing on his mind.

"Angela, I must tell this story to Field." Dickens's voice was firm yet gentle. "But he will be the only one. Wilkie and I will never utter a word of it to anyone else. There have been no hints of this very private information in any of the threatening letters, so I do not think that this man is their source. I feel this elusive night guard from the bank is our man, but one never knows. Please do not worry. Field will do everything that he can to put these troubling crimes to rest. In the meanwhile, however, you must be very careful in your handling of the other policeman, this Collar. Miss Ternan is presently his prime suspect and I fear we must leave him with that ridiculous misapprehension for now. Wilkie and I must go do some work for Field today, but we shall keep you well informed. Keep Thompson close by; he is a good man. And, for God's sake, do not get yourself all upset about some ghost out of twelve years past. That man has probably been shot by some angry husband years ago." And he ended his lecture with a mischievous chuckle.

Both Angela Burdett-Coutts and I could not help but laugh. Dickens had a talent for doing that, for inserting a comic twist into even the most serious considerations. We left Miss Burdett-Coutts much more composed than she had been when we arrived, when she was still bearing the burden of her secret past alone.

It is strange though. After that, after hearing her secret, I could never think of Angela Burdett-Coutts in the same way again. After hearing her story, she seemed so much more human to me, much less intimidating (as I think I had held her to be as the master of the greatest bank in England). And then, years later, whenever I thought of her secret story, I always thought of Dickens's own Miss Havisham, his bride left at the altar. But no one could ever accuse Angela Burdett-Coutts of shutting herself off from the world. She had dedicated her life to the women of London.

STRANGE INTERVIEWS

ৼ

(August 12, 1852—Afternoon)

Sleepy Rob, sitting outside of Coutts Bank on the box of his double hansom cab in his perpetual doze, seemed oblivious of the oppressive heat of the day. A tap of Dickens's walking stick to his wheel awakened him. With his long face and his slow eyes, he looked like a reluctant hound.

"Yes guv, 'ere and waitin'," he assured Dickens. "Where will it be now?"

"Macklin Street. Miss Ternan's lodgings."

At the Macklin Street house, we pulled up behind a black police post chaise sitting abandoned at the curbstone. Even as we were stepping down, Inspector Collar and his man with the foreign and unpronounceable name emerged. We had proceeded there in hopes of finding either Miss Barbara Leigh Smith or Miss Evans, or both, at home. We had not expected once again to have to deal with the annoying Collar.

"Mr. Dickens, Mr. Collins . . ." Collar addressed us in that curt idiom of martinet clerks speaking to their inferiors of the public. "We seem to be making all o' the same stops today."

"Yes, don't we," Dickens humoured the man. "We came here in the hope that Miss Ternan and Mr. Collins's secretary,

Miss Sheehey, had returned." But he could not leave it at that. His resentment got the better of his judgment. "I had hoped to find them here so that I could warn Miss Ternan of your absurd suspicions and advise her to consult with you immediately."

Collar visibly flinched when Dickens pronounced the word "absurd," but he immediately recovered himself. He, clearly, was not used to dealing with a person like Dickens, who could be a commanding presence when he chose to be. Collar was a mean little toad of a man with eyes too big for his face and a bullying arrogance which perhaps worked well on the poor and downtrodden of the streets, but which had no effect whatsoever upon an adversary like Charles Dickens.

"No help for you here, I'm afraid." Collar grinned stupidly. "She hasn't come back, and those two don't know nothin' about it."

"Ah, good, they are at home. Good day, Inspector." And Dickens swept by him in dismissal, leaving me marooned in the company of those two stunned policemen.

Then Collar did a rather peculiar thing, perhaps as a way of saving face, perhaps as a warning to Dickens not to treat him so cavalierly. With a simple extension of his arm as if it were a gate, he detained me for a moment from following Dickens in, and solemnly took me into his confidence.

"I have heard that some eighteen months ago," he began in a low conspiratorial voice, "Miss Ternan wos the prime suspect in a quite similar murder. Of a theatrical man? Stabbed in the back with a sharp object?" He paused for that bit of evidence to sink in. "And Inspector Field, who wos investigatin' the case, did not think there wos evidence enough for the bench to proceed against Miss Ternan. Now why wos that, Mr. Collins?"

"Why, why, I'm sure I, I, I haven't the slightest . . . ," I stammered. I simply was not suited for this sort of intrigue. I was incapable of lying credibly. Even as my tongue was stumbling about in its clumsy attempt to evade Collar's interrogation, my body was breaking through that flimsy barrier of his upraised arm and fleeing into the house.

118

The inner door of the three women's lodgings had been left open for me. I caught up with Dickens in the front parlor, where he was just seating himself in a small overstuffed chair directly opposite Miss Barbara Leigh Smith and Miss Marian Evans, who shared a small settee pulled up to a low table covered with blue books and literary journals.

"Fetch yourself a chair from the kitchen, Wilkie," Dickens ordered, not even looking at me.

Our interview with Nellie's two housemates took place in a bright, pleasant room befitting the residence of three young ladies. The drapes were open and the sunlight poured through the windows, making the pinks and yellows of the flowered wallpaper dance as if the room were in the middle of a meadow. Similarly, the two women were dressed in summery colors, Miss Smith in a white ruffled blouse, very feminine, over a quite ample light brown skirt that flowed to her booted ankles, and Miss Evans in a pale blue dress. Miss Evans was a tall, horsey girl. Conversely, Miss Smith was a robust, freckled, sunburnt outdoorswoman, who looked to be of the rough-and-tumble school. It was she who, with a note of complaint, opened our conversation.

"Honestly, Mr. Dickens, those policemen have done nothing but harass us for the last two days."

"That is true, sir," Miss Evans added, in her deep thoughtful voice. "I feel as if they have been camped on our doorstep like wolves, waiting for that poor girl to return."

"It is bad, Mr. Dickens," the lively Miss Smith chimed in. "All they can see is Nellie as their murderer. I'm sorry I had to tell them, but they waved that scarf in our faces and we both knew it was hers. But that does not make her a murderer, does it?"

"Oh, sir," the shy, thoughtful one in her husky deep voice spoke from the heart, "we are so worried about Nellie. She has not been home now for two nights. Maybe she is murdered, too."

Both women stared at him, wondering, I am certain, how he could be so confident of Nellie's safety, so unmoved by her disappearance.

"Mr. Collins and I believe that the best and only way to help Miss Ternan allay the suspicions of the Protectives is to find the real murderer of Eliza Lane"—their eyes widened at this—"and we need your help."

"Yes, of course, anything." Barbara Smith nodded her head fervently in the affirmative.

Dickens was in fine form and full control of the interrogation; the amateur detective who fancied himself a professional was on full point. I sat there like a statue trying to think of some way I could assist him.

"We need to know more about the murdered woman," Dickens mused. "What was she like? Who were her friends?"

I saw my opening. "Meg told me there were three factions in the Women's Emancipation Society," I spoke up, "the riches, the witches, and the wenches."

Barbara Leigh Smith giggled at that.

The less lively Miss Evans glared.

"Miss Lane was one of the witches. What can you tell us about them?" As I finished, even Dickens was staring at me in mild surprise.

"Eliza Lane was troubled, angry," Miss Evans began. "She had been abused by her husband."

"He beat her, used her in perverse ways." Miss Smith showed no reticence toward revealing these uncomfortable facts. "That is why she fled her husband. She was terrified of him. She has some relatives, an aged aunt I think, with whom she lives. She is . . . was . . . a very confused girl."

"How was she confused?" Dickens pressed.

A look passed between Miss Smith and Miss Evans then, as if they were silently asking each other whether they should go on, as if they were somewhat embarrassed at what they were about to say. Dickens caught it immediately, read it in an instant.

"Please, ladies, this is not just idle gossip," he assured them. "We need to know all about this poor dead woman, her habits, her company, the confusion of her mind. It is the only path we have to her killer."

His little speech seemed to ease their misgivings.

"She turned to women, she did," Barbara Smith blurted out. "Said right out in a meeting that she never wanted to be with a man again."

"She fell in with Sydney Beach and Marie de Brevecoeur," Marian Evans took up the narrative. "They both dress like men, in imitation of the French writer, George Sand. Marie is from Paris. She has said so. Sydney Beach is a very quiet, retiring woman, but Marie de Brevecoeur—"

"Is a monster!" Barbara Smith cut in.

Both Dickens and I stared at that accusation.

"—seemed to us"—and Miss Evans looked at Miss Smith briefly, though not in admonition—"somewhat sinister in her attentions both toward Sydney Beach—"

"Who I think is a true feminist even though she argues for free love," Barbara Smith interrupted again.

"—and toward Eliza Lane."

"Do you feel . . ." Dickens hesitated, his mind working to rephrase what I guessed must be a rather delicate question. "Miss Ternan told Irish Meg that Eliza Lane made unnatural advances toward her," Dickens began again. "Do you feel that Eliza Lane was involved in that way with Miss Beach or Miss de Brevecoeur?"

"No doubt of it," Barbara Smith declared.

"I do not think Eliza Lane knew what she wanted," the more analytic Miss Evans said. "I think she fell under the power of those women."

"What do you mean 'power'?" Dickens once again jumped alertly on point.

"I don't really know. They were strange women. It was as if they were . . . I just don't know."

"Sometimes they were normal," Miss Smith tried to resolve Miss Evans's judgmental reticence, "but other times it was as if they were, well, drugged or enchanted, saying things, doing things, that they wouldn't normally do. Wild things."

"No, not wild really. Elizabeth Siddal does wild things," Miss Evans corrected, "but strange, uncalled-for things. Once they kissed each other on the lips, to shock the other women in the room. But we do not shock easily. In fact, we all feel this reigning discomfort with sexuality to be one of the most prominent flaws in our society." Miss Evans, in an extremely quiet voice, spoke with a seriousness that gave evidence of a strong inner feeling struggling with a powerful intellect.

No wonder she is gaining such a reputation as a freethinker, I thought.

"Drugged, you say? Or enchanted?" Dickens leapt to that possibility.

"I don't know." Miss Smith tempered her judgment, and Miss Evans nodded in agreement. "Now, Lizzie Siddal talks openly about taking drugs, but neither Sydney nor Marie de Brevecoeur ever did. For them it was sex, for Sydney only with women, she said as much, but for Marie de Brevecoeur, well . . ."

"I received the impression that she was interested in both women and men," Marian Evans finished Barbara Smith's sentence.

"Did those two women ever make any unnatural advances toward either of you?" Dickens asked, no longer embarrassed, it seemed, at any turn that this exceedingly frank conversation might take.

"No."

"No."

"Then why Miss Ternan?"

I could see that it was a struggle for Charles to ask that question, but he forced it out.

"I do not know," Miss Smith said, and she seemed suddenly quite tired of this conversation.

"I do not know, either," Miss Evans agreed, but one could perceive her interest in the problem. I think she, this fledgling novelist who in later years would even become Dickens's equal, had a bit of the detective in her. "But . . ." She hesitated, thinking on it one moment longer. "But I think it was some sort of initiation rite which perhaps the others had imposed upon Eliza Lane; perhaps they had challenged her to seduce a new young woman into their unnatural circle, or perhaps it was because Nellie was an actress and on occasion wore men's clothes onstage. She has just such a part right now in *The Taming of the Shrew.*"

"You ought to talk to Lizzie Siddal or Flory Nightingale," Barbara Smith suggested. "Those two were the most interested in Marie de Brevecoeur's philosophies. I think I remember actually seeing one of them, or maybe both, going off with the witches after a meeting. That's all I can remember." And with that Barbara Smith seemed to be signaling the end of her interest in this interview.

Dickens apparently picked up her cue: "We cannot thank you enough for all the help you have given us. We have a much clearer picture now."

That last was, certainly in my case, not true at all. In fact, I was probably more confused now than I had been before we commenced our interview with these two ladies. These unsettling revelations seemed to be flooding upon us as if this murder had opened a weir.

Miss Evans, however, even as Dickens was rising to take his leave, still seemed inclined to pursue the case of these daughters of Lesbos. "I would go and talk to Lizzie Siddal and Flory if I were you, Mr. Dickens. They move in different—shall I say, more open—circles than do Bobbie and myself. We are really homebodies. They are not. Eliza Lane, Marie de Brevecoeur, would talk more openly to them than to us. Flory is a nurse. She works all over London. God knows where you might find her. But Lizzie Siddal lives in Rossetti's house, the painter. She is his model."

"Thank you. We shall try." And with that we left Nellie's two housemates sitting in their parlor wondering what this affair was really all about.

THE MAN WITH THE MUSTACHE

(August 12, 1852—Midafternoon)

I t was almost three in the afternoon when we came out of Nellie's Macklin Street house. The heat pressed down upon us like a huge steam iron, flattening out all of our senses.

"Where shall we go next, Wilkie?" Dickens made a sincere plea for guidance.

Whether it was the sudden heat or the unpleasantness of the previous interview I do not know, but I was utterly incapable of making a decision.

Dickens waited, but when I said nothing he pulled at his dandified goatee and held counsel with himself for my benefit: "We must see Miss Siddal and Miss Nightingale, but one we have no way of finding, and Rossetti's house is all the way down on the Chelsea Embankment. I have been there." He informed me of all of this as if I were his valet. "Now Browning's house is but two or three streets over. Why don't we try them before we go abroad looking for the others?" With that decided, he rapped smartly on the box of Sleepy Rob's cab, causing that worthy to loll himself into consciousness, and ordered him, "To Eagle Street. I'll tell you where to stop when I see it."

We trotted across High Holborn toward Eagle Street just off Red Lion Square, where, Dickens informed me, Robert Browning, the poet, had taken rooms with his invalid wife, Elizabeth Barrett Browning, the more famous poet, in order to be close to her doctors.* As we moved slowly in the press of foot traffic trying to cross High Holborn, I had sufficiently recovered my wits to the point where I remembered to tell Dickens of my unsettling exchange with Inspector Collar. He listened intently to my description of the man's threats against Miss Ternan, set his jaw for a brief moment in anger, and then tried to scoff those threats away with bravado.

"The man is a climber, Wilkie. He likes the notoriety of this case, the rich and famous people he is meeting. He wishes to eclipse our friend Field in reputation. The only problem is that he is a fool and Field, when he wishes, will make him look like one." Then, with a quick movement, Dickens stuck his head out the window and shouted, *"Here! Pull up!"* at the top of his lungs.

The Brownings lived in a high, gabled brick house whose stoop had been removed in favor of a dark wooden gangway which formed a gentle incline from the curbstone to the front door. That wooden walkway was clearly an accommodation for an invalid's chair, which could be pushed up without lifting in order to allow entry through the front door of the house.

"Elizabeth Browning sometimes must go about in a chair," Dickens advised me as we were getting down. "She experiences extended periods of sickliness. But she is not crippled. She can walk. And her intelligence certainly suffers no debility."

Robert Browning, in his shirt and braces, with his bush muttonchops squeezing his angular face like furry bookends, answered Dickens's sharp knock upon his door.

*Mrs. Browning's fame, in 1852, rested upon her authorship of "The Cry of the Children," a poem of social outcry which championed the cause of the London poor.

"Why Charles." Browning, though somewhat flustered, seemed genuinely pleased at Dickens's intrusion.* "Hallo, good morning, I mean, afternoon. Please come in. You must excuse me. You have caught me at my desk."

"No, Robert, no, you must excuse us for intruding unannounced." Dickens was all apologies even as Browning was ushering us into the foyer. "I know how annoying it is to be interrupted while one is trying to write, but we need to talk to Elizabeth on some rather pressing business."

At that last, Browning visibly stiffened, even became somewhat suspicious. I do not know whether his reaction was precipitated by a jealous sense of his wife's literary prominence being more widely established than his own or by a husband's protectiveness. I would like to think that it was the latter.

"What is it, Charles?" Browning seemed startled. "In what pressing business could Elizabeth be involved?"

"If we might just speak to her, Robert." Again, Dickens was all conciliation. "It is, indeed, rather urgent. It involves the murder of a young woman of her acquaintance."

"Oh my God!" Browning's hands leapt to his face and cupped his bushy muttonchops. "We read of it in the *Times*. That poor woman at the bank. But Elizabeth barely knew her."

"Yes, I know. Miss Burdett-Coutts told us. This, by the way, is my colleague at *Household Words*, Wilkie Collins." Dickens introduced me as a necessary afterthought. "We are helping the Metropolitan Protectives in the investigation of the case." For some reason, Dickens's rather far-fetched portrayal of us as detectives on a case seemed to appease Browning.

"Why, of course, I'm sure that Elizabeth will be glad to see you. She is reading in the library. But you must not overly shock or excite her," he solemnly cautioned us, "and you must not tax her for too long. She tires very easily."

"Of course, Robert, we have only a few questions to ask

her." Dickens could not have been more reassuring. "Really, it is so good to see you. I don't think we have been together since Alfred's presentation of his great poem to the queen."* Charles made charming literary talk as Browning escorted us to the library.

Elizabeth Barrett Browning was sitting reading in a high-backed brown leather chair beneath a gas lamp which bathed her in an enchanted circle of light. Upon our entry she turned her head alertly and rose to her feet. She was not at all the invalid I had expected.

Tall and slim, with long grey hair undone and flowing to her shoulders, wearing a dark brown dress which provided sharp contrast to her exceedingly white, almost translucent face, she was quite striking in appearance. She was older than I expected, older than the voice I had pictured from reading her impassioned poems of love translated from the Portuguese.† When she spoke, her voice was thin and fragile as stemware.

"Why, Charles," she said with a smile, "what a pleasant surprise. Please, sit down. What is it? You look so grim." And she motioned to a small couch which faced her chair even as she was sinking back down into her cushions.

"Yes, Elizabeth, it is so good to see you. I was just telling Robert that we need to have another literary evening soon with Alfred and William and Macready and some of the others."‡ Dickens entered quite the charmer, not yet ready to shock her with tales of murder.

"Oh, Charles, I would love that." Her dark brown eyes above those pale ghostly cheeks fairly burnt with enthusiasm.

"Yes, we shall do it," Dickens assured her. "But this is my col-

---

*Dickens must be referring to a ceremony fully a year earlier, in 1851, when Tennyson presented a leather-bound copy of his long poem *In Memoriam* to Queen Victoria.

†Elizabeth Barrett Browning's *Sonnets from the Portuguese,* published in 1850, only two years before the events of this particular Collins narrative, were purported to be translations, and many of her contemporary readers, evidently including Wilkie Collins, were taken in by this ruse of a literary convention.

‡He refers to Alfred, Lord Tennyson, the poet; William Makepeace Thackeray, his fellow novelist; and William Macready, the greatest actor of that day and artistic director of Covent Garden Theatre.

league, also a writer, Mr. Wilkie Collins, and we are here on a much sadder business."

"It is about the murder of poor Eliza Lane, isn't it?"

"Why yes, it is."

"It is all I have been able to think about all morning," Elizabeth Browning informed us as we took our seats, "since Robert read it to me from the news at breakfast."

"We"—and he implicated me as his accomplice—"are working with the Metropolitan Protectives to try to find her murderer. Angela asked us to do so. We feel that you might be able to help us."

"What can I do? Please tell me."

"Can you tell us anything, even the slightest perceptions, about Eliza Lane or Sydney Beach or Marie de Brevecoeur?"

"Only that I hardly knew any of them. My only acquaintance with them was at the Women's Emancipation Society meetings. They were so different that they almost frightened me. They spoke of love between women, sexual love. I must admit it seemed unnatural to me. I am forty-six years old and I have barely learned to love a man," she said, and smiled gently at her attentive husband.

"Is there anything that you can remark about the night of the murder which might be helpful in our investigation?" Dickens made one last plea.

She thought for a long moment.

"Only that . . ." She stopped to think again, as if trying to visualize something.

"And . . . ," Dickens gently prompted.

"I remember seeing Eliza Lane, just a glimpse of her, I think, the night of the last society meeting," she said, then faltered. "It couldn't be important."

"What did you see?" Dickens pressed her.

"It was just a glimpse because I was in such a rush, and Robert was pushing me in the chair. She was talking, I think, to the guard outside the front doors of the bank before Robert summoned the man to help carry me in the chair up the steps. I did not speak to her because I was late and I was scheduled to read my poems to the meeting that night. I do not think she was still there when we reached the top of the stone steps and entered the bank."

"What did the man look like?" Dickens was relentless.

"He had a very large mustache, I think. Robert, do you remember?"

"Not at all, dear," he replied, even as he was elbowing Dickens as a signal that the interrogation had gone on too long.

Dickens rose to his feet in quick respect for Robert Browning's wishes. He thanked Mrs. Browning for her help and we took our leave of her. In the foyer before departing, Dickens again thanked the husband for allowing us to intrude.

"It was Barsad in his mustache," Dickens exulted as we sat in the standing cab, which was not moving because, in his excitement, Dickens had failed to give Sleepy Rob any direction as to our next destination. "He was on the door that night, and he was talking to Eliza Lane outside just before she broke into that meeting and cursed all of those women. Don't you see?"

I must have been staring at him with an exceedingly bewildered look upon my face because he stopped talking and stared back at me as if I were an idiot.

"I am sorry, Charles," I confessed, "but I don't see. We already know he was there, or at least supposed to be posted on the front doors that night."

"Yes, I know." Dickens moved slowly through his explanation, adopting the pace and tone a parent would take with a slow child of two or three years. "But this puts the two of them together just before her strange outburst, and he is a mesmerist, I am certain. Don't you see, he cast a spell upon her with his ring and sent her into that meeting to frighten those women, to drive them away so that he could get in and have a free run of the bank."

I followed his whole line of reasoning, nodding my head up and down like a pump handle. But I did not really have a chance to answer or join in Dickens's enthusiasm for this particular version of the conspiratorial events because, at the very moment that he finished spinning out his scenario, Sleepy Rob's sour voice barked down from the box: "Are you gents gonna sit 'ere in this blasted 'eat all afternoon or are we bound for somewheres else?"

"Yes, of course," Dickens answered, and stuck his head out the window again to deliver Sleepy Rob's instructions: "To the Chelsea Embankment. When I see the house, I will know it."

Dickens never ceased to amaze me. He protested that he barely knew Rossetti, yet he knew exactly where he lived and could recognize his house by sight. Dickens knew his city as a sailor knows every inch of the channel of his home port.

In the cab trotting across Piccadilly and into Sloane Street heading for the Chelsea Bridge Road, Dickens continued to exult in our discoveries: "Oh, Wilkie, don't you see? This is how it is done. This is how Field does it. With every interview we gather another piece of information, fit another piece into the puzzle, and all of it leads to this Barsad. Who is he?"

INTO THE HAREM

(August 12, 1852—Late Afternoon)

D ante Gabriel Rossetti, the painter, lived in a high
sprawling brick house that overlooked the stinking
Thames. By the time we arrived at number 16 Cheyne
Walk it was all of four by the clock and we were both quite
prickled by the heat. Rossetti's establishment was fenced in
wrought iron and gated, but the gate opened to our touch and
we traversed a short path through a tiny grass yard to the
front door. Two stone dogs, whippets by their lean and hungry look, sat on the edges of a small, square brick porch,
guarding the front door. The facade of the house was smoth-
ered in coarse brown vines bearing small blue flowers, wiste-
ria I believe, and the door was a solid oak affair buried in the
foliage like the overgrown entrance to some secret garden.
Dickens clacked the brass knocker twice.

The door was opened by a youngish woman in a linen peas-
ant smock holding a baby. She looked at us pleasantly enough,
even smiled slightly, but she was busy with the child, who was
wrapped in a pinkish blanket. This doorkeeper did not immediately say anything. I wondered if she was a mute. That
proved not the case.

"Good day," Dickens greeted her cheerily. "I am Charles Dickens, an acquaintance of Mr. Rossetti, and I, we, are here to see Miss Siddal on a rather urgent matter. Might we come in?"

"Mr. Charles Dickens, my goodness, I am delighted to meet you, sir. I have read every number of *Bleak House* thus far, and *David Copperfield* is my favorite among your many writings. Oh yes, please come in. I know that Danny will be delighted to see you." If this speech were evidence, the Rossetti household employed the most well-spoken and literate housemaids in the nation. "Oh please, do come in, gentlemen," she finished. "I will run right up and tell them you are here." And with that she handed the blanketed baby to Charles and scurried excitedly up the steps.

Charles seemed rather intimidated by the responsibility which had been so precipitously thrust upon him, but the child seemed rather amused by the whole affair, as if being passed around like a basket of muffins was a rather common occurrence in her young bohemian life.

After long minutes of dandling the infant, shifting our feet on the tiles of the entrance foyer, and gazing at the many paintings which hung on the walls of the hallway leading to the steps up which that young woman had disappeared, she finally returned with a sheepish smile.

"Oh, Mr. Dickens, in my hurry to tell Danny the news, I just, out of habit, handed Lolly to you. We tend to pass her around here like a beach ball. I am sorry. He and Lizzie are in the studio. You know, the late afternoon light and all. He said for you to come right up."

"Why thank you," Dickens said, handing her back her pink bundle, and with that we followed her up.

After ascending to the second storey of the house, she led us down a long corridor, our footfalls muffled in lush oriental rugs, our eyes feasting upon the glut of brilliant original paintings which covered every available space on the walls. When she opened a door at the end of that hallway for us and bid us go in, we realized what she had meant by the artist's need to take advantage of that late-afternoon August light. That carpeted art gallery of a hallway was in no way dark or dim, but when that young woman opened the door to Rossetti's studio, a rich golden light flooded out upon us. It was a brilliant light though textured and soft, and in no way a violent shock to our eyes. What we encountered, however, when we entered that studio, was, indeed, quite a shock and stopped us dead in our tracks just inside the door on a small landing two steps above the sunken room.

It was a large high room of half-circular shape. From the entrance on that small landing where we stood staring, the walls, totally windowed, curved in a gentle arc out away from us. The room was all wide windows and skylights, and the late-afternoon sunlight streamed through and bathed everything in a golden glow. But it was neither the graceful arc of the room nor the mythic light which had so captured our attention.

At the far end of the room, on a simple cream-colored divan set into the deepest curve of the windows, reclining in a pose of total abandonment, was an utterly naked woman. She did not move when we entered. She seemed blissfully, even innocently, unaware of our very presence in the room. I was transfixed by her beauty, and Dickens must have been as well, for we both stood there gaping down at her, utterly unaware of anyone else in the room. Lying there on her back bathed in that golden light with one arm and her head thrown back in total abandon, her eyes closed, she was a figure out of myth. Her other arm hung helplessly to the floor as if trailing in some limpid forest pool. She was Psyche; she was the Eternal Muse; she was the Lady of Shalott. The golden sunlight danced across her alabaster skin and caressed the gentle curve of her breasts. Her legs were open in beckoning submission, one dangling helplessly over the end of the divan, the other trailing heedlessly to the floor, and the golden light set afire the dark red triangle which adorned her mound of Venus. She was a nymph out of the Golden Age (certainly not of our age) waiting in languid expectation for the satyrs to return for their sport. It was Elizabeth Siddal, who by Dante Rossetti's brush would become the icon of female sexuality for our age. Oh, Lizzie Siddal was an exotic beauty indeed. I could not take my eyes off of her.

"Thank you, Sarah," a somewhat bemused voice broke our enchantment. Turning my head too quickly in embarrassment, I realized that it was a tall thin man at an easel dismissing the woman with the baby who had been our guide into this enchanted world. Rossetti was tall and clean featured, with shiny black hair brushed back from his forehead and a thin Frenchified mustache adorning his upper lip. The woman with the baby shut the door as she left, and Dickens stepped forward to greet Rossetti.

Standing at his easel, which held a large canvas upon which his study in golden flesh was in progress, with a large dirty palette in one hand and his brush in the other, Rossetti looked more like a banker on holiday than a famous painter or notorious bohemian. He was wearing a somber and buttoned black suit, with his white shirt open at the neck sans cravat. He just didn't look like a painter. I guess I expected some sort of long flowing paint smock and an extravagant straw hat.

"Charles, I am delighted to see you again. It was the benefit dinner for John Overs, that poor poet, that last brought us together, was it not? I attended with Carlyle, who lives just two houses down the Walk."* Rossetti placed his brush and palette on a high work table beside his easel and greeted Dickens with an outstretched hand.

"Dante"—Charles took his hand warmly—"I am so sorry to intrude. Please finish your work. We shall wait outside until you are done. I would never have broken in upon you unannounced like this if it were not urgent."

"Nonsense." Rossetti smiled a gentle understanding smile. "We all work too hard at this mad thing we call art. No one works harder at this than you. We read each new number of *Bleak House* aloud, you know. Poor Jo has become all of our

*John Overs, the workingman poet, wrote a small book titled *Evenings of a Working Man* which Dickens helped to publication just before Overs's death of lung disease in 1844. Since that time Dickens had adopted Overs's family as one of his personal projects by arranging annual benefit dinners for their support and education. It is surely one of these dinners to which Rossetti refers. Thomas Carlyle, Dickens's close friend and the author of *Sartor Resartus, Past and Present,* and *The French Revolution,* who was Rossetti's neighbor in Cheyne Walk, had also been a friend and supporter of Overs.

child. We mourned his death as though we had lost one of our own."

"But you are working. You shall lose your light, your model her mood."

"Not at all." With a sweep of his arm Rossetti took in the whole room. "I welcome the interruption. In fact, I live for the interruptions. This art, this composing, is such hard work. The light will come again. And as for Lizzie," he laughed, "she has been drinking most of the afternoon. She is in the land of the Lotus Eaters."

He delivered that speech in an almost lilting voice full of amusement and philosophical disdain. His allusion to Tennyson's poem seemed altogether fitting. Miss Siddal did, indeed, look as if she were drugged. She reclined there in her pose of naked abandonment even as we spoke about her.

Suddenly, however, I was startled by the model's abrupt movement. Miss Siddal sat up and stared, rather blankly, at us. She made no attempt whatsoever to cover her nakedness. She just looked wonderingly up at us as if *we* were the curiosities, the rara avis in that room. I, of course, immediately averted my eyes.

"Miss Woodruff said that you were accompanied by a second gentleman, Charles." Rossetti's laughing voice drew my attention away from that awakened nymph. "I don't believe that I have had the pleasure," he said, and moved toward me with his small hand extended.

"Wilkie Collins." Dickens made the perfunctory introduction, but I noticed that his gaze also had been arrested by the sudden movement into life of the naked Miss Siddal. "Wilkie is my colleague in *Household Words.*"

"Mr. Collins, I am pleased to meet you." Rossetti was all charm and ease. But that mood was stridently broken in an instant.

"Are they here to paint me, too?" Miss Siddal demanded in a harsh voice clearly returned from Lotus Land. "Or have you just invited some of your gentleman friends in to watch you work"—and a mischievous grin stole across her face, giving her teasing away—". . . *and me pose.*"

"Actually we are here to see, uh"—Dickens paused, momentarily flustered at his own poor choice of words (for a word-man) — "to speak to you, Miss Siddal."

At that, the woman rose and reached for her wrap. I watched her every movement even as she covered herself in a flowing green silk robe. Having done so, she walked to a wide, flat worktable at the side of the room against the only unwindowed inner wall, and refilled a stemmed wineglass with an emerald green liquid which matched the color of her robe in the dying sunlight.

"Would you like a glass of absinthe, gentlemen?" Rossetti took his cue from Miss Siddal. "It has a very pleasing effect upon one in the late afternoon."*

Dickens waved off that offer of seductive hospitality and I demurred as well, but I must say that I found the afternoon surprise, the *différence* as the French call it, of nude models and decadent drugs decidedly stimulating.

Miss Siddal resumed her seat on the creamy divan and looked up at us expectantly while Rossetti pulled up two high, plain wooden stools, of the sort that clerks in countinghouses are chained to, for Dickens and me to perch upon. Her eyes were wide with the drug, or perhaps with curiosity at these two birds of prey who had descended upon her, but she seemed perfectly capable of conversing.

"What is it you wish of me?" she asked.

"We are involved with the investigation of the murder of Eliza Lynn Lane of the Women's Emancipation Society." Dickens got down to the business of the moment. I was always amazed how, even in moments susceptible to great distraction, he was able to maintain his concentration upon his task. "Could you tell us anything about her or about the night of the murder?"

She thought on that for a moment as Rossetti looked on rather bemused, sipping from a glass of absinthe which had magically appeared in his hand.

"Actually, not much," she finally answered. "I was there at

---

*Absinthe was a powerful liqueur popular in the Victorian era, almost a drug, reputedly able to cast one into a trancelike, hallucinatory state; hence the comparison to Tennyson's "The Lotus Eaters."

our meeting that night when she burst in and threw her cat fit." She grinned happily at the memory. "But she just screamed a lot of silly things and ran out. Most of the women were shocked, though I thought it rather funny."

"How was it funny?" Dickens pressed her.

"Well really," she laughed, "imagine Eliza Lane accusing us of all those terrible things. It was like casting the first stone. And, anyway"—she became a bit more thoughtful—"those things she accused all of us of doing were the very things we often discussed in those meetings, things like the freedom to love and take your pleasure just as men do."

Dickens decided to move on with his interrogation. "So you didn't see anything unusual or significant that night which might reveal why she was murdered and by whom?"

"No. Not really."

"Anything? Any small thing?"

"No. No sir. She seemed especially angry at Miss Angela and at Nellie Ternan . . ."

At that, Dickens perceptibly recoiled as if he had been struck in the face by a small stone.

". . . but why I certainly do not know. They are two of the sweetest, kindest women in that group. But now that I think on it, your name was mentioned along with Nellie's." At that, a light seemed to come on in her distracted mind. She grinned vacantly. "Oh, that is why you are doing this, isn't it?"

Again, Dickens was momentarily taken aback, but he hid his embarrassment and quickly recovered.

"What about Miss Lane's friends? Miss Beach and Marie de Brevecoeur." Dickens struck off in a new direction. "Do you know them at all?"

At this question, Elizabeth Siddal glanced quickly at Rossetti as if for permission, as if she was uncomfortable with the question and wanted him to help her to answer. He did nothing. He sipped from his fragile glass and smiled benignly at Dickens as they both waited for the answer.

"I do not know Sydney Beach, except for talking to her at the meetings, but . . ." And again Miss Siddal paused and her eyes leapt to Rossetti in a plea for help.

This time he answered her with a slight, almost imperceptible nod downward of his head. What he gave her permission to say proved the most shocking revelation of any of our interviews thus far. Little did we know that we were entering a world where the aesthetics of the body tangled themselves with the rough commercial perversions of the night streets.

"Marie de Brevecoeur has been here," Elizabeth turned back to us and almost triumphantly declared, "and we tried to make love right here on this divan."

"And I tried to paint them," Rossetti added quite congenially, "but it did not work out. I got only a few preliminary sketches."

This revelation managed to break even Dickens's concentration.

"What do you mean? I, I, I don't understand," Dickens managed to sputter.

"Shall we say that Marie de Brevecoeur expressed a, shall we say, intimate interest in Lizzie," Rossetti, still quite amused, began to explain.

"She asked me to sup with her after one of the Women's Society meetings." Elizabeth Siddal took up her own story as a woman quite used to speaking for herself. "But we never went into the coffeehouse. In the cab on the way, she talked of free love. She said that she and Sydney Beach were daughters of Lesbos. She asked me if I knew what that meant and I said yes, because I did, because Danny is always talking about it since his paintings are mostly of women. Then she started touching me."

She paused to drink, and I looked quickly at Dickens, who looked quizzically at Rossetti. Rossetti just nodded solemnly as if to say *Be patient and she will tell you all.*

"I was somewhat surprised," Elizabeth resumed her narrative, "but she was saying very nice things and she was very gentle, in no way threatening. But I was confused. I told her that I was Danny's lover, that I had only been with men and I was very happy as his mistress and model. When the cab stopped outside of the eating place, I broke away from her and told her that I needed time to think about what she had been saying."

"What had she been saying?" Dickens miraculously seemed to have found his voice.

"She told me that she had fallen in love with my body from Danny's paintings, that they had inflamed her desire and that she would like to make love to me, but, even more than that, she would like Danny to paint us making love. I told her I would think about it and I had to leave. She was utterly accepting of my decision. She made me take the cab. I left her standing there in the street before the coffeehouse. I never had any sense that she was forcing herself upon me as men have so often in the past, before I met Danny."

Again she stopped, only this time not to drink. Rather, she waited, as if her part of the story was over and her partner in crime (though neither of them exhibited any guilt) was expected to take it up and bring it to conclusion.

"Naturally, I was quite intrigued by this story and this woman's proposition." Rossetti took up the narrative without the slightest hesitation.

"Naturally." Dickens said it somewhat wryly, in a voice approaching sarcasm.

"Yes, quite naturally actually," Rossetti answered with that same heedlessness that was beginning to remind me of Tally Ho Thompson's eternal knowing grin. "I told Lizzie that the whole idea spurred both my carnal curiosity and my aesthetic desire. I told her that I would enjoy both watching and painting her and this woman making love here in the studio. We discussed the whole project at length and Lizzie seemed quite as curious as I. The upshot is that she invited the woman to come, the woman came to the house in the late afternoon on a day much like this, but it just did not work."

"What do you mean 'it did not work'?" Dickens could barely contain himself as Rossetti seemed, by stopping, to be signaling the end of his story.

"I didn't really like it. I felt uncomfortable," Elizabeth Siddal resumed the narrative. "I thought it might be a lark, a new experience, the freest of free love. But when we were naked"—her voice slowed as she remembered—"and we were kissing"—she spoke as if she were in a trance, reliving a dream—"of a sudden I felt very frightened and confused. I was afraid and wanted to escape her caresses."

The telling of this intimate tale had completely broken Miss Siddal down. She struggled from her seat on the divan, tears streaming from her eyes, overturning what was left of her glass of absinthe in the process, and fled to Rossetti, burying her head in his chest. "Oh Danny, Danny, I'm sorry. It would have been such a picture."

"It upset her greatly, as it still does, as you can see." Rossetti, quite composed, finished speaking for her. "She was not really able to do it, you see, to open herself to that other woman in the way that woman was demanding she do. She sought shelter in my arms just as she is doing now. I think it confused her mightily," Rossetti finished in classic understatement.

"And you were trying to paint them?" Dickens, who had recovered his composure, pressed for more of the tawdry details.

"Yes. I tried." Rossetti seemed to be getting bored with the subject. "But they weren't at it long enough for me to get anything down, just a few scrawled sketches." He stopped a moment to think. "But the woman's idea was a good one, and she has helped me to execute it. Actually, she was very nice about that whole affair."

"Oh she was wonderful, so understanding." Lizzie Siddal, still in tears, raised her red face from Rossetti's chest. "She didn't mind that I couldn't make love with her. She said that I probably wasn't right for women, not all women are. She said she was sorry and she hoped she hadn't frightened me. She said once more how beautiful I was, that I was"—and a desirous wistfulness seemed to float like a flower in a still pool into her voice—"the most beautiful woman of our age and that was why she so wanted to touch my beauty."

I was stunned at the simplicity and depth of her narcissism. I was moved by it, I think, not only because she so believed in it, but because the wistfulness in her voice gave off the scent of mortality. She knew how fleeting was that beauty upon which she had built her whole existence.

"But I was caught up in the idea, you see, of painting two women making love." Rossetti seemed to have rekindled his interest in our conversation. "And I asked Miss de Brevecoeur, before she left us that day, if I might paint her making love to another woman."

Rossetti clearly had none of the woman's compunction about following his art for art's sake philosophy wherever it might lead.

"And what did she answer?" Dickens was utterly captured by the strangeness, the utter frankness of Rossetti's distanced, purely aesthetic view of this act which our century and every other century condemned as unnatural.

"She answered that yes, it was quite possible, but I would have to pay for the privilege and do my painting in a much different, less congenial light."

"What did she mean?" Dickens pressed.

"You really ought to talk to Flory about her, about Marie." Miss Siddal, wiping her eyes and trying to compose herself, broke out of Rossetti's arms like a frightened bird fluttering frantically about a closed room. She crossed to the worktable to pour a fresh glass of her calming absinthe. "Talk to Flory Nightingale. She is almost obsessed with Marie. She seems to think she can save her. But then, she wants to save everyone . . . even me."

"Save her from what?" For the first time Dickens's voice betrayed confusion. Those two, the utterly composed artist and his model in frantic disarray, volleying this conversation back and forth like a shuttlecock, seemed to have thrown him off.

"From selling herself to men," Miss Siddal said; then she drank deeply of her numbing liqueur and collapsed onto the divan.

"But I thought she only went with women?" Dickens was lost at sea, adrift in this maelstrom of contradictions.

"That is true," Rossetti, maddening in his equanimity, averred. "That is what I was about to tell you before Lizzie felt compelled to introduce *her*"—and the cold emphasis his voice placed upon that pronoun clearly signaled his dislike for its referent—"friend, Florence Nightingale, into our conversation."

He smiled and extended his hands, palms up, out to the sides in a small gesture asking if we wished him to proceed with his explanation.

"Please, I really do not understand all of this," Dickens begged him to go on.

"Marie de Brevecoeur told me that I could still paint her, but I would have to pay."

"Pay whom?"

"Kate Hamilton."

"Who is Kate Hamilton?"

"She is the keeper of a house of, shall we say, out-of-the-ordinary entertainments."

"And?"

"Marie de Brevecoeur told us that she worked in that house."

"As a whore for men?"

"In a sense."

Rossetti was so detached from the monstrous reality of what he was describing that I began to feel a genuine dislike for the man. I later learned that Dickens did not trust Rossetti, either.

"What do you mean?" Dickens patiently waited for Rossetti to explain.

"She is not a whore for men in the usual sense." He warmed to his story in the way that a painter enjoys showing the subtle play of light and shadow over his subject. "You see, Kate Hamilton's is a specialty house, in Mayfair, rather elegant actually . . ."

I found myself remembering Lady Godiva's, which Dickens and I had visited two years before in the course of the Ashbee Affair.*

". . . which only indulges a single male obsession."

The man paused. He was taunting us. I must credit Dickens with not rising to his bait, waiting.

"Voyeurism," Rossetti went on after a long, dramatic sip from his glass of absinthe, "specifically that of men who desire to watch women make love to other women. There are private shows gotten up for this purpose."

*Lady Godiva's House of Gentlemen's Entertainments was a rather elegant Mayfair brothel which Dickens and Collins had occasion to visit for the purpose of gathering information for Inspector Field in the case of "the Macbeth Murders" as recounted in *The Detective and Mr. Dickens.*

"Marie de Brevecoeur does this for money?" The shock in Dickens's voice was genuine.

Rossetti was undeniably pleased with the reaction he had elicited from Dickens. That was when I realized what fueled Rossetti's existence. He was in the business of shocking people. His art, his life, his intercourse with the world at large, was that of the incendiarist. He wanted to blow up all that was conventional, narrowly moral.

"Yes, and I must say, she is quite good at it, quite elaborate and dramatic in her presentation, as a great actress would be on a different sort of stage."

"So you went there and saw her?" The wonder in Dickens's voice was so that of a naive child that I began to wonder if he, too, was not playing a game with Rossetti, counterfeiting his shock and moral indignation in order to draw the man out.

"Yes, we did"—Rossetti was eager to paint this picture in all of its lurid detail—"Lizzie and I. And we took Miss Nightingale along. She seemed enormously interested in what she called 'the social phenomenon.' I think she just wanted to see this Marie with her bloomers off."

That last comment betrayed Rossetti more than any of his other affectations had. Saying it, he raised his eyebrows lewdly at Dickens and me.

"It was all extremely useful for my purposes, you see," Rossetti went on. "I have been there three times to sketch. I have captured it all. If only I can recapture it in paint."

He sounded like some triumphant hunter brandishing his bag with the bloodlust still upon him.

"When does she do this, put on this performance at Kate Hamilton's?" Dickens was no longer the naive country bumpkin marveling at Rossetti's urbanity. He had what he wanted. His voice had changed and sounded almost like Field's in its grim efficiency. Rossetti noticed this change of tone and his equanimity was momentarily shaken.

"Why, she . . . uh . . . once a week, on Friday evenings," Rossetti answered, looking strangely at Dickens. "We would be happy to take you there." Rossetti was desperately trying to regain what he thought was his hold over Dickens's curiosity.

"Oh no, no need, I think we can forgo the pleasure. Good

day." And Dickens brushed him off like a piece of lint from his sleeve, turned on his heel, and was out the door of that studio, which suddenly seemed very dim and dark. The afternoon light certainly was gone.

"I CANNOT GIVE HER UP!"

(August 12, 1852—Evening)

We must go straightaway to Bow Street, Wilkie," Dickens informed me as we emerged from Rossetti's high house and crossed the Embankment to Sleepy Rob's waiting cab. "We must apprise Field of the intelligence we have gathered this afternoon."

"Just what intelligence have we gathered?" I asked in all innocence as we settled into the overstuffed seats and Sleepy Rob began his monotonous trot across the town.

"Good lord, Wilkie!" Dickens's exasperation at the obtuseness of my deducive powers was both visible and audible. "All of the pieces are starting to come together."

I just looked at him in incomprehension, not willing to further embarrass myself by asking another stupid (at least in his eyes) question.

"Don't you see, Wilkie?" he finally said to me, as if I were a child. "We know that the murdered woman was abused by her husband and turned to other women because of it. We know that these women were daughters of Lesbos and that Marie de Brevecoeur had the strongest influence upon Eliza Lane. Then Elizabeth Browning saw the Lane woman talking to the mustachioed French night guard, Barsad, outside the bank the night she was murdered. Thus, Marie de Brevecoeur, the murdered woman, and the mustachioed Frenchman are all connected. Perhaps they are the gang that Field thinks committed these crimes."

"But the landlady in Lambeth told Field that it was four men meeting with Barsad," I continued, quizzical.

"Good lord, Wilkie!" Dickens's exasperation at my blockheaded myopia toward what he evidently saw so clearly would have been comical if he hadn't been so intent upon displaying his own detectiving skill. "These women all dress as men. Except for Barsad, the whole gang could have been women."

I did feel somewhat stupid at not having seen it at first, but that did not stop me from trying to salvage my dignity by poking yet another hole in Dickens's little deductive jigsaw puzzle.

"All well and good"—I nodded my head enthusiastically in the affirmative as if agreeing with Dickens's smug reading of this lesbian conspiracy text—"but that is only three members of this mythical gang. Who is the fourth? The landlady said there were four men meeting with Barsad. And why? Why the threatening letters? Why murder one of their own?"

I am happy to say that those petty questions stopped Dickens in his arrogant tracks. He stared at me, wrinkling his forehead as he strained mightily for an answer or two. I am sorry, but the temptation to taunt him was simply too much for me to resist.

"Perhaps this fourth was Miss Ternan's mother." I winked comically at him, but he did not see the humour at all in my speculation. Luckily, at that very moment, we pulled up in front of Bow Street Station and Dickens disembarked without badgering my obtuseness any further.

Field and Rogers were less than enthusiastic when Dickens came bursting through the door of the bullpen and interrupted what, from all appearances, seemed a rather silent moment of pipes and contemplation in their wing chairs before the cold hearth.

Field rose somberly as we entered. "Gentlemen, you look as if you have had a good day." He said it, however, with a decided lack of engagement and sank listlessly back into his chair.

But even this cold reception could not dampen Dickens's high spirits and elevated sense of his own detecting skills.

"A good day, indeed," Dickens burst upon them. "We have gathered what I think is some valuable information. I think we have identified at least three of the members of this bank-robbing gang." And with that preface, he poured out his narrative of the afternoon's interviews complete with all of his theories about spousal abuse leading to lesbianism and women disguising themselves as men to walk around the city hatching plots. For some reason, discretion I presume, he chose not to mention Angela Burdett-Coutts's rather startling revelation of her ill-starred marriage to James Barton, even though she had expressly commissioned him to do so to Field. But I did not question his judgement. No one in England was more conscious of the vicissitudes of reputation than Charles Dickens, and for that reason, I presumed, this was one of those times when he chose to keep his own counsel.

"You have certainly been much more successful than we have been," Field glumly admitted after Dickens's euphoria had subsided. "We have not been able to turn up a single lead as to the whereabouts of our French friend, the professor. He and his mustache, if he even has a mustache, have temporarily gone to ground."

Dickens thought for a moment. "Do you think," he began, clearly viewing himself as a full partner of Field in the planning of the strategy for the solving of the crime (or crimes, as it were), "that if we could find this Frenchwoman, this Marie de Brevecoeur, that she would lead us to Barsad? He certainly seems to be the puppetmaster who is pulling the strings."

"*Cherchez la femme,*" I said, quite wittily I thought.

The other three looked at me as if I were a drunken fool who had intruded upon their solemn deliberations speaking a foreign language.

"Uh, follow the woman," I stammered lamely by way of translation.

They just ignored me and went back to their plotting as if I didn't exist in their real detectives' world. The result was a

147

plan to seek out, the following day, the nurse, this Florence Nightingale, whom both Barbara Leigh Smith and Lizzie Siddal had advised us to consult.

"It seems, perhaps," Field confided, "that Miss Nightingale might lead us to the others, or at least set us on their trail."

"It is worth a try," Serjeant Rogers grumbled out of a blue cloud of pipe smoke.

We all agreed that enough detective work had been done for one day, and that we would meet again in the morning and try to find Miss Florence Nightingale. With that, Dickens and I got up to leave, but Field stopped Charles for one last word.

"In the morning you must do something about Miss Ternan." He spoke gently to Charles in the voice of a friend and advisor. "It is too dangerous for both you and me for us to continue to hide her. You must give her to Collar; then we will be free to clear up this mess without his interference."

"But she is innocent," Dickens protested. "She will go to Newgate."

"I know . . . we all know . . . with complete certainty, that she is innocent," Field consoled him, "but this is necessary so that we can prove her innocence without her appearing to be guilty. She must give herself up or the Queen's Bench magistrates will find her guilty just for runnin' away."

"I cannot give her up." Despite his assertion, a look of doom haunted Dickens's face.

"Collar will persist, I assure you," Field reminded him, rather gently I thought. "The longer she stays in hidin', the stronger he shall suspect that she is his murderer."

"I know that. I know." Dickens's voice was desperate. "But don't you see, I simply cannot cast her into Newgate. It is a fearful, hellish place. I have been there."

"Yes, but we cannot keep her out of the way forever."

Rogers and I stood silently in attendance to this quiet battle of wills.

"I know that as well, but if we could only catch this Barsad, sort out this whole mess of the murder, then Miss Ternan will be a moot point," Dickens argued.

"Moot? Perhaps. But we can only keep Collar away for so long." Field was shaking his head negatively the whole time he was speaking. "And, Miss Burdett-Coutts will have to report that robbery soon as well."

"Not if we recover that ten thousand pounds before anyone even knows it is gone." Dickens sounded like a solicitor arguing his client's case. "Do you think that Miss Burdett-Coutts wants the whole world to know that her bank's security was penetrated for ten thousand pounds?"

"No. I don't suppose so." Field said it slowly, contemplatively, as if weighing the idea for the first time which I am certain was not the case. "All we are sayin', Charles"—and Field glanced quickly at Serjeant Rogers, whose head nodded dutifully in support—"is that if Miss Ternan turns herself over to Collar voluntary-like, then things will most assuredly go better for her and we shall gain some time to sort this all out."

"Without that Collar's constant interference," belligerent Serjeant Rogers punctuated his master's point.

Dickens was sorely outnumbered and he knew it. His eyes were desperate as he looked grimly from Field to Rogers, hoping for some reprieve. But their faces were like stone. Finally, he relented.

"I will take her to Collar in the morning," Dickens begrudgingly assured them, "but we must find this murderer. That is the only way we can save her."

"We know that, Charles." It was Inspector Field's turn to be consoling. "And we shall get it done. We shall find out wot happened that evening of the murder and we shall find the man"—and he paused for a quick pull at his pipe—"or woman, who did it."

Dickens blanched. "Woman?" he repeated. "But you do not think that . . . ?"

"No. No. You misunderstand me." Field was all reassurance. "All I meant was that there are so many women dressed as men poppin' up in this case that any of them could be our killer."

"Oh." But Dickens still sounded suspicious, as if he did not trust Field's expression of unequivocal belief in Ellen Ternan's innocence.

Out in the street in front of Bow Street Station, Dickens still looked stricken.

"Wilkie, I must see her tonight." A sadness had overtaken

his countenance, which was truly pitiable. "I know that I must, but I just do not think that I can give her up."

In the cab on the way to Hawkins's den in Leicester Square, I tried to turn his attention to more practical considerations. In short, I attempted to rehearse him in a fabricated story to tell Collar to account for Miss Ternan's whereabouts over the previous two days. We agreed that after Nellie left my flat the morning after the fateful night of the murder, she went off to visit her mother in the country and upon her return had gone to Dickens, who immediately escorted her to St. James Station and Inspector Collar.

"Oh, Wilkie." Dickens's voice struggled in pain as Sleepy Rob's cab rolled to a gentle stop at our destination. "How can I tell her that I am going to betray her?"

"You are not betraying her, Charles," I tried to reassure him. "It is simply what must be done, the best, the safest path to take."

NELLIE BETRAYED

❦

(August 12, 1852—Evening)

At the shooting gallery, the situation was directly opposite of what we had expected. Nellie seemed quite composed, almost resigned to her fate, while Irish Meg was all aflutter.

When we arrived, Nellie was fast asleep on a small pallet behind a flimsy partition. Irish Meg, however, was pacing the floor and smoking one of Captain Hawkins's rum-soaked cigars.

"Oh, Wilkie, I hates it here," she confided after taking me aside as soon as I walked in with Dickens. "It's so dark and dirty and closed up, and that twisted little man with his filthy parrot gives me the frights."

I tried to calm her, but she would have nothing of it. She poured out her complaints in a torrent, ending with how terribly frightened Nellie was, how fearful of Newgate and the gallows. "I'm so afeared for Nellie," Meg confided. "What are we to do?"

"Our only concern is for doing what is best for her," I assured Meggy with greater certainty in my voice than I truly felt.

Thus was I able to calm her, which was not such a burdensome task owing to her great devotion to Dickens's Nellie. In fact, in the time since Nellie's liberation from Miss Burdett-Coutts's Urania Cottage, she and my Meggie had become almost like sisters.

When we had entered, Dickens's disappointment that his Nellie was sleeping had registered upon his face. But, while I engaged myself with the pacification of Irish Meg, he had contented himself with exchanging pleasantries with Captain Hawkins, Broken Bert, and the parrot. It was probably the loud, bawdy chirping of the parrot that awakened Miss Ternan from her slumber.

She came out from behind her sleeping partition with a lost look on her face.

"Oh, Charles, what is it? I was sleeping." She smiled in confusion when she saw him.

"It is nothing, my dear." But there was an undeniable tension in his voice. "I just stopped here to see you, that you are well . . ." And his voice trailed off in his own confusion.

We were so awkward, the two of us, in the presence of these women who ruled our lives and whatever emotions of love we thought we possessed. We were two feckless men who had cast ourselves under their spell.

"But we have really come for your help in solving this case." Dickens's voice broke my reverie and brought me back to reality. "We wish to talk with Miss Florence Nightingale. What can you tell us about her? Do you know where we might find her?"

"Wot do you want with that witch?" Irish Meg used a term that ladies seldom apply to one another.

"We are in search of Marie de Brevecoeur. Field thinks that she is at the center of this whole affair. We have been told that Florence Nightingale knows her better than anyone."

"Flory thinks she knows everything," Irish Meg remarked sourly.

"She would be at one of the hospitals during the day," said Nellie Ternan, who with a finger to her pursed lips had put her mind to the problem. "She would either be at the asylum for madwomen, Bethlehem on the Lambeth Road, or at the lying-in hospital, St. Mark's in Claremont Square."

"Madwomen?" I exclaimed.

"Women who don't have no one. Mostly whores sick from the streets or girls up from the country or wives broken by their husbands. Women whose heads don't work no more. They goes to Bedlam to die." Irish Meg explained it all to us with angry patience.

"Flory works there many days to help make the poor things comfortable. She says she's a public nurse," Nellie added.

"Wotever that is!" Irish Meg seemed angry at us, at Florence Nightingale, at the whole world at that moment.

"We must find her tomorrow," Dickens said. Then he took both of his Nellie's hands tenderly in his own and bent to her to whisper something.

"This will all be over soon, Meggy," I tried to reassure my love, but she spit back at me like a cornered animal.

"It better be, Wilkie! Or I'll be in that Bedlam for mad-women meself!"

"Tomorrow morning!" Ellen Ternan suddenly exclaimed, stepping back from Dickens in alarum, her hands fluttering like frightened birds to the sides of her face.

"Wot is it, Nellie?" Irish Meg rushed to her side as Miss Ternan's body began to quake with uncontrollable sobs.

Dickens turned to me with a look of pain and helplessness on his face that spoke volumes. He was terrified that he was giving his beloved up to the gallows and that she could never forgive him for this betrayal.

As she rocked the stricken young woman in her arms, Irish Meg's eyes shot sharp daggers of recrimination right at me.

Dickens also stared helplessly at me as if begging for me somehow to set things right.

Everyone seemed to be looking at me, blaming me for this violent overflow of emotion, demanding that I do or say something that could make all of this pain subside.

I was momentarily struck dumb. I had no idea what to say, how to calm her, to bolster him. I struggled to gather my wits, but I never had the chance.

At that very moment came a powerful, insistent pounding at the shooting gallery's barred door.

"Open in the name of the Metropolitan Protectives!" shouted a voice of authority through the locked door. "Open, or we'll have to break it down!"

It was not Inspector Field's voice.

DICKENS PLYS HIS TRADE

(August 12, 1852 — Evening)

My God, it is Collar!" Dickens found both his voice and that reckless power of mastery over threatening situations which had momentarily abandoned him in his distress over his beloved Ellen's plight. He moved purposefully to the door as that relentless pounding persisted. Without hesitation, but to all of our horror, he opened it.

The door opening inward caught Collar's man, Serjeant Mussbabble, in midpound. That worthy tumbled comically into the room as if toppled off a perch. Behind him, framed in the doorway, stood Collar, glaring at the lot of us.

"Inspector Collar, come in." Dickens greeted him jovially, as if this angry policeman was a late arrival at a dinner party. "Come in. This is indeed fortuitous. I am so glad that you are here. We were just talking about you."

Dickens was nattering on so rapidly that Inspector Collar had no opportunity to reply. He stared wide-eyed at Dickens with the same amazement which had turned all of us to statues.

"Miss Ternan has just this evening arrived back in the city and we have been trying to decide whether to come talk to you about this whole unfortunate affair tonight or to wait until morning."

Dickens was smiling warmly at the overmatched policeman, who still had not uttered a word.

"It seems you have solved our dilemma for us. Come in, come in please. This is Miss Ellen Ternan." And he ushered Collar right to Nellie's side.

As if on cue, she looked pitiably up at him with tears streaming down her face.

Collar drew himself up on tiptoe. "Miss Ellen Ternan, you are under arrest for murder," he blurted out, but with none of the violent authority that Field would have put into it. In fact, Collar seemed almost intimidated either by Dickens's equanimity or by Nellie's torrent of tears.

Of course, Collar's blunt, gruffly spoken charge sent Ellen Ternan into further paroxysms of sobs.

"Really, Inspector Collar, that is a bit harsh, is it not?" Dickens was still smiling as if this were all some trivial parlor game, charades or hide the handkerchief. "You said that you merely wished to talk to Miss Ternan about the murder. You gave us no sense of such great urgency. Is there some reason for such a serious charge?"

Collar looked like a volcano about to erupt. He spewed forth his charges in a garbled explosion of words: "You've been hidin' her. You've known where she was all the time. You've all been lyin' to me. I'll not be fooled with."

"Please, please, Inspector Collar"—Dickens never changed his hospitable manner and smiling equanimity—"nothing of the sort."

"Nothin' of the sort, nothin' of the sort," the policeman sputtered like a boiler on the verge of bursting. "Everything of the sort!"

And Collar would not be pacified.

Dickens spun out the story we had concocted in the cab, but Collar refused to be swayed by this latest fiction which Dickens spun out so adeptly on the spot.

"I'll tell you wot I think." Collar, who as Dickens spoke managed to somewhat compose himself, still glared at Dickens as if seriously contemplating arresting him as well (and probably all the rest of us) for harboring the tender fugitive. "I think you've all been hidin' her, that she's been in this hole-in-the-wall of a shootin' gallery all of the time."

"Oh, Inspector Collar"—and now it was Dickens's turn to be chagrined—"that is a serious charge and simply not true."

"True or not true," Collar backed down from Dickens's stern chagrin, "we are takin' Miss Ternan tonight. This is a murder case"—he raised himself up against the gravity of it and stuck out his chest as a mark of his own importance—"and she must be remanded to the custody of the bailiffs."

With a nod to Mussbabble, Collar ordered Nellie taken up.

Dickens never ceased to amaze me. He could create characters on the spot and then play out their parts in the scene as if the whole world were no more than a novel that existed inside his own active imagination. Even as Collar's Constable was stepping forward to take Nellie in hand, Dickens was smiling once again and graciously entering into negotiations with Collar. Realizing the inevitable, he chose to hide his pain and fears for his Ellen's well-being and attempt to make the best of a certain setback. "Must Miss Ternan be taken up tonight? It is so late."

As were all the rest of us, Inspector Collar seemed momentarily unmanned by Dickens's concern.

"Miss Ternan will present herself in the morning," Charles pressed. "I will take full responsibility for her appearance. Surely you cannot think she will flee if I am her sponsor."

"I knows my duty." Collar's words rasped like cutlery being drawn across stone. "She'll be in the holdin' rooms at St. James's tonight and she'll go before the magistrate in the mornin'."

Dickens's face fell. I think it was only then that he realized that the man was not going to listen, that he could not write this particular chapter in the Dickens style but would have to settle for Collar's inferior version. He turned to his Ellen and, when their eyes met, the pleading in his caused the tears to rush forth once more in hers.

After a moment of silent suspension in time, Dickens

turned back to Collar, his features under perfect control, his voice steady: "May I have a moment, Inspector, alone with Miss Ternan? To prepare her."

"Let her go." Collar nodded to his familiar. "One minute," he cautioned Dickens, "then we take her away."

It was one of the longest, tensest minutes of my memory.

Dickens retired to the back of the dim shooting gallery with Nellie.

Collar and his swarthy constable stood waiting with faces of stone by the door.

Even Broken Bert's parrot seemed momentarily awed and was uncharacteristically silent as those two old inseparables lurked in the shadows on one side of the cold hearth.

Captain Hawkins stood leaning against the hearthstone with shadows bisecting his smooth-shaven head and a bemused look upon his face, as if this were all just a Sherwood Forest game and he was just waiting for Dickens to give the signal so that he could spring into action like some latter-day Little John and rescue us all from the terrible pall that Collar's intrusion had cast over the dingy premises.

As for me, I stood frozen in the viperous gaze of Irish Meg. She looked at me with utter disgust, as if I were the arresting officer, as if I were the informer who had led Collar and his man to the shooting gallery and had given Nellie up to them.

It was one of the most uncomfortable minutes of my life, but it finally ended when Dickens returned, leading Nellie, her tears dried, her countenance resigned to being taken away by those two glowering policemen.

And take her away they did, without another word from either side.

Dickens followed them out into the street, but Collar packed the girl into his black post chaise with little ceremony and drove off.

When Dickens returned, it was as if his whole demeanor had caved in upon itself. Where he had been urbane, conciliatory, hospitable, and even jocular with Collar, he was now anxious, worried, helpless, and guilty in our presence.

"There is nothing more we can do tonight," he finally announced after a long moment of all of us looking to him for guidance and him looking into the blackness of the cold hearth and thinking on it. "I think he believed enough of our story that there will be no repercussions upon you and Bert, Captain. I think the best thing *we* can do is go home now," he said, turning to Irish Meg and me. "It has been a hellish day, Wilkie. Damn, he must have followed us from Bow Street. We should have been more careful."

Out in the street, with Irish Meg already handed into Sleepy Rob's cab, Dickens took me lightly by the elbow for one last word.

"You take the cab, Wilkie. I need to walk all of this off tonight. I will see you in the morning early. There is so much that needs to be done." And then he paused for just a moment, thinking, my elbow still in custody. "It is all topsy-turvy, Wilkie," he finally said, letting me go, "but as novelists it is our task to make it all work out."

"Tell that to Irish Meg!" I replied over my shoulder as I climbed into the cab. We left him standing there in the feeble gaslight in front of the police station, all alone, bearing the full weight of the whole affair.

BEDLAM!

(August 13, 1852—Morning and Afternoon)

T he next morning dawned much too soon, and when I arrived at about half ten at the *Household Words* offices, it appeared that Dickens had enjoyed every bit as rocky a night's sleep as had I. First, I had been forced to deal with all of Irish Meg's resentments toward both of us for leading Collar to Miss Ternan and then giving her up. In addition, I had proceeded to toss and turn all night, haunted with guilty fantasies of daughters of Lesbos and nude artists' models writhing in my fevered brain.

As for Dickens, it did not take a phrenologist to intuit that in his anxiety for his Ellen he had not slept a wink.* However, we had been given our assignment by Field, and nothing was going to stop Dickens from carrying it out.

Honoring me with but the most perfunctory of greetings when I arrived, Dickens unceremoniously spun me around, out the door, and into Sleepy Rob's cab. With that, we were once again off to play detective.

---

*In Victorian England, phrenology was the young science of measuring people's heads with calipers in order to speculate upon their mental capacities.

Our first stop, however, was at St. James Station, where Dickens attempted to see Miss Ternan, and was apprised that he could not see her until after her arraignment before the magistrate, which would not occur for yet another day because of the heat and the magistrate's inability to deal with its excesses. In other words, the magistrate had decided that it was simply too hot to hold court and had most probably retired to the country to go fishing on some shaded waterway. Dickens, of course, was irate. But since neither Collar nor his man Mussbabble was in attendance, he had no one to vent his wrath upon except a poor illiterate constable just emigrated from Scotland, who must have been the only person in the British Isles who had never heard of the inimitable Charles Dickens. Needless to say, Charles was sorely frustrated. Thus, it was good that we had our task to perform for Inspector Field. Nonetheless, Dickens was fuming as we set off on our search for Miss Florence Nightingale.

The Bethlehem Lunatic Asylum is located across the river by the Lambeth Bridge just off the Lambeth Road near that hot and dusty neighborhood where we had first gone looking for our French friend Barsad. "Bedlam" is the name by which it is popularly known. The heavy day was moving into sluggish afternoon by the time we got to that stage of our "investigation," as Dickens called it ("chasing phantoms" seemed to me a more accurate description).

We were fortunate, upon inquiry, to find Miss Florence Nightingale at work in the women's wing of that horrible place. As we traversed the corridors in search of her, the sounds of madness assaulted our ears. Through doorways and out from behind flimsy partitions, wild animal sounds, growls and grunts and barks and screams, shrill shrieks and deep guttural moans, bleats and brays and long painful groans mixed and formed themselves into an angry mob which seemed to be bearing down upon us at every turning of our journey through that terrible labyrinth of a building. It was like walking through a zoo in which all the animals were aroused.

We found Miss Nightingale. She was working in a long, low-ceilinged, dimly lit ward which was windowless. In the August heat, this room was an airless, stifling place, cursed with the vilest of smells, of unwashed diseased bodies, of incontinence, of lingering death. It was hard even to breathe in Bedlam.

Florence Nightingale was tending to two women simultaneously when we came upon her. One of her charges seemed dead from her injuries already. With a face swollen by large yellowing bruises, she lay still on a narrow bed. She wore an utterly blank look upon her wide-eyed face as she stared silently up at the ceiling. The other patient was directly the opposite. Her arms and legs tethered tightly to the bedposts, she writhed angrily against her restraints and cursed and ranted madly in some utterly unintelligible language whose lexicon existed solely within that poor woman's broken mind.

"Good Lord," I exclaimed to Dickens in an alarmed whisper as we came upon Miss Nightingale and her charges. I had not intended for anyone but Dickens to hear me, but, as I was to perceive upon further acquaintance, Miss Nightingale missed very little of what went on about her.

"Good Lord, indeed," she wryly critiqued my exclamation of surprise and shock at the conditions of her two patients. "The Lord wasn't very good to these two. All we can hope is that he makes up in some other life for the way he has treated them here."

"Miss Nightingale, I am Charles Dickens and this is Mr. Wilkie Collins. We desperately need to talk to you on a matter of some urgency."

"You may talk all you wish, and I shall try to answer, but I must care for these two poor souls because there are others waiting to be tended to." The woman, though slight of stature, had a directness about her that asserted a clear control over this conversation. In her sense of realistic priorities, those two helpless women had unarguable precedence over these two intruding gentlemen.

"How on earth did they get this way?" Dickens's curiosity overcame his delicacy.

"That one has been beaten by her husband regularly for years. It's laudanum in heavy doses makes her sleep like that with her eyes wide open. She is only eighteen years old."

"And this one?" I asked timidly.

"She is in the last stages of a brain sickness caused by

162

syphilis. She'll be gone within the week." Even as she finished, I was drawing back in shock and revulsion from that poor tethered madwoman, as if I might catch her terrible disease simply from bending over her bed.

"Good Lord," I muttered again.

"But what do you two want of me?" Her directness again brought our conversation out of the realm of idle curiosity and placed it firmly into the realm of distasteful reality. "I know who you are. Nellie Ternan and Meg Sheehey have spoken well of you. I presume they have put you onto me, have they not?"

"Yes, yes, of course they have," Dickens stammered, rather taken aback by the aggressive directness of this young woman who never ceased in the bathing of her poor bruised patient as she spoke, "as have Miss Elizabeth Siddal and Mr. Rossetti."

At their mention, Florence Nightingale did pause in her ministrations to her patient. "Those two sent you here?" There was suspicion in her voice.

"Yes," Dickens answered.

"Just what do you want of me?"

"Miss Siddal said that you know Marie de Brevecoeur better than anyone, that you could help us to find her," Dickens explained.

Miss Nightingale raised her eyebrows in recognition and glanced quickly from one of us to the other as if trying to decide whether to trust us or not.

"It is about the murder of Eliza Lane, isn't it?" she finally said. "Marie would never do that."

"We know. We know," Dickens hastened to reassure her. "We think that the murderer is a man with whom she keeps company, a tall, French-speaking man with a mustache called John Barsad."

"He is the evil one, that's certain." Miss Nightingale nodded her head. "If I could get Marie loose from his influence, well . . ." She let her wishful thinking trail off as she bent once more to her patient.

Dickens did not press her. We waited in silence as she completed the bathing of the bruised limbs of her drugged patient and turned with her sponge and basin to her more difficult charge. Surprisingly, whether because of the light touch of her hand or the coolness of the water on the sponge, the tethered madwoman seemed to calm under Miss Nightingale's gentle ministrations. By the time the bath was finished, the poor woman had dropped off into a fitful sleep.

"This is important work that you do," I overheard Dickens whisper to Florence Nightingale as we followed her out of that airless ward and into a smaller workroom, which housed a drain and a water pump. "What has brought you to it?"

"I first tended to my father, who was a very kind man, in a hospital when he was dying." Though somewhat surprised at Dickens's interest, Miss Nightingale answered quite forthrightly. "It gave me satisfaction to tend to the sick. It gives my life direction."

As I eavesdropped upon their conversation and observed Dickens as he listened to this young woman, I could clearly perceive the powerful impression she was making upon him. This was no Mistress Quickly of a nurse, no gin-tippler of the sort that Dickens himself had described.*

"I went to Alexandria two years ago to work in a hospital with the sisters of Saint Vincent de Paul," she continued, warming to her subject. "Those nuns taught me that nursing was a profession, like that of doctors and solicitors and clergymen. Unfortunately, nobody in England seems to agree." She finished with a shrug of frustration.

"Perhaps you can change that," Dickens said, and smiled at her.

"Perhaps." She looked strangely back at him, no longer distrustful, but almost grateful that he had taken the time to listen to her. That was, I must admit, one of Dickens's great strengths. He was a wonderful listener.

"I have other patients to tend to this afternoon," Florence Nightingale turned our conversation toward its conclusion.

"Can you help us to find Marie de Brevecoeur?" Dickens pressed.

"Perhaps." She paused and looked hard at Dickens. "I will have to look into it. I do not know where she lives. I have only

*Such as Sarah Gamp in his novel *Martin Chuzzlewit.*

met with her in public places. But she confides in me. She makes money for this Barsad."

"How?" Dickens pursued Miss Nightingale when she attempted to flee the subject.

"As an actress," she resigned herself to answering, "in private performances."

"What sort of private performances?" Dickens was relentless in his questioning.

"At Kate Hamilton's and in séances. I have attended séances twice. They are, shall we say, 'different.' "

"Kate Hamilton's?" Dickens repeated the name as a question.

"You have been there and seen her?" Florence Nightingale spoke in an alarmed voice, and looked sharply at Dickens.

"No, we have not, but Miss Siddal mentioned that establishment."

"Then you know that men watch women make love to other women there?"

"Yes."

"But that is not all. Some men bring their wives there to be molested. All is not always what it seems there. Some women taunt their husbands by performing there. Eliza Lane has performed there, with Marie de Brevecoeur. Did you know that?"

"No, we did not." Dickens was utterly thrown by this revelation. I think he really believed that he knew what was happening in this strange sexual underworld. But, as we were to find out, none of us, not even Inspector Field, fully understood the twisted motives of this case. London in those days was so like that; nothing was ever what it seemed.

"Kate Hamilton's productions are not Marie de Brevecoeur's best performances," Florence Nightingale declared as a means of changing the subject.

We both stared at her in dumb show.

"It is Wednesday, is it not?" She seemed serious in her question, as if she had absentmindedly lost connection to time and space owing to her voluntary confinement in this madhouse.

"Yes," Dickens answered, puzzled.

"There is a spirit rapping on Thursday nights, a private séance," she explained. "Marie serves as hostess for the

165

medium. You must pay to attend. Perhaps you will find her there."

Dickens stared questioningly at her, and his wondering look actually amused her.

"Oh, I don't believe in such silliness," she laughed, "but Marie seems to. Here, I shall write down the address. I will be happy to attend with you if you wish. I would like to see Marie freed from this man Barsad's influence."

With that, our conversation came to an end, except for one last private exchange which I observed between Dickens and her just as we were about to leave. A rather thick packet of bills passed from Dickens's hand into the pocket of her work smock. He had found yet another charity to support.

As we drove away from the Bethlehem Lunatic Asylum, Sleepy Rob stopped once just before the Lambeth Bridge to check his horse's bridle. Then he stopped again on the Victoria Embankment to climb down and walk all around his cab before climbing back up and continuing on to Bow Street. When we pulled up in front of Bow Street Station to deliver our report to Inspector Field, Sleepy Rob apprised us that we had been followed by a black coach drawn by two horses ever since we had left the lunatic asylum. He was sure, however, that it was not Collar's Protectives coach, which seemed right since Collar believed that he already had his killer.

But if it was not Collar, who could it be?

NELLIE IN NEWGATE

(August 14, 1852—Morning)

I was sitting next to Dickens in the Kensington Magistrate's Court the next morning when Ellen Ternan was led in. She did not look much the worse for wear despite having been forced to spend two nights in the holding room at St. James Station. Much to Dickens's relief both Field and Rogers had joined us in the gallery of the courtroom just before Miss Ternan was brought in.

Her hair was a bit tousled, but she had clearly been allowed to make a complete morning toilette, and she looked clean and fresh despite her ordeal. Of course, that sort of appearance comes easily, even under stress, to persons of Miss Ternan's youth. If I had been forced to sleep in gaol two nights running, I would emerge looking like a disgruntled porcupine.

The magistrate was a Mr. McWhelply, who exhibited all of the gruff disinterest of his Scottish ancestry until Miss Ternan was announced and the word "murder" raised its viperous head in his courtroom. The word caught his (and everyone else's) attention. A murmur buzzed through the courtroom as if a hive had just been whacked. All eyes flew to Dickens's Ellen as she was escorted into the dock.

Magistrate McWhelply made quick work of her.

"For murder? A woman? Worst kind," he pronounced, and turned to Inspector Collar for an explanation.

"Yes sir." Collar, a model of fawning respect for the court and bloodless protector of the civil peace, addressed the high justice like a true martinet. "The affair at Coutts Bank, Your Honor, murder of another woman it is."

"Evidence?"

"Yes sir." Collar produced the green scarf. "Belongs to the accused and was used to strangle a Miss Eliza Lane at the previous mentioned bank."

"Quite so. Thank you, Inspector Collar." And that seemed to close the case for Chief Magistrate McWhelply. However, as a necessary afterthought, he stared off into space as if contemplating a beckoning trout stream and asked no one in particular: "Is there anyone present here to speak for Miss"—and he consulted his charge sheet to find her name—"um, Ternan?"

"Yes, Your Honor, indeed. Here to speak for the accused, your honor. Jaggers of the Middle Temple, Your Honor. Council for Miss Ternan, Your Honor." He had heaped enough toadying "Your Honors" upon the magistrate that that worthy seemed almost buried under them.

Dickens had wasted no time in retaining the formidable Jaggers. That worthy's name immediately caught Magistrate McWhelply's attention, and, for the second time that morning, a knowing buzz spread through the courtroom. I guess in those parts the words "murder" and "Jaggers" had come to be synomomous.

Jaggers is a bulky, bald specimen who bludgeons his way through the frail gate that bars entrance from the gallery to the small stage before the bench where the legal theatrics are acted out.

Jaggers is incredulous.

Jaggers is incensed.

Jaggers is intense.

Jaggers is aghast that such meagre evidence and malicious

168

hearsay would even be considered in such a fair and univer-sally esteemed court of justice.

But, unfortunately, none of Jaggers's theatrical exertions are enough to carry the cause this day.

"Thank you, Mr. Jaggers." Magistrate McWhelply nods knowingly as he looks around for his mallet of justice, which has somehow been misplaced. He proceeds to dismiss Ellen's lawyer with a wave of his hand in lieu of a good gavel pound, as if that worthy were a piece of lint that had landed annoy-ingly upon his sleeve.

Jaggers withdraws reluctantly, his face flushed from his en-treaties, his unargued brief clutched in his troubled hand.

"Bound over to the Queen's Bench," McWhelply growls, still swiveling his head in search of his missing gavel. "Take her away. She will be remanded to Newgate." With that dreaded pronouncement, Magistrate McWhelply finally found his wooden mallet and gave the table a resounding bang even though it was too late. From the tragic look on Charles's face, the magistrate might well have been pounding the last nail into Ellen Ternan's coffin.

Dickens rushed to the front of the courtroom to try to get a final word with his Ellen, but the constable hurried her off so quickly that he could not speak with her. Frantically, he fol-lowed her outside, but by the time he fought his way through the indolent crowd of court hangers-on, she was already pad-locked into the closed prison cart and he could not even catch a glimpse of her as that tumbril rumbled off.

We—Field, Rogers, and myself—caught up with Dickens, standing, utterly forlorn, in the cobblestone street. But before we had even a chance to plot our next move, Collar and his man descended upon us, no doubt to gloat. Field, however, never gave him a chance to lord it.

"Inspector Collar, congratulations. It is in the hands of the courts now, it is." The tone of Field's voice gave all evidence of his having washed his hands of the case.

"Yes," Collar said with a smirk, "I am sure, and the court ob-viously agrees, that we have got our man."

"You mean 'woman,' " Field corrected him with a congenial grin.

"Yes, of course, 'woman,' " Collar corrected himself with a knowing laugh of the sort men exchange amongst themselves in the privacy of their clubrooms.

I was afraid that Dickens was going to step up and strike the man, but he restrained himself. To all of our relief, Collar decided not to tarry to discuss the case, but with a patronizing salute continued on with his man in tow to their waiting police post chaise.

"Bloody twit!" Serjeant Rogers cursed him in a stage whisper as soon as they were out of earshot.

"That he is, foursquare," Inspector Field agreed, "but the good is that he is out of our hair." And with that Field turned to Dickens, more to cheer him up, I think, than to plot any startling new strategy. "Which means that we have an open field."

"While Miss Ternan pines away in Newgate." Dickens was a portrait of despondence.

"There is no good to be gained in feelin' sorry for ourselfs," said Field, turning deadly serious. "We have no choice but to keep turnin' over rocks till we find our murderer."

Field paused to let Dickens think on that.

"I have a good feelin' about your Miss Nightingale." Field's gravity seemed to pull Dickens out of his depression and back into the detective's game. "If she can lead us to this Frenchwoman who dresses like a man, then I will wager we'll find our friend Barsad close by."

"This spirit rapping, then, may be our best chance," said Dickens, grasping eagerly at the hope that Field held out like some poor shipwrecked mariner grasping for a spar.

"Yes, and tonight we shall see where Miss Nightingale's phantoms will lead us." And with that Field nodded to Rogers and turned to leave.

"But I fear there is another possibility," Dickens said, stopping them.

"And wot might that be?" Field's crook'd forefinger shot to the side of his right eye.

"Angela Burdett-Coutts has apprised me of a man out of her past, a seducer of women, who she fears might be involved in this confusing affair."

"And who might that be?" Field's sudden anger was nearly palpable, smoldering beneath his dark eyebrows and the grim set of his mouth as he spoke.

Dickens told the whole story, of this James Barton and the false marriage, to Field and Rogers right there in the street. It was information Dickens should have imparted (in fact, was directed to by Miss Angela herself) to Field before.

Field held himself under admirable control, I thought. He did not admonish Dickens for holding back the story to this late hour, but it was clear that he was displeased.

"Perhaps, and perhaps not," Field finally said when Dickens had completed his revelation. "But we must follow the signs that are the clearest, and for now this Barsad and his gang of women is our best chance. Tonight at Bow Street."

And with that curt order, Field turned on his heel and was gone.

MEETING THE
PUPPETMASTER

(August 14, 1852—Early Evening)

Miss Nightingale had promised to escort us to the private séance that evening, and she proved as good as her word. She appeared at Bow Street Station at six and informed us that the spirit rapping would commence at eight in private rooms on Southwark Bridge Road across the river. Strangely, almost every turning in this case seemed to take us across that pestilent river and into those hot and dusty neighbourhoods of Lambeth and Southwark, where the greater part of London's population seemed to be so busily constructing the railway.

When we set off from Bow Street to follow Miss Florence Nightingale's lead, we were in two coaches. Dickens rode with her in Sleepy Rob's hansom. I joined Field and Rogers, who was on the box, in the black Bow Street post chaise. It was slow going through the streets at that busy time of the evening, and it took us a good while to wind our way through the pedestrian mobs to the base of old Southwark Bridge. There, at Field's expressed suggestion, we stopped to dine at a riverside tap. Field fondly called it the Old Bridge Coffee House, though the paint on its sign hanging over the door was so faded and cracked that none of us could verify whether that was truly the public house's title or not.

Throughout that whole tedious journey through the crowded London streets, all of us, in both coaches, had kept a sharp eye out for that sinister coach which Sleepy Rob had assured us was on our track that afternoon. Despite our vigilance, however, no such coach was observed moving in our wake. Either, we speculated, it was staying far back, or it had been replaced by a less identifiable mode of surveillance, or it had never existed in the first place. But Sleepy Rob was hardly an alarmist, and both Dickens and I agreed that if he felt strongly enough that we were being followed, then the chances were quite good that we were.

At the Old Bridge Coffee House, the five of us dined on beer, ham, and fluffed potatoes, plotted our course, and were offered a full description by Miss Nightingale concerning what to expect at this séance. At half seven we resumed our coaches and proceeded across Southwark Bridge and into Southwark Bridge Road led by Dickens and Miss Nightingale, who knew the proper house. It had been determined over dinner that Miss Nightingale, accompanied by Dickens and me, would attend the séance while Inspector Field and Serjeant Rogers would wait outside on the chance that our French friend might appear and invite confrontation.

The house which Miss Nightingale pointed out and before which Dickens and she alighted (Field and Rogers pulling up directly across the way, for me to disembark and join the two principals), was a high, narrow brownstone utterly indistinguishable from any of the other high, narrow stone fronts which lined both sides of the wide thoroughfare leading to the bridge. On closer inspection, its only distinguishing mark was a small white card tacked to the frame of the front door and lettered thusly in black ink:

MADAME FONTANELLE
MEDIUM
SÉANCES—THURSDAY EVENINGS

We knocked and the door was promptly opened. Miss Nightingale had thoroughly prepared us for the superstitious theatrics we might encounter during this spirit-rapping session, but she had not prepared us to be greeted at the front door of this spiritualist establishment by none other than a demure and glassy-eyed Marie de Brevecoeur herself.

Florence Nightingale confessed to us later that no one was more shocked than she to be greeted by the very object of our search. "Marie had always been in evidence as a sitter at séances," Miss Nightingale declared, "but she had never revealed herself as a member of the establishment previous to that night."

Having never seen either Dickens or me in person, no recognition showed in her face when she opened the door. In fact, she did not even seem to recognize Florence Nightingale, who greeted her openly—"Marie, good evening"—as soon as she opened the door. She looked upon us with a strange, uncomprehending blankness, as if she were one of those faceless plaster heads upon which wigs are displayed for sale. Florence Nightingale, raising an eyebrow at the strange emptiness of her acquaintance, introduced us, using our own names, as two curious gentlemen desirous of being admitted as sitters to that evening's séance.

"Are either of you gentlemen seeking correspondence with a particular spirit from beyond the grave?" Marie de Brevecouer, eyes downcast, asked in an utterly emotionless voice.

Dickens looked at me, and I at him.

With a quick touch of her hand to his wrist, and a subtle shake of her head, Miss Nightingale prompted Dickens's answer.

"Ah, why no," Dickens stammered. "We would, ah, just wish to sit and view the proceedings if we might."

"Very well," our empty-eyed hostess replied in that same dead tone, as if she were already herself a member of the spirit world. "You are welcome to sit at the table and observe, but you must maintain silence and not address any of the spirits who may appear, even if they are recognizable to you."

It was clearly an oft-rehearsed speech, but it gave Dickens pause.

"To us? How could you conjure spirits who are known to us?" Dickens actually stepped back from her in alarm.

"Madame Fontanelle does not control the spirit world, sir," Marie de Brevecoeur replied languidly. "She only serves as a medium for those spirits who wish to contact one of the sitters at her table. There is a three-crown sitter's fee for the séance," she concluded, and waited discreetly with her hands folded at her waist for us to pay.

Upon payment of our fee, our guide ushered us down a long and narrow, dimly lit corridor with closed room doors spaced at intervals on our right-hand side. She stopped before an open doorway, hung in beads, at the back. That portal offered admittance to a large, low-ceilinged room, so dimly lit that one could barely make out its walls. As we passed through those strings of hanging beads, our guide faded back into the dim corridor behind, and disappeared. This momentarily stopped Dickens in his tracks, probably because he wanted, above all, to keep her within his sight, but at the prompting of Florence Nightingale, by means of yet another discreet push to Dickens's shoulder, we vacated the doorway and entered the séance room.

The stage was set for the performance. In the middle of that darkened room was a large cloth-draped table. Already seated, by my quick count, were seven other sitters. In the center of the table sat an ornamental oil lamp in the shape of an angel with outspread wings which provided the room's only shadowy light.

We seated ourselves at the table. Dickens and I sat together at one side while Florence Nightingale took a single empty seat directly across from us. Our presence effectively filled the seats around the table, except for one thronelike wooden chair which had been purposefully left unoccupied by the sitters. Looking around the table, I encountered the curious stares of a rather motley collection of séance sitters: two gentlemen in somber black suits whose faces floated above the table like severed heads; a workingman in a rough country jerkin accompanied by a voluminous woman, presumably his wife, in a lumpy country bonnet pulled down around her ears; a sad old lady with grey hair and resigned eyes; and two military-looking men who upon questioning afterward turned out to be customhouse officers drawn on a lark to this spiritualism by their shared hatred of government bureaucracy and their shared liking for hot rum cordials.

In that exceedingly dim light, we examined one another with equal curiosity as we waited, silently, quite expectantly, for that exotic event to begin. At exactly eight sharp, we were startled to attention by the loud sounding of what must have been a Chinese gong secreted somewhere in the darkness. In fact, that sound so startled some of the gentlemen, Dickens and myself included, that we leapt to our feet upon its intrusion into our silent waiting.

With the receding gong as her processional, a tall, commanding woman of severe visage muffled completely in Arabic veils, shawls, and flowing skirts materialized out of the darkness and beckoned for us to seat ourselves in order for the séance to begin.

She took her seat in that elaborate armed chair and placed her two hands, palms down, upon the table. Bowing her head almost into the oil lamp, she began to chant in what, I am sure, was supposed to be some theatrical imitation of some mystical incantation.

This Madame Fontenelle, upon her appearance out of the darkness, had looked somewhat familiar to me, but muffled up as she was in all of those harem veils, I could not place her immediately. As soon as she began to speak, however, I looked sharply at Dickens and he at me. The recognition was clear and instant in both of our faces: that voice, that singsong cadence so reminiscent of the opening incantation of the witches in *Macbeth*. It was none other than old Peggy Ternan, Ellen's unscrupulous actress of a mother, wrapped up in that exotic mufti, playing this new role in this different incarnation of theatre.*

In the dimness of the room with her head down upon the

*In the case of "the Macbeth Murders" as described in *The Detective and Mr. Dickens,* Peggy Ternan had actually played one of the witches who opened the famous Covent Garden production of *Macbeth,* which was Macready's farewell performance to the London stage.

table, I am sure that she had not yet recognized Dickens and me, but we certainly had recognized her. We had, however, no time to ponder our discovery, for even as her unintelligible chant began to heighten in intensity, sharp rappings seemed to emanate from the table before us, and that very table seemed to take on a life of its own, moving, jumping, tilting, bouncing, to the point where every single sitter around its maniacally animated border had instinctively placed his hands upon it in a vain attempt to calm and steady its startling palpitations. It was moving about so roughly that I feared the oil lamp might fall over and set us all on fire.

In a moment, however, the rappings and thumpings and joltings of the table calmed, but for an occasional paroxysm when it would suddenly lurch upward, then settle back. As the spirit rappings subsided, our muffled medium, Madame Fontanelle, took center stage.

"Keep your hands upon the table," she commanded in her strong clear actress's voice. "It calms the spirits, helps them to escape the charmed circle of the table's circumference and show themselves singly to us."

As she spoke, she slowly unwound the veil which circled her head and freed her face for the conjuring of the spirits. With the unveiling of her face, I was certain that she would recognize Dickens and me, but, to my surprise, she did not. Instead, she gazed straight ahead into the flame of the lamp with a fixed stare as if she were mesmerized by it. It was that same sort of empty, unquestioning look which had haunted Marie de Brevecoeur's face when she had opened the door.

"Who is it that we wish to contact tonight? Whom do you seek? To whom would you speak? The souls of the living and the souls of the dead are both restless in this room tonight. I can feel their torment, their longing to reach out." She chanted in a flat, dead singsong her rehearsed litany of conjurations.

"To my daughter Mary," the grey-haired old lady begged, "gone these two long years."

"Aaiiieee!" our medium screamed as she leapt to her feet with her arms outstretched. "She is here. She is here. I can feel her presence in the room."

177

With that, the old lady herself jumped back in her chair as if burnt and cried out, "I felt her touch. She is here. I know she is here."

Slowly, in a far corner of the room a light seemed to rise up out of the floor. That light fluttered in shadowy waves up the walls like wavering candle flame and drew the attention of everyone at the table. But nothing happened, and that eerie light slowly subsided.

"I can feel her presence," our pseudomedium kept up her chant. "She wishes to walk amongst us."

"Oh where are you Mary Macalester? Where are you?" The old lady's voice seemed to take on the incantatory cadence of the medium's chant.

At their prompting, that eerie light began to rise once again in the far corner of the room, except that this time the figure of a young woman in a flowing white gown walked in the fluttering shadows.

"It is she," the old lady moaned. "It is she."

Suddenly that light died, and that ghost disappeared, and Peggy Ternan's voice recaptured all of our attentions with its incantatory litany, which in turn set off another round of table rappings and jumpings. It was all we could do to subdue the buckings of that possessed object by pressing our palms upon its surface.

"Whom else do you seek? To whom would you speak? Who is there? Who is there?" Our medium seemed caught up in the fervor of her delirious connection to the loose spirits prowling the room.

Imagine how startled I was in that shadowy darkness when right next to me Dickens raised his voice to request an audience with one of those restless spirits.

"Is Miss Eliza Lynn Lane there?" he inquired. "Recently murdered."

This last elicited a gasp from more than one of the sitters about the table, and brought a hand up to cover the mouth of the large countrywoman in the bonnet. But Dickens's request did not in the least interrupt the fervent incantations of Madame Fontanelle. It did, however, elicit a reaction from a different quarter. Quick muffled sounds of panic suddenly erupted out of that far side of the room where the ghost had just so recently walked in that eerie, shadowy light.

A chair overturned.

A woman screamed.

A body fell.

Footfalls.

A door slammed to.

"Come on, Wilkie"—Dickens was up and moving away from the table, which suddenly, inexplicably, ceased its rappings and lurchings—"we must get to the bottom of this."

Simultaneously, that old witch Peggy Ternan seemed to emerge from her incantatory trance and recognize us.

"Aaiiiee!" she screamed. "What are you two doing here?"

Dickens was up and moving across that darkened room in the direction of where that ghostly girl had walked.

When I caught up with him in the darkness, he was tangled in a hanging silk curtain behind which the theatrical effects had been staged. Groping his way through the curtain, he kicked over a bucket of sand, in which we later found three candles of differing lengths embedded; bumped into a hanging gong, sending ripples of sound off over the darkened room; and tripped over an upturned chair while further tangling himself in a series of thick hanging strings which seemed suspended from the low ceiling. As Dickens blundered about in this chaos of disrupted objects in the thick darkness, I tried to follow him as closely as I could, reaching out in an attempt to right him as he fought his way through these unseen obstacles. He must have finally reached the wall of the room because, cursing, which he rarely did, the blunt objects which had barked his shins and the hanging strings which had wrapped themselves like snakes around his head, he groped his way along until he found, quite by chance, a doorknob. He flung open that door, and moonlight from a small first-storey porch suspended over a dark mews poured into the room. Sitting on the floor of that small porch, her arms hugging herself and her eyes wide with fear, clad in a flowing white gown, was Marie de Brevecoeur. When Dickens burst through that door and came upon her, both of her hands leapt to her mouth in fear.

"Where is he? Where has he gone?" Dickens demanded.

"There." She pointed. "He is making for the horses in the stable." It was not the voice of that blank-eyed, mesmerized thing which had answered the door earlier in the evening. It was as if she had awakened or been set free from some evil spell.

Following her direction, Dickens leapt down the rickety stairway that led to the ground and set off running after whomever, Barsad I presumed, he was pursuing. I, too, descended and started after him, but I immediately thought of Inspector Field and Serjeant Rogers. I turned back and ran toward the street to alert them. But Field and Rogers were on their toes. I met them at full run coming around the corner of the building.

"There," I said, pointing. "Charles is after him. They ran off that way."

Field took stock of the situation in the quick pulse of a moment.

"Rogers, secure the witnesses in that room," he ordered, pointing to the open door beneath which the ghostly Marie de Brevecoeur lay dazed. "Let no one leave till we've talked to them. Collins, show me where." And he set off running down that moonlit mews.

"The stables, she said," I shouted after him, trying to keep up, hoping that might give him some direction.

We ran the length of that dirty corridor of dustbins, splashing through dark puddles where drainpipes from the tenements emptied their foul refuse to the ground. When we reached the intersection with another crossing mews, however, we met Dickens coming back, alone, out of breath, and dismayed.

"He got away from me," Dickens confessed as if he had committed some grievous sin. "I chased him to the backs of those buildings over there"—he pointed to a block of high, wooden tenements looming darkly over the street—"and then he just seemed to disappear into thin air."

This Barsad was proving a will-o'-the-wisp. Always before, in our other cases on duty with Inspector Field, the villains—

Lord Henry Ashbee, Palmer the poisonous doctor*—had been full-blooded, red-eyed devils whose crimes had been confronted in all of their perverted reality. This Barsad was of a different sort. He seemed able to shift shape, to control minds, to appear and disappear at will like some magician.

"He could be anywhere," Field consoled Dickens, "lyin' low in some dark corner, off over the rooftops. But he is on the run now, and we can still catch him. I will put our constables at every way out of the city, on the high roads. He may try to escape back to France with the money. Or he may rely on his disguises, his multiple identities, to sustain him here. He moves quickly from place to place. We must set our men in the railway stations and we must watch the river. He cannot fly away. We shall circulate his description and stop every man of his height, mustache or no mustache. The river police will help us. My men will take the railways."

Our heads were spinning at Field's whirlwind plan.

"He is our man, 'elst he wouldn't have run," Field added as he brushed past us and headed back to the rear door of the spirit-rapping room.

Back in the phony spiritualist's rooms, Rogers had all the witnesses, including old Peggy Ternan and Marie de Brevecoeur, who was in tears and being comforted by Florence Nightingale (ever the nurse), seated around the now docile and ordinary table. He had found the gas and had lit the room's two jets, flooding with light that room which had before been so dark and mysterious.

The evidences of Barsad's spiritualist artistry were unmasked. The table was ingeniously suspended on three invisible wires which at ceiling level were attached to three ropes which ran through wooden pulleys across the ceiling to that corner of the room where Barsad controlled his effects. The eerie light had been produced by the candles of different sizes and lengths shining through a shimmering, transparent

*These were the criminal minds that Dickens and Field had confronted in Collins's previous secret journals, published under the titles *The Detective and Mr. Dickens* and *The Highwayman and Mr. Dickens*.

silk curtain. Marie de Brevecoeur had, of course, been the woman in white who had walked in such a ghostly way behind that selfsame curtain. Almost literally, these evidences of his handiwork proved Barsad the puppetmaster, as Field had suspected all along. He pulled not only these real strings which made the table move, but so many others. His sinister mesmeric meddling with the minds of his company of female puppets had produced these exotic entertainments.

Each of the other sitters at the séance was questioned and sent home. All proved either legitimate mourners of lost loved ones, or simply curious dilettantes in search of a taste of the unusual. That left us with old Peggy Ternan and Marie de Brevecoeur.

Both women were visibly shaken by their abandonment by Barsad, to whom they seemed curiously bound.

Inspector Field started in on Peggy Ternan right away. His anger this time, I am quite certain, was not of his usual theatrical sort. I actually feel that he hated this desiccated woman who always claimed that someone else was responsible for her criminal acts.

"You have been in it with him all along, haven't you?" Field moved close to her and spat the words.

"No. No. I did what he told me, that is all," the woman said, cowering before Field.

"And wot wos that?"

"These séances and . . ."

"And wot?"

"That is all," she lied. One could see the panic in her face. "He hired me to be an actress in his little plays. 'People pays for this spiritualism, and I gives it to them,' he said."

"You lie, you wretch!" Field flogged her with his accusations. "You are in it for the blackmailin' of Miz Burdett-Coutts, for the harassin' of your own daughter, for the robbin' of the bank, and for murder."

"No. No." The woman's voice was desperate, which signaled that she might be getting closer to telling the truth. "Not for murder. We weren't there, were we, Marie? He sent us off didn't he?" She turned pleadingly to Marie de Brevecoeur for corroboration.

182

All of our eyes turned to Marie de Brevecoeur for her answer, but that poor confused woman burst into tears and buried her face in her hands.

Field did not care a whit. He bore down all the harder upon old Peggy Ternan.

"You wrote the blackmail letters, didn't you?

"You followed your own daughter and threatened her with exposure, didn't you?

"You became his familiar and put on these séances, didn't you?

"You helped him murder her and rob the bank, didn't you?"

Field pounded the questions into her cowering form as if he were trying to beat her to death with a hammer.

"No! No!" she screamed back. "I did the blackmail and the séances, that's all. The one to get my daughter back wot they took from me, and the other to make money to live. Ellen is mine, you see, and they"—she pointed vaguely at Dickens and me—"put her in a house of whores."

" 'E made us do all of zose things." The small voice of a sobbing Marie de Brevecoeur interrupted this onslaught. She spoke as if she was emerging from a strange haunting dream. " 'E had a great power over all of us. 'E could make us do anyzing."

This unexpected outburst left even Field at a loss for words.

"What was his power?" Dickens stepped into the exchange in a much quieter, almost cajoling, voice.

"Zee power of zee ring." Marie de Brevecoeur, frantic, turned her face to him in flight from Field's violence.

"Yes, the ring. It was the ring," old Peggy Ternan, that opportunistic harridan, agreed, with the oily glibness of one happy to pass the heat of Field's scrutiny on to her partner in crime.

"How did he use the ring?" Dickens pursued his quiet line of questioning with an almost scholarly curiosity. His tone of voice seemed to calm Marie de Brevecoeur.

"Zee ring led us down zee steps into ourselves."

"Steps?"

" 'Close your eyes,' 'e would say. 'Close your eyes and see zee steps, zee steps going down into zee cave.' Zen 'e would tell me to open my eyes and see zee ring, his blue ring, would be zere before me, on his finger, moving slowly back and forth as if drawing me toward him. 'Now walk down zee first step,' 'e would say, and zee ring would draw me toward him and I would walk down one step and zen anozer, and anozer, and all zee time zat voice would be luring me deeper and deeper into somewhere or somezing until I did not know where I was, did not care, could do only what zat voice told me to do. It was as if I had drunk laudanum or eaten lotus, as if I was floating utterly in its power, willing to do anyzing zat was bid of me."

"Extraordinary!" Dickens pronounced in an awed whisper.

"Claptrap!" Field barked, breaking the quiet spell that the woman's words had cast over the whole room.

"No. It is true. I believe her." Florence Nightingale leapt to Marie de Brevecoeur's defense in the face of Field's harsh skepticism.

" 'Tis true. It is, it is." The Ternan hag was quick to jump to this excuse. "He could make us do anything once he cast his spell."

"And all you did paid him very well, didn't it now," Field growled, silencing her with a murderous jab of his brutal forefinger.

Old Peggy Ternan glared back at him with her best actress's hatred: "He paid us with promises," she hissed. "He promised these girls, Liza Lane and Marie, he would free them from this world of men, free them from the beatings, the humiliations, the ill use."

Hers was a powerful speech, worthy of a professional actress who had played Shakespeare all her life. It was a speech coated in anger and filled with the venom of one who had herself always been ill used and exploited, and had learned to fight back with her own machinations of exploitation. What a novel power the man must have exercised, to turn these women's lives to his own perverse purposes. I could see that Dickens was utterly spellbound by their story, and Florence Nightingale, who had taken the sobbing Marie de Brevecoeur in her arms and was consoling her as a mother would a frightened child, was in full empathy with them.

184

Only Field remained undaunted.

"He is a thief and a murderer, and you are his familiars," Field charged in a voice as hard and unyielding as the stone steps of Coutts Bank.

Marie de Brevecoeur's body was quaking with sobs as she tottered in Florence Nightingale's arms. But suddenly, as if desperately trying to pull herself back up one more time from the depths into which she had descended, she screamed out in a voice as fragile as blown glass.

"No! 'E didn't kill her. I was zere zat night and 'e didn't kill her! It was zee other who did zat."

And, as if that desperate shriek of truth had drained every drop of resistance from her quavering body, she fainted dead away.

THE STALKERS

(August 14, 1852—Night)

W ot?" Her desperate pronouncement brought up
short even the redoubtable Inspector Field.

"Didn't kill her?" Serjeant Rogers, his jaw fallen,
echoed his master's consternation.

Dickens blanched, went as white as an altar cloth, stood
looking fearfully down at Marie de Brevecoeur's fallen form
as if she had just placed a death sentence upon his beloved
Ellen's head. I could almost see his thought processes at work.
He feared she was going to accuse his love.

We all stood by, staring in utter confusion.

"Water. Find water," Florence Nightingale ordered as she
adeptly ministered to the stricken woman, rubbing vigorously
at her cheeks, forehead, and wrists, twisting open a small glass
vial magically extricated from some hidden pocket in her voluminous skirt.

I quickly surveyed the room and spied a closed door in the
corner where Barsad had set up his curtain, candles, and
ropes for the séance. To my good fortune, it led to a small
pantry where a Toby jug half-filled with water sat in its basin
on a small dry-sink. I returned at a run with my prize to find

Miss Nightingale applying restoratives from her tiny glass vial, some sort of smelling salts I presumed, to Marie de Brevecoeur's nose, causing that worthy to begin twitching convulsively back into consciousness. Tearing the jug from my grasp, Florence Nightingale poured the water onto her own hands and applied it to the faint woman's cheeks. It was this cooling application which restored Marie de Brevecoeur to life.

I could see that Field and Dickens could hardly contain themselves as Miss Nightingale helped the distraught woman to a chair at the séance table and nursed her with further applications of water, both internally and externally, back to lucidity. After some minutes passed on this road to recovery, Field could no longer restrain his impatience. But he began quietly, cautiously, not wishing to frighten her into an excess of emotion which might occasion a reprise of her fainting spell.

"You said that this Barsad did not kill Miss Eliza Lane," Field gently coaxed her to attend. "Who murdered her then?"

We all waited a long moment as she tried to marshal her wits for the story that we all knew she must tell no matter how fragile her condition.

"I do not know." Her voice was little more than a whisper, but seemed slowly to be gaining strength. "I do not know who killed Liza Lane, but I know zat John did not."

Her voice faltered, but Inspector Field would not let her drift away upon the flood of frightened tears that were streaming down her face.

"You are certain?" Field pressed. "You are certain he could not have killed her?"

" 'E and I found Liza with zat scarf choked around her neck outside zee door of zee bank. She was already dead. When we came out of zee bank with zee money, she was lying zere behind one of zose high stone columns, strangled. John dragged her back inside, and we left her zere."

"Wot was she doin' at the bank? Why was she outside the door?" Field pressed his advantage before the woman collapsed into another faint, which she gave all the appearances of imminently doing.

"She was to keep watch for us, to warn us if anyone came

while we were at zee cupboard with zee ripping chisels. Her duties were to get ze society out of zee bank by upsetting zere meeting, and zen to stand watch while we emptied zee day strongbox. But somebody killed her while we were at it."

"Who?" Field snarled at her, brutal, angry.

"I do not know, I tell you. Please, I do not know."

We were about to lose her and Field knew it. He was casting about for anything that would keep her talking. He needed some change of tone or topic that would send us in some new direction now that the prime target of our suspicions, John Barsad, seemed to be absolved (at least in her mind) of the murder.

"Who else knew of this robbery of Coutts Bank?" Field cajoled her now in a voice oiled by desperation. "Was there a fourth man in your gang? We have been informed that a fourth person, a man, or a woman dressed as a man, we do not know which, met with Barsad in his Lambeth rooms. Is that true?"

Field's memory, his mastery of the smallest detail, the briefest mention, was amazing. My mind raced back through all the evidences that we had gathered in the case. It was the amorous landlady at Barsad's abandoned rooms in Lambeth who had mentioned that she thought she had seen four men meet with Barsad at different times.

"Oui, oui." Marie de Brevecoeur's voice was little more than a quaver. " 'E put John onto zee robbery in zee first place. 'E found zat John worked at zee bank. 'E was all ears. I met him only once. 'E was shy of meeting eizer me or Liza." Her voice faltered badly. " 'E planned zee whole zing. 'E told John how to do it. 'E . . . 'E . . ."

"Who?" Field was only a breath away from her tear-stained face. "Who?" he hissed at her in a barely controlled whisper.

But the beleaguered woman fainted dead away in Florence Nightingale's arms before she could answer Field's desperate plea.

After a long moment, Field regained his voice and broke one of his cardinal rules of detecting.

"But why?" he asked. "How in heaven did this happen?"

Field had once told Dickens and me that he had no concern for the why of any of the crimes he investigated, but only for the who and the how. He called it reading the book of the case. Unfortunately, no more reading of this case was to be done at the moment. Marie de Brevecoeur was shattered and unconscious. It was abundantly clear that this interrogation could not, and should not, go on. If Field had any inclination toward pursuing it further, one look at Miss Nightingale, who had enfolded the unconscious witness in her protective custody, scotched that idea.

ANGELA ABDUCTED

❦

(August 14, 1852—Night)

I'm not sure I believe any of this"—Field turned to the rest of us, his crook'd forefinger scratching at the side of his right eye in the deepest concentration—"but for now, till we can talk further with this woman, we must find this Barsad."

"Why do you not believe her?" Dickens, ever curious, inquired.

"For God's sake, who knows if she is tellin' the truth. She is this devil's familiar. She would probably say anything to save him." Field's frustration resounded in his voice.

"I believe her," Dickens said, risking Field's wrath.

"So do I, damn her," Field grudgingly admitted, "and it makes everything that much more difficult."

"That it does." Rogers had to put in his tuppence as a contribution to the proceedings.

"But no matter if we believe her or not," Field galloped straight onward, "we must catch this Barsad and catch him now. He will run. He will dart for France. That is where they came from, he and his Marie de Brevecoeur. We must do what I said, close down the city, cut off his escape."

"But how?" Rogers voiced what all of us were wishing to ask.

"We must put men at every way out of London. On the river. At the railway station. On the high roads."

"But sir, we've never done nothin' like that," Rogers said skeptically. "We don't have enough men at Bow Street."

"We will get Collar to help, and the River Police." Field was carried away with the grandeur of it.

"Collar?" Rogers dumbfounded.

"Collar?" Dickens skeptical.

"Collar?" Me wondering if Field was serious.

"Yes, Collar, for God's sake," Field barked at all of us in frustration. "I will talk to him. He will go along. Now, Miss Nightingale, you go with Rogers and me in the post chaise. We will take this woman to Bow Street Station for safekeepin' until she can tell us more about this Barsad cove." He turned to Dickens and me to explain. "And you two follow along to Bow Street. Barsad will try to run. We must close down the city tonight. Close it tighter than a Scotsman's purse."

With that, Field and Rogers ushered their charges out and left Dickens and me to follow along.

When we arrived at Bow Street, Field's plan was already set in motion. He had dispatched a constable to fetch Inspector Collar from St. James and was in the process of sending Rogers out in the post chaise. That worthy's charge was to collect all of his constables from off the streets and to roust the others out of their off-duty haunts. Collar arrived within the hour. Dickens and I listened with great curiosity to their exchange.

Field earnest: "Inspector Collar, thank you for coming. I need your help."

Collar suspicious: "Help for wot?"

Field eager: "For catching John Barsad, who I suggest murdered the woman in the bank."

Collar defensive: "I already have my murderer."

Field helpful: "I think this Barsad is a better choice."

Collar adamant: "I have solved that murder. The woman strangled her with her personal scarf."

Field cajoling: "But can we ever be certain? I have evidence, equally strong, that Barsad could have done it."

Collar interested: "Wot evidence?"

Field relieved, in the knowledge that the hook is set: "A new witness."

Collar very interested: "Wot new witness?"

Field triumphant: "Marie de Brevecoeur, this Barsad's whore. The woman who dresses as a man."

Collar confused: "Dresses as a man?"

Field moving on: "Yes, but we must move quickly. I propose to close off the complete city of London so that Barsad cannot escape. I need your help, all the men in your station."

Collar flabbergasted: "Close off London?"

Field impatient: "Yes; listen, you must marshal your men. We will need every one of them."

Collar utterly at sea and sputtering: "Close off London? Close off . . ."

Field losing patience rapidly: "Yes. Can you not see? The Protectives have never done anything like this before. It is a first in our line. We are goin' to close off all the ways out to catch our killer."

Collar reluctant: "But I have already got my killer."

Field the rationalist: "But wot if you do not? There is nothing to lose. At worst, we catch an accomplice in the murder, or another witness. This can only help your case."

Collar again confused: "Accomplice? Wot accomplice? Wot witness?"

Field, whose face was reddening at this absurd functionary's obtuseness, and who was beginning to look like an anxious teakettle, started to answer, but was interrupted by a furious pounding at the outer door. Since Rogers had taken the desk constable with him, I hastened to answer those insistent knocks.

Tally Ho Thompson burst in upon us, breathless, bleeding from the nose, and sporting a darkening bruise on the side of his face.

"He has taken her," Thompson exclaimed, collapsing into one of the chairs by the cold hearth.

He looked to have run halfway across London with his cryptic message. He was utterly blown, yet his voice was all chagrin and apology. It was unlike Thompson. He was completely serious.

"He surprised me at her door when I answered his knock and hit me with a stick. He has taken her!"

"Who, man? Who?" Collar, as usual, had not perceived what Field and Dickens and I already knew with dread.

"Miz Angela. He took Miz Angela and left this on the floor." Thompson was holding his head with one hand, in obvious pain from the blow, and listing heavily in the chair. With his other hand he passed to Field a hastily scrawled note on a scrap of foolscap.

Field read it aloud: "I have the stone bank bitch. Free passage to France with the money or I'll throw her into the sea."

"Wot money?" Collar was beginning to sound like Broken Bert's parrot.

We ignored him and looked to Field.

"She is his hostage," Field said as he stared at the note, reading it again, and yet again.

" 'E is all zee zings you zay," Marie de Brevecoeur pleaded feebly, "but 'e is not a murderer!"

Inexplicably, she chose that moment to rouse herself from her faint and defend her master and exploiter.

"No, he is not a murderer." Field silenced her with a grim look upon his hard face. "But if this is to be believed"—and he waved the scrawled note at us— "he threatens to become one."

Once again Field read the note slowly, aloud, not for our enlightenment at all, but for the triggering of his own deductive processes.

"He is makin' for France, he is." Field was thinking aloud. " 'Throw her into the sea. Throw her into the sea,' " he repeated the words of the note.

He thought a moment, his crook'd finger scratching thoughtfully at the side of his eye. Once again he was reading the text of the case.

"Bloody hell! That's it!" He finally saw what it all meant. "He's makin' for Dover. The sea. To get across to France. We must cut him off before he gets out of London."

"He left his horse tied in front of Miz Burdett-Coutts's house when he run off with her," said the guilt-stricken Thompson, trying to be helpful. "I rode it here, but it broke down only halfway and I had to run the rest."

"He is on foot with Miss Burdett-Coutts in tow." Field, as if in some sort of deductive trance, was thinking aloud again, putting it all together. Suddenly, he turned on Collar like a wolf baring his fangs. "We must seal off the city, Inspector Collar. We must block the Dover road and all other roads that feed into the Dover road outside the city. Can your men do that?" His voice was so grim that his last query was more a challenge than a question.

Collar coughed nervously twice and then answered, "Of course," as if this sort of desperate exercise were something they did every day and for which they were prepared.

"My men shall cover the railway stations," Field informed him. "He may try to escape tonight by coach on the high road, or he may try tomorrow to go by the Dover train. It leaves the Victoria Railway Station at nine in the mornin'."

"But what about Angela?" Dickens's voice was heavy with concern. "Good lord, he will be using her as his shield. Your men"—and he turned from one to the other, leaving no doubt that he was addressing both Field and Collar—"must be extremely cautious. You must make certain that no harm comes to her."

"He will not harm her, and neither shall we," Field reassured Charles. "He will mesmerize her if he can, to make her docile, but he will keep her close, he will. She is his safe passage!"

BARSAD'S REVENGE

☙

(August 15, 1852—Midnight)

T he plan laid out for the closing tight of the entire city completed, Field ushered Collar and his silent serjeant out, offering a few final suggestions about the immediate placement of troops and the communication between outposts.

When he returned, Thompson was sitting disconsolate on a bench by the wall nursing his head, and Marie de Brevecoeur, with Florence Nightingale watching her closely, was sputtering back to some semblance of equilibrium. Rogers had not yet returned with his constables, and we could not set the plan in motion until he did. It was Dickens's ever-present curiosity that broke the expectant silence.

"Miss de Brevecoeur"—Dickens spoke very softly in addressing her so as not to raise the ire of the protective Nightingale—"why is your . . . this Barsad . . . doing this? Abducting Miss Burdett-Coutts?"

Marie de Brevecoeur looked at Dickens as if she did not understand; then her eyes, like a frightened animal's, moved from Dickens to Field to me and finally came to rest, pleadingly, upon Florence Nightingale's face.

"Marie . . . Marie, how did this all happen?" Florence Nightingale broke that circle of men pressing around that shaken woman. She sat next to her on the arm of the over-stuffed chair and took her hand. "They need to know what happened, then I shall take you home to bed." At that half promise, Miss Nightingale had to silence Field with a stern look. It was painfully clear in his face that she was not going home, that her next residence would be an English gaol. Marie de Brevecoeur, in her confusion, however, did not seem to notice. "What happened, Marie?" Florence Nightingale coaxed.

" 'E took her because 'e hates her and her bank." The shaken woman's voice took on a brief renewal of strength, fired by passion, I presumed. I think she really loved the mes-merizing Barsad, was, in a sense, a willing participant in the strong hold that he had upon her. "It was her bank, in Paris, zat drove him from his place in zee university. I was his stu-dent."

"He taught in university?" Field almost seemed intimidated by this revelation, as if he was reassessing his opinion of Barsad's capacities.

"Yes. Literature and zee sciences. 'E knew so much. But 'e gambled, at cards and on boxing matches."

"And how does Coutts Bank figure in all of this?" Dickens gently asked.

" 'E borrowed money from them. 'E put up his small house. When 'e lost it, and could not pay, they took his house, and zen zey hounded him at zee university. 'E was but a poor scholar, but zey wanted his wages to go direct to zee bank." She stopped, and Florence Nightingale rose to cut off the inter-rogation, but Marie de Brevecoeur, with a touch of her hand to her protectress's wrist, signaled that she would go on. "Zee professors called him in. Zey would have no scandal. Zey told him not to return. Zat his students would go to other profes-sors. 'E blamed it all on zee bank."

"And how did you get to England?" Dickens's voice was soft and seductive. It was as if this woman was under his spell and was compelled to tell the whole story to him.

"We came on zee channel boat, and all zee way 'e drank wine and plotted against zee bank."

"And then he went to work there?" Field took up the questioning, but in the same quiet tone that Dickens had used and which was working so well. Nary a tear had fallen in the course of her complete narrative.

"Yes. When we came to London, it was zee only work 'e wanted. 'E had zis obsession with zee great stone bank. 'E hated it, and zen 'e came to hate her."

"Miss Burdett-Coutts?" Field asked, though he need not have; we had all assumed the woman's meaning.

"Yes." She raced on as if trying to escape her whole story, as if it were some sort of prison. " 'E said she slighted him when she came through zee doors zat 'e guarded. 'E said she was a toff and a haughty bitch who had ruined his life and would not even deign to look at him."

"And all this time he was plotting to rob Coutts Bank?" Field coaxed her further along her narrative path.

"Yes, 'e wanted to hurt zee bank, to ruin eets reputation, but 'e didn't know how to do it." Marie de Brevecoeur surprised us all with this answer. " 'E was waiting for his chance, until zat man, zat gambler, put him up to it."

"Who is that man?" One could hear the excitement in Field's voice as he got closer to solving the mystery, but he kept his voice in check and posed the question in a way that Marie de Brevecoeur felt no threat.

"I do not know who 'e is," she answered. " 'E is a gambling man zat John met at Kate Hamilton's one night when Liza and I were performing. John was playing at cards with him. I only saw zee man once."

"Performing at Kate Hamilton's?" Field did not know this small tidbit of information which Dickens and I had gleaned from our conversation with Rossetti and Elizabeth Siddal. "Both of you?"

"Yes." Marie de Brevecoeur seemed resigned to telling all. "We performed private shows for men to watch through peepholes in zee walls. John made us do it. 'E used zee ring."

"Marie, you do not have to . . ." Florence Nightingale, ever the protectress, tried to stop the interrogation, but Marie de Brevecoeur wanted to go on, as if she was trying to absolve her sins by exposing them to the light, as if by way of the truth she was trying to flee the enchantment her master had cast upon her.

"But I must. Yes, we performed for men's eyes. But Liza and I were lovers. John made us so. 'E liked to watch us, at home. When Liza visited, 'e used zee ring and we made love for him. For a time, she even moved in with us. And then John found us work doing private shows at Kate Hamilton's casino. I was still his lover, and hers, but zis money supported our household. Zen, 'e met zis man, and zey made zee plan to rob zee stone bank."

"And this man, this gambler, it was his plan to rob the bank, not Barsad's?" Field became almost clinical in his questioning, slow, quiet, like a physician asking a patient for her symptoms. "But Barsad liked the idea? Was an enthusiast?"

"Yes, from zee very first word. 'E was so excited. 'E came to me and Liza telling us zat it was his chance to have his revenge on zee bank and zee woman. 'E was obsessed with her."

"Why did he hate Miss Burdett-Coutts?" Dickens was naive enough to believe that there might be some rational explanation.

Marie de Brevecoeur thought a long moment on that question.

One could see the impatience in Inspector Field's eyes as he shot a sharp look at Dickens which warned: *No more questions! This is my witness!*"

But Marie de Brevecoeur wished to answer Dickens's question.

" 'E hated her because she was a woman of great power and 'e could not accept zee control she exercised over his life. 'E felt she had robbed him and 'e was determined to rob her back."

"He is mad!" Dickens could not contain himself.

"No." Field was speculative, his forefinger scratching at the side of his right eye. "He is a thief and a whoremaster."

"And a mesmerist," Dickens added.

"A man of strange powers." I heard myself adding my judgement to their listing of this shape-shifting phantom's occupations.

Marie de Brevecoeur sank back in her chair and seemed to be resting.

"He hates women." Florence Nightingale interrupted our dissection of his elusive character. "He could not stand a woman possessing that sort of control over his life. He hated her because he could not control her."

Only now, after twenty years, as I remember this whole bizarre episode, am I beginning to understand what it was all about. It was about possession, the devil's own possession, and all of the different kinds of possession which we Victorian gentlemen desired over our women. *Our women*—how ironic that I should still, twenty years later, choose that phrase. John Barsad possessed these women with his mesmeric trances. His was a tangled web that Marie de Brevecoeur was trying to escape with her telling of the truth of the story.

"But who is this other man?" Field demanded, his voice hard again, knowing that he had it all from her and this was the only piece left in the puzzle.

Marie de Brevecoeur's head shot up as if she had been dozing or dropping back into a trance.

"I do not know," she answered softly, apologetically. "John never told me, never gave him a name. 'E was just zee man from Kate Hamilton's who will help us make our fortune, who will tell us when zee money is zere. Liza wanted to know his name, too, but John would not tell us."

At that moment, Rogers entered with a disheveled lot of constables. Some were, by the order of their dress, clearly on duty, and the others, by the evidence of their various attitudes and attires of unpreparedness, had been collected from their off-duty entertainments. With that turn, Field cut off the interrogation of Marie de Brevecoeur, still unresolved, and went about the deployment of his troops.

The woman, under the care of Miss Nightingale, was put away for the night on the pallet bed in the unoccupied cage of the bull pen.

Field wrote out the descriptions of Barsad and Angela, and the assignment for each and every constable individually. It was a requirement of the Protectives that every constable know how to read, but from the manner in which these men turned their assignment pages about, hither and yon, upside and down, I wondered how stringently that regulation was being enforced.

Field forcefully warned them of the man's penchant for disguise and phantomlike elusiveness. He emphasized Barsad's height as the bellwether of identification. All that done, he sent them off to their posts.

As for Dickens, Thompson, and myself, Field sent us home until morning; Thompson to nurse his cracked head, us to get some sleep. His last order to us was to meet at Victoria Railway as early as possible in the morning to help watch for the fugitives at the departure of the Dover train.

THE DUEL

ℬ

(August 15, 1852—Morning)

Victoria Railway Station in the morning was a humming swarm of milling people going about the business of empire. Victoria was the new stepping-off point for England's international commerce, the gateway to the Continent, from whence stern bankers and men of business embarked to buy and sell, barter and bargain and best their commercial counterparts in France and Spain and Italy and beyond. The days of the Dover stage, which Charles would fondly remember in *A Tale of Two Cities*, were gone forever. Everyone went by train. At that time, there was no other railway terminus like it. Waterloo, which was just then being built, would ultimately surpass it in size and splendor, but in 1852 Victoria was the only gateway to the south coast by rail.

Field's men had been in place at Victoria since two in the morning. Field and Rogers themselves had been there most of the night. Field's men were stationed at the barrier. The only problem was that the barrier was not the only point of entry to the platforms. Coaches and pedestrians could drive up or walk in right off of either Eccleston Street or the Belgrave Road, and proceed directly to the trains. Cabs could deliver their passengers almost to the doors of the railway coaches. The Dover train left at nine. Dickens and I arrived at half eight.

As we rode across London from the Wellington Street offices, our summer-long imprisonment in that suffocating heat was finally broken. We entered the cab under a dark and glowering sky, and as we turned into the Strand headed for Trafalgar Square lightning flashed dramatically over the dome of St. Paul's. In brief moments the rain came in waves off the river, beating down upon us in torrents, pummeling poor Rob as he sat unprotected on the box, turning the streets into rushing streams flowing around the horses' hooves and drowning the trudging boots of the foot passengers. But through it all Sleepy Rob drove on and delivered us to our destination.

The Dover train stood at platform 1 wheezing and belching steam and smoke as its boilers were slowly brought up to running pressure. The platform itself resembled Covent Garden Market. It was crowded with porters wrestling luggage about, with victuallers peddling pastries and sausages, Scotch eggs and country pies, loaves of bread, slabs of cheese, and flasks of cheap wine. Trainmen officiously consulted their pocket watches. Young gentlemen, dandies in frock coats, loitered smoking. Stern men of business, checking their repeaters, anxious to get on with the ruthless machinations of commerce, waited impatiently. Gay families in bonnets and parasols off on holiday to Provence or the beaches of southern France rushed about. And in the midst of this madding crowd waiting to board the Dover train stood Field, like a lighthouse in the deepest dark, his gaze sweeping steadily over that roiling sea of faces, bags, carts.

Dickens and I stood for long minutes in Field's company before he ever noticed our arrival. We watched as his eyes searched the crowd for our two fugitives. When he finally acknowledged our presence, there was an edge of frustration in his voice.

"Damn, there are too many people out there," he complained to Dickens. "They could be anywhere, in any sort of disguise. He is probably watchin' us right now, waitin' for his chance to get aboard."

"He won't get past us," Dickens assured Field with a confidence to which I am not sure he fully subscribed. Field confessed later to Dickens and me that the whole affair was bungled. It was, after all, Field rationalized in retrospect, the first time he had ever attempted, or for that matter even considered, closing down the whole city to keep a fugitive from escaping justice.

As we stood at the barrier watching Field's relentless gaze sweep the bustling crowd, I felt a sudden sense of the futility of his efforts. This scene before us was out of his control. It was too big a stage with too many players. There were too many people coming from too many directions in too many various forms of conveyance.

"Look sharp!" Field turned to Dickens and me with his plea for help, which in his inimitable way turned out to be a gruff order. "We are lookin' for a couple, tall man with a woman. He will surely be in disguise. She will be led against her will."

At Field's command, Dickens and I redoubled our surveillance of the platform. It was no use. This day's train seemed completely booked with couples of all shapes, sizes, colors, and enormous configurations of luggage that they all seemed to be quite conveniently hiding behind.

I tried to make some sense out of that crowd of milling passengers. As my eyes moved from one departing couple to the next, desperately searching for some telltale sign of a disguise, of resistance on the woman's part, or of anything out of the ordinary, the whole platform suddenly deteriorated into a chaotic swirl, all ran together in a whirling dance.

They could be anyone, I thought. *We are undone.*

Then Field proceeded to exacerbate my sense of confusion and futility.

"The train leaves in three minutes," Field barked. "He could already have her on board for all we know, or he could be waitin' to make a rush just before the train pulls out when the mob is the most dodgy. We must git out amongst them. It is our only chance now." And he pushed his way through, making for the train.

"Charles, Collins," he spat our names back over his shoulder as his pace picked up to a trot, "you take the platform on that side of the train. Rogers and I will get this side." As we came abreast of the first railway coach, which was, of course, the last coach on the train, Field punctuated his order with a fierce stab of his commanding forefinger to the right; then he broke off down the left side of the straining, steaming train.

"All passengers on board!" Two conductors, each consulting his official pocket watch, standing on each side of the small metal porch mounted on the rear of the train, leaned out and shouted down the crowded platforms on either side of the coupled line of railway coaches.

I followed Dickens around to the right of the bellowing trainmen as he broke into a run at Field's command. However, as we came around the corner of the coach and the platform opened up before us, he suddenly brought himself up short and I, rather clumsily, ran right into his back.

"Sorry," I said stupidly, and then I realized why he had come up of a sudden so short.

"Good God, Wilkie." He was staring into what was now an uncontrolled mob eight railway coaches long all struggling to board the waiting train through the more than sixty or so carriage doors on this side alone. "We'll never find them in this mess." It seemed like a declaration of despair, something I had never before heard Dickens utter. "But we certainly must try." He immediately righted himself and plunged into the crowd.

I waded in after him wondering how on God's earth it had come to pass that I was here doing this and feeling such a terrible burden of responsibility for something so far out of my ken or control.

Charles ran up to an elderly couple tottering, the man with the aid of a cane, slowly toward the train. He blocked their way and without saying a thing peered hard at them, then reached out and pulled at the man's beard. Satisfied, he hastily said, "Sorry, sorry" and continued on, leaving the stunned couple utterly mystified if not terrorized.

I accosted a tall man handing his young lady down from a carriage which had just trotted in off the Belgrave Road.

"What is it, sir?" the man, startled, turned to me when I rather rudely grabbed his shoulder so that I could turn him to see his face.

"Sorry, sorry," I apologized, "I thought you were someone else." And I fled down the train looking for another unsuspecting couple.

In my haste, I, almost, once again, ran right into Dickens's back. Abandoning his frantic darting from one unsuspecting couple to the next, he had stopped suddenly in the center of the platform and was turning slowly in a small circle for the purpose of intently surveying the crowd.

I stood staring at him rather stupidly as he did his slow pirouette. I should, however, have been taking stock of the crowd myself, but I had so surrendered to the habit of observing him that I tended to forget my own humble responsibilities. Suddenly, he burst off at a run back toward the rear of the train, away from the steam engine belching forth those steady streams of smoke which signal its imminent jolting to life followed by its immediate departure in an explosion of sound and cinders and speed.

I watched as Dickens ran up to a tall, mustachioed porter pushing a coffinlike crate on a wheeled handcart toward the mail coach, which was the second to the last coach on the train. When he accosted this tall burly chap, the man took one step back in perfectly normal surprise, then bristled at Dickens in temporary anger. I was too far away to hear their exchange, but the man was clearly and demonstrably unhappy at this unwelcome interruption of his labour. Dickens, however, was undaunted. Ignoring the man's growled words, which, though I was just coming up to them and didn't hear them all, sounded like they were pronounced in a thick Scottish burr and said, in translation, something like "Wot in 'ell you doohin, you bloody gorp," Dickens first peered hard into the Scotsman's face and then knocked hard two or three times on the side of his large box. Only then did Dickens's shoulders sag in frustration and defeat, and his voice turn to the unpleasant task of apology. To this day, neither Dickens nor I know what a "gorp" is.

That possibility having proven yet another embarrassment, and the train mere moments from pulling out, Dickens stood, rather forlornly, looking to me for some sort of direction. All I could manage was a clueless shrug.

"Wilkie"—Charles's hand was on my shoulder—"either they have found some other conveyance out of London, or they have somehow eluded us and are already on that train."

But even as he spoke, something caught my eye back down the length of the platform toward the rear of the train. All of the final "All aboards" had been shouted up and down, and the engine was mere moments from dragging its cargo off into the driving rain. As a consequence, the hurrying crowd on the platform had somewhat calmed and cleared. There were still a goodly number of people about, waving farewell to friends and relatives, lovers and husbands, some joyfully, some tearfully, but the crowd was not nearly so dense, nor moving so animatedly. In this momentary calm, and, in a strange, almost mesmerizing way, as if time and motion had momentarily slowed so that I could see more clearly, my eye focused upon one shard of movement out of the darkness of that storm-tossed street across the platform toward the train. For some reason, which to this day I still cannot fathom, I instinctively knew that it was them. I am neither sharp of eye nor acute of perception, and yet I knew, and with a certainty which I have rarely felt about anything in my hapless blunder-about of a life.

"Charles, there!" I pointed excitedly, though he was right at my elbow.

Perhaps it was the size, or the timing at that last moment, or the hurried motion toward the train that drew my attention. I honestly do not know. However, as soon as Charles sighted down my pointing arm and picked them out in their movement toward the train, he was as utterly certain as I.

"Yes, Wilkie, it is them," he said in a low, awed whisper as if he were looking at a beatific vision. Without any hesitation, he leapt off at a run down the platform just as the train began to move.

What had caught my attention was yet another odd couple,

two women in black, wearing veils (perhaps it was the veils that gave them away?), a towering nurse awkwardly pushing an invalid in a chair toward the last coach of the train. A single small valise was their only luggage, and it sat in the lap of the invalid patient as she was wheeled across the platform. As we watched, one of the trainmen threw open the rearmost door, jumped down, handed the valise up to one of his colleagues, and helped the female nurse lift her charge out of the chair and onto the train; then, most obligingly, the trainman helped wrestle the bulky chair on board. He managed to get them accommodated just as the train started to move. It was at that moment, as she handed the chair up onto the train, that the nurse saw Dickens burst into a run down the platform toward her, but his shouts for the trainman to stop her from boarding were utterly drowned out by the screech of the steam whistle as the train got under way.

The nurse was startled. Moving too quickly and powerfully to be either feminine or innocent, she jumped aboard the moving train and slammed shut the compartment door.

Seeing this, Dickens stopped short and, without hesitation, changed direction and ran for the moving train. Because it was still moving slowly enough for Dickens to catch it, and because an observant and obliging gentleman who spied him running for it pushed open a compartment door and grabbed Dickens by the shoulder as he dove though it, Charles was able to get on board rather easily.

"Wilkie, for God's sake, come on!"

I had not moved, but Dickens was shouting for me to once again take my life in my hands and leap onto this smoking behemoth which was rapidly picking up speed. Inexplicably, I ran for that open door and leapt for Dickens's outstretched hand as the train jolted by.

He pulled me in and we were off in hot pursuit.

"They are behind us on the train, Wilkie." Charles had stopped to puzzle it out. "At all cost, we must not let them get by us. He will try to secrete her and himself. He may even change his identity once again. He has seen us. He knows we shall be searching for him. We must go slowly and look not only for him and his charge, but for any sign of his passing or his hiding. If we are blessed with good fortune, he will immediately abandon his hostage and attempt by whatever means to save himself. Once Angela is safe, he is no more our concern as I see it. We can leave him to the authorities in Dover when the train arrives."

I was certainly relieved to hear that last, and to realize that Dickens was not recklessly seeking violent confrontation with this phantom.

"Where the devil is Field?" leapt from my mouth as, I thought, a quite natural reaction to our dilemma of being aboard a speeding train in pursuit of a confirmed bank robber and possible murderer. "Should not he be conducting this search?"

"Quite possibly he did not even board the train, not knowing, as we did, with certainty, that our friend Barsad had gotten on board."

"Oh, Charles, I do not like this. What if he has a pistol or some other dangerous weapon? Innocent people could get hurt. We could get hurt!"

Dickens, that heedless idiot, actually broke into a grin and chuckled at my alarum. "No one is going to get hurt, Wilkie," he assured me condescendingly in the tone a beekeeper might use to a skeptical child.

When we had vaulted into the train, we landed right in its midsection. But it was a long train, for those days, and we were still probably some four coaches from the rear, where our kidnapper had boarded with his hostage.

"We must search slowly through every coach, Wilkie," Dickens proclaimed as he set off to do just that. In each coach, a narrow corridor with a window every ten feet or so ran down one side while the windowed (and window-shaded, which somewhat complicated our task) inner compartment doors formed the interior wall and opened inward from the corridor. Of course, the outside of the train was all lined with compartment doors out of which Barsad could leap into the dark and the storm at any moment, provided that he decided that the risking of life and limb by ejecting oneself from a swiftly moving train was his only means of escape.

I, of course, followed at Dickens's heel like the faithful bulldog that I have always been. One after another we opened the compartment doors to intrude upon startled travelers and importune them for information that they did not possess concerning our two fugitives.

Dickens would fling open each door and interrogate the startled occupants of each compartment. "A tall man or woman with an invalid woman in his charge. Have you seen them? Have they passed by you?" All was happening so fast that he did not have time to realize how absurd and confusing his questions must have sounded.

Repeatedly the compartment passengers would stare wide-eyed at this lunatic who had so rudely burst in upon their slumbers, or their reading, or their quiet contemplation of the rainy night speeding by outside their windows, and then would shake their heads in the negative in astounded silence. But by the time any spokesman could muster a protest or a curse, Dickens would be gone, lunging for the next compartment, accosting the next lot of unsuspecting travelers.

In this haphazard way we progressed through two coaches. Ignoring the drawn shades, he broke into one compartment and surprised a young couple who had progressed well past the preliminary stages of the act of love. In another, he burst in upon a congregation of Jews in shawls chanting around a lighted candle. In yet another, and by far the most dangerous, he interrupted a rough man cleaning his fowling piece, and, I am sure, if that weapon would have been loaded, Dickens would have been shot on the spot because the man, by animal reflex, raised it toward us to hold us off.

In this manner, we made our way toward the back of the train until we entered the mail and large baggage coach which stood immediately forward of the last, into which Barsad and his charge had boarded. It was in this mail coach that we finally picked up the trail.

When we entered that wide, open coach stacked high with portmanteaus, crates, and all various sizes of shipping boxes, we at first thought that it was unoccupied, but as we progressed to the rear and reached the mailbags piled high atop one another, we heard the low moaning of a man painfully returning to consciousness.

The mail clerk was sitting propped up upon the bags which served as his rough pillow and holding his head gingerly as if it were a cracked egg.

"She burst in, she did," the poor man groaned as Dickens bent down over him, "and smashed me square in the face."

"Where did they go?" Charles shook the man's shoulder with a gentle urgency. "The tall woman who hit you, where did she go?"

"There wos two of them," the mail clerk sluggishly remembered as Dickens helped him to regain his feet. "There, up there." He pointed unsteadily toward the ceiling in the corner of the coach. "The one dragged the other up that ladder." And he pointed once again even as he collapsed back down onto the mailbags. Evidently, his weakness from the blow to his face had reasserted its wobbly governance over his knees.

Dickens, so solicitous but a moment earlier, abandoned him like a burdensome relative and scrambled over the mailbags into the shadowy corner toward which the man had pointed. Attached to the dark wall, a wide ladder rose up to a hatchway in the roof of the coach. When I arrived, clawing my way over the mailbags, Charles was already halfway up it, climbing to the top of the train. The hatch at the top was open and Dickens disappeared through it as the violent dark clouds rushed past straight above. I, of course, was damned to follow no matter where my personal demon led. Why I remained so recklessly faithful to his lure of becoming a novelist no matter what the risk, I simply do not know.

When I emerged into the driving air atop that speeding railway coach, Dickens was recklessly in the act of leaping across the gaping crevasse between our mail coach and the next coupled coach toward the front of the train. As I steadied myself in the rushing air—thank God, it had stopped raining, though the deck of that speeding rooftop was still quite slick from the wet—I could see that Dickens was moving in pursuit of two shadowy figures progressing slowly over the top of the train toward the steam engine. In the rushing wind, with bright cinders spewing back all around from the engines like a swarm of berserk fireflies, those dark fleeing figures did, indeed, seem like phantoms.

Stooped low against the wind, Dickens steadily made his way along the roof of that coach in the wake of the receding figures. And then he leapt again, fearlessly clearing yet another crevasse between jolting, lurching railway coaches, and I realized that I could no longer just watch, holding hard to the safety of that open hatch. To my chagrin, I realized that I was cursed to follow Dickens along the top of that train straight to perdition.

As I timidly crept along, all that prodded at my mind was the image of my body being ground to mincemeat beneath the iron wheels of that speeding train. I don't remember jumping that first crevasse between coaches. I must have simply closed my eyes and done it, and done it again at the next coupled juncture and the next. I vaguely remember timidly scuttling forward, bent over with my hands steadying myself against the moving roof of that speeding coach, then actually crawling on all fours as low as I could possibly crouch in order to stay on. But though I was beyond comprehension of how I progressed, I did nonetheless progress to the point where I was within hailing distance of Charles and the two fugitives he was pursuing.

Landing after a frantic leap across coaches, I looked up and realized that I was on the roof of the same coach which Dickens and the fugitives occupied. It was the forwardmost passenger coach on the train, with only the coal tender and the steam engine mounted in front. At its far end, Dickens stood in direct confrontation with the two fleeing objects of our foolhardy pursuit. Even in the murkiness of the day and the rush of the train, I was able, to my surprise, to see and hear their exchange. The tall powerful veiled figure in the woman's black dress loomed above Dickens while the second woman had sunk to the roof of the coach. Dickens was standing with his back to me confronting this pair. The tall woman (or man), the criminal Barsad, faced Dickens defiantly, the valise clutched in his hand like a weapon. Angela Burdett-Coutts seemed either to have sunk to the floor in exhaustion, or have been thrown or pushed down there. She seemed inert, utterly submissive to her captor.

Strangely, I felt the train beginning to slow. *Perhaps the en-*

gineer has sighted this congregation of lunatics atop his moving train and is slowing down to insure that we don't fall off, I thought, hoping against hope that some reasonableness might still be in force in this murky, rushing, insane world I had found myself trapped atop.

Though I could not see very far ahead in the rain and mist, the train was pulling into a station. I learned afterward that it was Maidstone, a regular stop on the Dover run.

Dickens and Barsad were within mere feet of each other. The hulking man incongruously imprisoned in the woman's skirts made, however, no hostile move toward Charles. Angela lay in a bundle at his feet, and I was unable to ascertain if she was even conscious.

I crept closer to them over the top of the train.

A shuddering gust of wind accompanied by a brilliant flash of lightning illuminated the whole length of that slowing train and revealed the station coming up upon us. It blew aside the woman's veil, allowing the flash to reveal for the first time the face of that shape-shifting phantom whom we had been pursuing all over London for so long.

John Barsad's face was broad and rough with glowering black eyebrows, but bore no bushy mustache as had been described. There was a dominance in his face that bespoke the power he seemed able to wield over these women who came under his influence. Yet, as that flash of light illuminated his face, it also revealed a mere man who, it struck me then and I remember it now, seemed every bit as terrified as was I.

"There is no place left for you to go. You can't escape England," I heard Dickens shout as I crawled closer. "Let her go. You have not murdered anyone. If you harm her, they will hang you."

Suddenly, the man in woman's clothes thrust out his hand toward Dickens's face. I, at first, thought that he was trying to strike Dickens down. But that was not his intent. He was extending his ring, set with a large blue stone, out toward Charles's face as if it were a weapon.

"You see it, do you not?" this Barsad screamed over the dying hiss of the wind as the train slowed to enter the station.

"Stay back! You see the ring. Look at the ring. I will throw her off if you do not. Look at the ring."

His words seemed to freeze Dickens for a moment. I was afraid that he was actually being drawn under the man's powerful spell. But it was merely a brief hesitation on Dickens's part. He, almost immediately, did an equally bizarre and unpredictable thing.

Slowly extracting his gold repeater from his waistcoat pocket, Charles swung it on its fob in the air between himself and the desperate man.

"No. You look at mine," Dickens coaxed. "Follow it in the air. You see, follow it in the air."

This strange tactic utterly unmanned Barsad. He dropped his ringed hand to his side and stared unbelieving at Dickens. At that instant, a flash of lightning crashed overhead, illumining the strange scene. The train was almost to the platform, slowed to but a gentle crawl.

"You think you can mesmerize me, you fool!" Barsad laughed maniacally, drawing the stares of every waiting passenger on that platform as the train glided slowly in and jolted to a stop, throwing all of us atop it off our balance.

At that small jolt, the prostrate Angela came suddenly back to life and, in a quick, rolling scissors motion with her legs, cut the legs out from under her tormentor.

Barsad pitched heavily down onto his back on the roof of that railway coach and would have rolled right off of it had he not caught himself upon a small upthrust edge. His body toppled over the side and he was left hanging there, only a few feet above the platform, dangling precariously by one clawing hand. In his other, he still clutched that bulky black valise.

As soon as Miss Burdett-Coutts tripped him up and he went down, Dickens rushed to her. He bent down and took her protectively into his arms, but she shook herself free and scrambled to her feet.

All the upturned faces waiting on that Maidstone platform stared wide-eyed at this strange tableau atop their train.

"I am perfectly recovered now, Charles," Angela assured Dickens. "He cast his spell over me, but that jolt threw me against his leg and broke me out of its power. He has the money from the bank in that bag. We must get it." She started to move toward her hanging antagonist.

"No! Angela, stop! You are free of him." Dickens forcefully restrained her from advancing on Barsad. "Wilkie, don't just stand there, get the bag," he ordered me as if I were his valet.

Well, he was utterly insane if he thought I was going to pursue that dangerous criminal any further. Granted, the man was hanging by one arm over the side of the train, but I just stood there, frozen, completely unable to confront him.

"For God's sake, Wilkie, move!" Dickens screamed as he wrestled to restrain Miss Burdett-Coutts.

Inexplicably, I moved.

"You could never mesmerize me with a pocket watch, you fool," that dangling man taunted Dickens as I moved gingerly over the top of the train toward him. "You are a showman just like me. All is a show, but you cannot control your actors unless they fear you."

There was a strange, almost pitiful, desperation in his voice even as he taunted Dickens and hung there so incongruously over that startled platform.

I was within mere steps of him. I rose to my feet, traversed the last three steps to the edge of that railway coach where he hung, and stomped down hard upon his hand with my boot.

My theory was that in his fall to the platform he would both drop the valise and injure himself in a heap on the ground, thus making his apprehension by the local gendarmes quite an easy proposition. There always seems, however, a great discrepancy between theory and reality.

In reality, he landed rather lightly on the platform and, rolling over once, leapt with agility, for such a large man, to his feet. At his descent into their midst, that small congregation of waiting train passengers flushed like a flock of birds, some fleeing the platform altogether back to whence they had come, others fleeing to the waiting train, ripping the carriage doors open and launching themselves into the safety of its compartments.

As for Barsad, when he found himself on his feet, his legs all intact, his valise still clutched in his hand, he simply turned and ran down the platform past the steam engine toward the far end, where it jutted past the station house on the edge of a small grazing pasture where, in the flash of another lightning bolt, we could see horses enclosed.

"Halt for the Protectives!" a familiar voice barked at the fleeing man's back, and, much to my surprise as I viewed the scene from my stage-side box atop the train, the man actually stopped, and looked back to see who had the audacity to issue such a foolish order.

It was, of course, Field.

Field and Rogers had materialized out of the train and stood below us, confronting the fugitive.

"Halt and surrender!" Field ordered the fugitive, who immediately sneered at the very idea of it, shouted, "Be damned!" in answer, and turned tail to continue his flight, stumbling down the platform toward its end with his valise in hand.

With surprising speed for such a blunt and blocky man, Field leapt after him, with Rogers in close pursuit.

Dickens vaulted past me, lowered himself over the edge of the car, and dropped to the platform. I turned to look to Miss Burdett-Coutts, but her head was just disappearing down a ladder between the car and the tender. I had no real desire to further pursue the villain whose fingers I had just so recently stomped, but it seemed I had no choice. I, too, scrambled down in Dickens's wake.

The chase proceeded down the length of the platform nearly to its end before Field caught up with his fugitive and with a leap grappled him to the ground.

But Barsad rolled away out of Field's grasp and struggled to his feet, swinging the valise as a weapon at Field, who was still on his knees.

That heavy case caught Field on the side of the head and knocked him sideways to the platform.

"This is rightfully mine!" Barsad stood over his vanquished victim screaming. "She stole my life from me in Paris. She must pay for that!"

In his triumphant concentration upon his fallen adversary,

Barsad failed to see Serjeant Rogers advancing upon him from behind.

With one heavy swing of his truncheon, Rogers knocked Barsad away from his master. The man stumbled backward from the blow, lost his footing on the slick wet boards of the platform, and tumbled off onto the tracks, still clutching his precious valise.

At that very moment, to the stunned surprise of all of us on the platform, the train suddenly jolted into motion and began to pick up speed.

Barsad lay across the tracks, dazed by the fall, but still clutching the valise.

Rogers and Dickens were administering to Field, who was still down and seemed stunned.

The train was picking up speed and bearing down on the stricken villain, who lay across the tracks, not moving, as if mesmerized by the single Cyclopean eye of that onrushing behemoth.

The engine closed upon the poor man and I froze in my place staring in horror at what I was sure would be his complete dismemberment by that rushing, red-eyed, smoke-breathing devil.

But even as I stood anchored in my own ineffectuality, Angela Burdett-Coutts leapt past me over the edge of the platform and onto the railway line. *She is after the valise of money,* I thought. But I was wrong.

Miss Burdett-Coutts grasped the fallen Barsad by the ankle and dragged him off of the tracks in a hairbreadth before the train rushed by. It would have cut him to pieces.

Curious, how in such a frightening and heroic moment all I could think of was a literary reference. Angela Burdett-Coutts had saved Barsad from repeating Carker's death in Dickens's *Dombey and Son.*

As the train rumbled by, Rogers scrambled down and took the disoriented Barsad into custody while Dickens and I attended to Angela Burdett-Coutts.

"Good lord, Angela, why did you do such a foolhardy thing?" Dickens finally asked after he had ascertained that she was not hurt in any way.

"I wanted my money back and him caught, not dead," she replied with a mischievous twinkle in her eye. "No one believes in the Industrial Revolution more than I, Charles, but I do not think it should kill people."

BARSAD TELLS ALL

(August 15, 1852—Morning)

Inspector Field had been stunned when Barsad knocked him down, but he quickly regained his faculties and took control of the situation.

"Rogers, hire a coach with a driver that will take us back to Bow Street," he ordered. "We need to talk to friend bank robber here before Collar gets wind of this."

Barsad was utterly subdued. His left arm was broken from the fall onto the railway line and a large bruise with blood clotted all around graced the side of his face where Rogers had struck him with the truncheon.

"Inspector, for the sake of the bank," Angela Burdett-Coutts leapt to the pleading of her case almost as quickly as she had leapt off the platform to save this Barsad's miserable life, "could we leave the details of the robbery out of this?"

"That may be a difficult thing to do, ma'am," Field said skeptically.

"Could it not have been just a planned robbery or an attempted robbery? Must the whole City know that such a large amount of the depositor's money actually left the bank?" Not only was she pleading her case, but she was actually prompting him as to how to help her conceal from the public the robbery. She knew exactly what she was about, and so, I think, did Field.

"Perhaps, ma'am," Field acquiesced. "I shall try me best." And with that he bent to attend to poor Barsad, who was moaning in pain and holding his broken limb.

I was sent to find a local surgeon, who proved a quite competent practitioner and set the arm in a wooden splint after some painful manipulation of the broken bone right there on the Maidstone railway platform. By the time this was accomplished, Rogers had arrived with a large open post chaise and driver. We were back in London within the hour.

At Bow Street, the first thing Field did was to pour a generous quantity of gin into Barsad. Whether to dull the poor prisoner's pain or to loosen his tongue, I am not altogether certain. That accomplished, however, and the prisoner made comfortable in Field's own overstuffed chair, with the wounded arm resting on a large feather pillow, Field set about his necessary interrogation.

"We knows you was not alone in this," Field struck in, "so who put you up to all of it, the threatening letters, the bank robbery, the murder? We must know it all. Tell us and I can fix it so you will not hang."

Barsad was a beaten man, and he knew it. He saw that he had no choice but to make a clean breast of it . . . to his best advantage, I am sure.

"It was Lane planned the whole crack," Barsad began with the dodgy eagerness of a cornered animal.

"Lane?" Dickens exclaimed.

"Peter Lane," Barsad said, nodding, "poor Liza's husband she had run away from."

"Was it he killed her?" Field pressed.

"It had to be." Barsad winced as he said it, from the pain I am sure. "I think he meant to do it all along. That is why he did not want her to know he was in on the bank crack with me. He was going to get Marie and me out of the country with the money. He said all he wanted was his wife back."

"Wanted her back?" Field enticed him.

"He said he still loved her, but she had run off because of his gambling debts."

"She ran away because he beat her and treated her like a slave." Angela Burdett-Coutts rose up indignantly in the poor dead woman's defense.

"How did this all happen?" Field steered the prisoner back to the track of the story, fearful, I am sure, that Collar would arrive at any moment.

"He came to me at Kate Hamilton's. He's a gambler and frequents the gaming tables there. He saw Marie and Liza, his wife, doing one of their private shows there. He said he had been searching for his wife and had found her, but he could not approach her because of the circumstances."

"Not searching for her, stalking her! Do you not see how it was?" Angela was adamant. "He was the one who attacked us in the street, the one that Meg Sheehey drove off. You all thought he was after me, but it was Eliza Lane he wanted to kill."

Field and Dickens and Rogers and I all looked to each other, suddenly aware that Angela had struck upon a truth that we all had overlooked. For a moment, Barsad the prisoner was forgotten.

"That was a close scrape for him," Field ruminated on it. "He barely got away and it made him wary. He had to find a better way to kill her."

"A way that would not point to him as the murderer," Dickens took up the story that he and Field were collaborating upon. "He needed to put it off on someone else. What better than a falling-out among thieves."

"How did he get you to do this?" Field turned our attention back to Barsad, who looked in danger of fainting from the pain and Field's persistent badgering.

"He approached me at Kate Hamilton's, I tell you—oh." He hugged his wounded arm, which must have been throbbing with pain.

Field poured him a full tumbler of gin, which the man gulped greedily down.

"Please, just tell us all of it," Field cajoled him, "and then we will let you rest, with some nice laudanum perhaps." That seemed to give Barsad hope.

"He took me out of Kate Hamilton's so his wife would not see us together, then we went to some public house in Mayfair, a posh place, and we drank late. He asked all about his wife. I told him she and Marie were lovers. He found out about my gift, how I could trance them and make them do the private shows and the séances and all that lot to make us coin. It fascinated him. He said he would pay me if I would help him get his wife back. Then, a few days later, he came into the tap at Kate Hamilton's when Marie and I were there after a show Marie had done on her own. He said he needed to talk to me. We sent Marie home in a hansom."

Barsad stopped. He was running down like a clock.

Field saw it and knew he had to get the whole story out of him before he fainted away from the pain.

"Rogers, go for some laudanum," Field barked, "to the apothecary on the Strand."

Now I knew for a fact, and that blockhead Rogers (after some hesitation) figured out, that they kept laudanum right on the premises at Bow Street Station. Thus, this order to go out to procure the laudanum was but a ruse on Field's part to keep up the hopes of the poor beleaguered prisoner and to buy some time for the extraction of his whole story.

Pretending to obey, Rogers left the room.

Field turned back to the object of his feigned concern.

"Wos it then he put you onto the robbin' of the stone bank?" Field pressed.

"It was. I had told him I worked there and I was tryin' to get money out of the woman banker, her." His eyes went to Angela's face in lieu of pointing, which he was too weak to do. "I had told him about the blackmail notes that I had been buildin', usin' the things I had gotten from Marie and the women's meetings and from the Ternan hag. It was that night he gave me the plan."

"And what was this plan?" Field's voice was gentle, seductive. He knew that he almost had it all.

"On the night that the strongbox was full, I was to mesmer the two girls, Marie and Liza . . ." His voice faltered. He was fading fast.

"And?" Field coaxed.

"And . . . and send Liza in to drive out all those other women, then break into the strongbox with the ripping chisels. When we had the coin, I was to leave Liza tranced there, and tied up, for the Protectives to find while we got away. But he was to come in and save her, and that is how he proposed to get her back."

"But he murdered her instead?" It was Dickens's stunned voice this time.

However, before Barsad could make any answer to that, he fainted dead away.

"He killed her, Lane did." Field was as grim as a judge. "He killed her and meant for the whole thing to be hung on this one," and Field nodded down at the unconscious man slumped in the chair.

"It was all a ruse so that Barsad would take the blame for the murder," Dickens simply repeated Field's revelation as a way of understanding it. "He changed the plan. He did not care at all about the bank robbery. It was to murder his wife all along."

"He is a rich man," Angela added. "Liza said that he gambles, but he does not care about the money. Oh, he was so cruel to her when she was his wife. He made her hate all men."

"He is a dodgy one all right," Field agreed. "He had been stalkin' his wife and then he started stalkin' this Barsad when he found out about the power of that ring."

And all of our eyes were drawn to the ring on Barsad's finger as he sat unconscious in that chair.

Suddenly the quiet of the room was shattered by a terrible scream. It was Marie de Brevecoeur, standing clutching the bars of the cage on the far side of that long, low room, straining at the sight of Barsad slumped in that chair.

"Oh God, is he dead? Is he dead?" she sobbed.

She had awakened out of her drugged sleep only to see her lover and master lying unconscious before her terrified eyes.

Field started to silence her with a sharp command—"You there, be . . ."—but he gave off and thought better of it. Instead, he moved to the cage, unlocked it, and led Marie de Brevecoeur out, every bit as solicitous as Florence Nightingale had been when she cared for her the night before. He nodded for Dickens to rise and he gave her that overstuffed chair next to the unconscious Barsad.

"He is only sleeping. His arm is broken and he is in pain, but he has fallen asleep and that is best for him now," Field gently reassured her.

This was quite a new Inspector Field that I was witnessing. He spoke softly rather than murderously. He coaxed rather than threatened. He made himself out a friend to these captured criminals rather than their worst possible nightmare. But he wanted more from them, needed them on his side, at least for the moment. I had a distinct feeling that as soon as he got everything from them that he desired, as soon as they finished playing the roles that he had scripted for them, he would cast them into Newgate to rot without another thought. But for that moment, Field was a consummate actor playing against his type.

"But you can help us, Marie." Field's voice was utterly unthreatening, almost fatherly, as if she were no more than a slightly wayward child. "We need to catch the man who has caused all of this trouble. He is Peter Lane, poor Eliza Lane's estranged husband. He killed her. He planned all the while to put the murder off on you and your friend there asleep in the chair. He was using you, do you not see it?"

Marie de Brevecoeur, who was still dull under the influence of the drug that Florence Nightingale had administered to her the night before to calm her and make her sleep, looked up at Field with wide eyes and slow powers of comprehension.

Field waited.

"Her husband killed her?" Marie de Brevecoeur finally saw the light.

"Yes."

"She hated him. 'E beat her."

"Yes, we know."

"She told us 'e beat her." Marie de Brevecoeur seemed to be wandering in a cloud.

"He was the man you saw with John Barsad. You remember, do you not? You told us you saw him once."

"Yes, I remember now."

"Will you help us find him? Can you point him out for us?"

"Yes, I zink so. May I go back to sleep now?"

Field solicitously escorted her back to the pallet in the cage, and she slipped into sleep as easily as if it were a burial at sea.

"She is a wreck," Field observed in a low stage whisper when he returned from tucking her in. "Between the trances and the drugs, she barely knows who she is. But, unfortunately, she is all we have got. She is going to have to find this Lane monster for us."

"And how do you propose she will do that?" Dickens asked in all innocence.

"You and young Mr. Collins here are going to take her out on the town tonight, that is how," Field answered with a mischievous flick of his crook'd forefinger to the side of his eye and a devilish grin commandeering the upturned corners of his mouth.

"What do you mean by that?" Dickens was surprised. "You just said yourself that she was a wreck."

"Oh, we will paint her up and bolster her. Never you mind. It will be two fast gents out to the gay spots with their fancy whore," Field said with a laugh, but then immediately turned grim, his usual self. "This Lane, he is a gambler. He does not know that Barsad has been taken. We can find him in Mayfair by night, I know it. The wench will be our stalkin'-horse."

"But will he not recognize her?" Dickens was applying himself to the problem.

"Perhaps, but perhaps she can point him out before he recognizes her." Field seemed perfectly happy with his plan.

"I have a wonderful idea." Dickens voice leapt. "We will dress her as a man. It is how she dresses half the time, anyway. It will be three gentlemen making the rounds. He will never recognize her."

Field smiled at Dickens's enthusiasm. "Exactly," he said, "I should have thought of it. We will catch him at his own game.

Do you not see? That is all it was. The blackmail, the planned bank robbery, the murder, it all played into his hand. For this Lane, it was all nothing more than a game within a game within a game."

"And his game is almost over," Dickens pronounced the plan set.

"We will meet here at eight tonight," Field said, tidying up the details. "Mr. Collins"—and he turned gleefully to me— "you are closest to this woman's size; could you bring your tightest suit of clothes for her to wear, and bring Meggy as well, to dress her."

Unlike Dickens, I was less than enthusiastic about being so visibly included in this whole affair. The very things that so excited that madman Dickens tended to terrify me. All I could envision were dangerous fights, precarious chases, lethal gunshots. To my chagrin, I fear we, the amateur detectives, were off again.

But Dickens was off to Newgate first. With a letter of passage from Inspector Field, he hurried to tell his beloved Ellen the good news. He spent the afternoon with her at the prison while I went home to my Irish Meg.

THE FACE OF
THE PHANTOM

ॐ

(August 15, 1852—Night)

I t was a rather unwieldy group that gathered at Bow Street
that night. Indeed, there were so many of us that I feared
we might look like a traveling circus going down into Mayfair to apprehend our villain. Of course, Field and Rogers were
in charge, and Dickens thought he was. As for me, I was rather
reluctant, as always, to embark on yet another dangerous
nighttime adventure.

Irish Meg had come along as directed to help Marie de
Brevecoeur get ready for her work, but Florence Nightingale
had also appeared out of the night to inquire as to her patient's condition. She proved an especially calming influence
upon the fragile Frenchwoman. Angela Burdett-Coutts was
also present with Tally Ho Thompson in tow and serving as
her bodyguard, still concerned for the protection of her
bank's reputation, I presume. And Sleepy Rob was loitering
on the doorstep waiting to transport us and our charge down
into the depths of Mayfair.

My clothes were a bit baggy on Marie de Brevecoeur, but
with a dexterity I had no idea that she possessed, Irish Meg
tucked and pinned and belted them so that the woman made

for a passable man. All ready, we embarked for Mayfair at about half nine. We purposely went late, when the various festivities of debauchery would be well under way.

" 'E goes to zee gaming tables at Kate Hamilton's almost every night. We need look no furzer for him zan zere." Marie de Brevecoeur seemed alert and committed to Field's plan for finding our murderer.

"Rob, can you find a Kate Hamilton's establishment in Mayfair?" Dickens inquired.

"If I can't, I don't desarves to be no London cabman," Sleepy Rob replied in his usual confrontational tone, but there was the slightest note of surprise in his voice, which signaled that he knew full well where Kate Hamilton's was and what it was all about, and he wondered what his two personal gentlemen were doing going to such a disreputable place. But Sleepy Rob well knew his own place, knew that his was not to wonder why, and certainly not to judge the destinations of his best customers. "Kate 'Amilton's, it is," he growled as we climbed in, and with a sharp crack of his whip in the air above his business partner's ear we were off.

We jolted to a stop on one of Mayfair's darker, less populous streets. That is not to say that there were not street whores about and scattered gentlemen in Tilbury hats sporting thin summer sticks and stalking their night prey, but there was not the lusty press of some of the wider, better-lit Mayfair thoroughfares.

The house we had come to a stop before was deceptive in its dimness. Unlike the blazing brothels of Park Street or Upper Grosvenor Street, with their lurid torches and lanterns gaily beckoning, this high house, set back from the street behind a black iron fence, was utterly dark in its upper storeys and most negligently lit on its small square porch. It was as if it did not want to draw undue attention to itself. Suspicious, however, in the face of this unobtrusive exterior, was the significant number of coaches drawn up in front. There must have been five or six others, their drivers smoking, their horses pawing at the dusty street. We were, clearly, not the first gentlemen to arrive for the evening's entertainment. Somewhere behind us, in separate coaches, standing off like privateers but ready to move in at the first signal, were Field and Rogers with their coach full of constables and Thompson with his coach full of women—Angela, Irish Meg, and Miss Nightingale. These last were under orders to stand off completely until Lane was captured and in irons.

As the three of us stepped down from the cab, an extremely dark-skinned man (whether Indian or African or of some South Seas origin I could not determine in the dim light) in formal evening clothes materialized out of the darkness of a large bush and peered at us through the black iron gate. He was above the average height of an Englishman and so broad through his neck, shoulders, and chest that he looked like a block of stone waiting for the sculptor's chisel. He spoke not a word of greeting as we approached, and I found him quite threatening in both his bulk and his silence as he barred our way.

"We are gentlemen, and we have been directed here to Mrs. Hamilton's by Mr. Rossetti, the painter, to witness the evening's entertainment," Dickens addressed this dark monolith while reaching his hand through the gate and depositing a half crown in said gatekeeper's palm.

The man's demeanor magically changed. His bright white teeth bloomed into a wide smile and he opened the gate for us.

We escorted our charge across the dark lawn and climbed the tiny porch only to have the high front door swing open before us in the hand of another large, dark-skinned mute who ushered us down a short, dim hallway which ultimately opened into the large, well-lit casino. Well-dressed gentlemen crowded around the gaming tables and congregated at the bar, smoking, sipping champagne, and conversing in soft murmurs and hooting laughs.

"Gentlemen, welcome," the cool firm voice of a woman greeted us as we entered the casino. "I am Kate Hamilton and I welcome you to our gaming tables this evening. My barman and hostesses will be happy to accommodate you." She delivered this rehearsed little speech with all the formality and confidence of the hostess of a fashionable dinner gathering. "I hope you all enjoy your evening, gentlemen, and remember, private performances can be arranged in the upper rooms." With that parting invitation to further degradation, she demurely withdrew.

This Kate Hamilton was a quite attractive woman of some five and thirty years, younger than Dickens, but older than I. She was dressed tastefully in a floor-length sky blue dress adorned with long, formal white gloves. Her hair was golden, her eyes a striking green, and her skin as pale and rich as the oriental carpet which adorned her plush casino. She was not at all the desiccated bawd that I had expected.

In discussing that evening later, Dickens remarked upon Kate Hamilton that "she was so businesslike and in control, so direct in her mastery of her place of business."

"Let us get a drink then, Wilkie." Dickens turned to me and our silent companion.

"Zere 'e is," Marie de Brevecoeur gasped in a barely audible whisper, "at zee bar."

"Which one?" Dickens gently steered her by the elbow away from the bar to the safe spying place of a large pillar across the casino in a corner which was further protected by a large potted palm. Like three frightened explorers peering through the jungle growth at a tribe of savages whooping it up, we parted the leaves of the palm tree to identify our prey.

Marie de Brevecoeur pointed out a bulky, mustachioed man sitting at the bar. He was in the company of four or five other mustachioed or muttonchopped or vandyked gentlemen all railing at two light-haired hostesses in their midst whom they seemed to have shanghaied from their serving duties.

"Wilkie, I have him," Dickens ordered. "Take the woman out and give her to Rob. Send him off with her as if she is drunk and sick, then come back. Field will see you and will cover the doors. Do not arouse suspicion. You are merely sending a drunken gentleman home. Return quickly; I will do nothing until you are back."

Faithful bulldog that I am, I hastened to do his bidding. When I returned, Marie de Brevecoeur safely trotting off in Sleepy Rob's cab, but no sign whatsoever of Field and the Protectives, Dickens had infiltrated the circle of men around the two fair-haired whores. He was silently observing Mr. Peter Lane from a standing position at the bar just off that worthy's right shoulder.

At the very moment that I returned, the gruff Lane emptied his champagne glass, clapped it down on the bar, announced, "Enough of these whores, I am for play," and stalked off to a large and noisy dice table on the far side of the room. Waiting a discreet moment, Dickens followed him along, stopping on the way to purchase a supply of gaming chips from a card dealer who was presently occupied with only two players. Dickens told me later that he did that in order not to draw attention to himself when he joined the crowd at the dice table. He was a marvel, always two steps ahead of the game. I followed along, of course, for want of anything safe to do.

Dickens stationed himself directly across the dice table from Mr. Peter Lane, who was betting the various lines and numbers with the grim intent of the obsessive gambler. The croupier's stick maneuvered the dice around the green felt expanse of the table until, finally, they arrived at our Mr. Lane's station. I was watching him closely, as I am sure Dickens was, and when the dice arrived at his hand, a fire seemed to kindle in his eyes; his face came alive with the excitement of the risk and the game. He rubbed the dice lovingly between the palms of his hands, caressed them with his fingertips as if trying to feel their love for him, kissed them once before throwing them out upon that plush green field of chance.

"Stop!" That loud shout shocked and utterly froze everyone around that table. "Stop the game. This gentleman cheats!"

To my horror, it was Dickens whose voice had stopped time.

Every single member of the thick crowd around that table stared at Dickens. Some must have recognized him.

A heavy silence descended upon the entire gaming room.

Lane had been frozen in midroll by Dickens's loud order, the dice still balanced in his hand. His head came up to find his accuser as would the dangerous hood of a cobra poised to strike. "How dare you, sir," Lane hissed at Dickens, almost quietly.

"He changed the dice. Check them and you shall see." Dickens paid no attention to Lane, but turned to the stunned croupier. "The man is a brazen cheat. He changed the dice."

"I changed no dice. I will kill you for this!" Lane, in his rage, flung the dice at Dickens and started around the table to get at him. Lane flung people aside as he struggled through the crowd, which parted in alarum at the murderous look on his face. Halfway around the table, however, Peter Lane stopped, stared hard at Dickens, looked quickly around the room at all the other people frozen in tableau looking at him, and seemed to come to some realization which his anger had obscured.

"What is this? Who are you?" he slid the words carefully, suspiciously, across the table toward Dickens as if pushing them with the croupier's stick. "I did not cheat. Why would you say such a thing? To provoke me? Who are you?"

"A friend of your murdered wife, sir. Charles Dickens." Dickens actually had the audacity to smile at him as he said it. Good lord, Dickens was a cool customer.

A gasp of recognition and celebrity set heads nodding around that crowded gaming table as the two men stared each other down.

I hoped against hope that Lane had no pistol at the ready, for the look of cold hatred in his eyes bespoke murder.

"Damn you!" Lane burst out, but he knew that he was cornered. "Damn you!" he repeated, but his voice wavered in indecision. Dickens had drawn him out for certain, all the way to the end of his tether.

Suddenly, that curse still on his tongue, Lane leapt back and, flinging people to the side to clear his way, fled the room.

Dickens, who through this whole confrontation had never once blinked at that murderer's rage, moved swiftly to my side.

"Come on, Wilkie"—he motioned to me to follow as if we were merely returning to the theatre for the second act of a play—"we must drive him into Field's net."

The man had disappeared down a dim corridor at the rear of the room. We made our way quickly through the stunned assemblage, and Dickens plunged into that hallway, giving no perceptible thought to the fact that there might be a violent, cornered animal waiting for us in the shadows.

Dickens at a run traversed that corridor to its end, where we found a wooden door, conveniently ajar, as if someone had just recently passed through. It opened upon a sort of musty attic, a storage area whose center had been cleared to form a small makeshift waiting room. That open space in the center of the room accommodated a tall candlestick for the purpose of light, a nondescript overstuffed chair, and a small couch flanking a wooden table which held two pots filled with the butt ends of cigars. No persons were in attendance.

Dickens took in the appointments of this scrabbled-together waiting room in an instant.

"He is gone, Wilkie!" he fired back over his shoulder as he dashed across that cluttered space and disappeared into the darkness.

I scuttled obediently after him, much less eager than he. Down a corridor between rough and shrouded shapes (old furniture, perhaps, or odd stored objects hung with sheets), a door stood open upon moonlight. Standing in that open doorway, looking out, was a woman. It was Kate Hamilton, the proprietress.

When Dickens came up to her out of the darkness, she made a startled turn at the sound of his running footsteps, and then stepped forcefully into the doorway, blocking our egress into the moonlit courtyard.

"How dare you!" she challenged Dickens as he rushed up. "What are you doing? This part of the house is not open to visitors." And she attempted to block his passage through that doorway.

There have been certain times throughout our long friendship that the unconsidered rashness of Dickens's actions stopped me dead in my tracks. This was one of those times.

He tossed that protesting woman aside as if she were no more than a string of beads.

"Where has he gone?" Dickens shouted at the woman even as he was roughly pushing her out of his way and bursting through that door.

That rear door opened upon a dark, cobblestoned mews

bathed in ghostly white moonlight. As I stood in that doorway, stunned at Dickens's violence, gaping at that woman thrown so brutally aside, the whole eerie scene, so provocatively moonlit, spread out in front of me like a strangely familiar panorama.* It all rushed toward me in a series of fragmented images like a Turner painting torn into strips. A hackney coach waited in the mews. Lane was, at that very moment, climbing into it. Dickens, with his arm upraised in a hail, was running after him.

"Stop!" I heard Dickens shout.

But I did not hear the rest because at that moment a terrible pain shot through my right leg and I toppled hard to the stones. Kate Hamilton had picked herself up off the ground and kicked me sharply in the shin.

"Who are you?" She stood over me screaming. "What right have you got to break in here?"

Fearing further retribution from her and smarting from the sharp pain, I rolled quickly away, picked myself up, and began limping painfully after Dickens.

The startled cabman could not arouse his horses quickly enough. Dickens reached the coach and ascended its step before they could get under way. Limping as quickly as I could toward them, I saw it all play out as if time had slowed.

"Stop! You are trapped," Dickens shouted as he hung in the window of the coach just getting under way.

Suddenly, a large fist shot out of the coach window and caught Charles flush in the face, knocking him backward into the air and down to the stones as the vehicle began to roll away.

When I came up to him, Charles was still stunned from the blow and the fall, but as I knelt to tend to him he rolled over and sat up. Together we watched as Field's dark post chaise blocked the mouth of the mews and the cab was forced to pull up.

*A similar scene, on a Thames waterfront street, as described in Collins's first commonplace book, *The Detective and Mr. Dickens,* provided the backdrop for the climactic confrontation of the Ashbee case. This, perhaps, accounts for the familiarity to which Collins here refers.

Lane leapt out and tried to run, but Field was upon him in an instant and dashed him to the ground with his murderous policeman's truncheon. The phantom was brought to bay.

"FRILLY BEGGARS
AND FROTHY 'ORES"

꙳

(August 15, 1852—Night)

S eems! I know not seems," our Shakespeare wrote.* The
truth is that nothing is ever what it seems. Barsad was
not our murderer; that role fell to the jealous husband.
The murderer was not our bank robber; that role fell to the
charlatan mesmerist. The blackmailer was not the angry
hoyden; she took the unenviable role of the murder victim,
while the actress-mother helped fill the role of the blackmailer. And the women—Ellen Ternan, Irish Meg, Angela
Burdett-Coutts—survived it all. In this strange adventure on
duty with Inspector Field, villains upon villains seemed to
arise† until the crimes and criminals seemed to swirl us all into
a confusing vortex.

Seeming, indeed. No, nothing is ever what it seems, and that
should be the first commandment of this exotic business of

---

*Collins here is misquoting Hamlet's speech from act 1, scene 2 of that
Shakespeare tragedy. Addressing his treacherous mother, Hamlet actually
says: "Seems, Madam! Nay, it is; I know not 'seems.' "
†Here, Collins is paraphrasing Alexander Pope's famous phrase "Alps on
Alps arise" from *An Essay on Criticism* (1. 232).

detectiving. What one comes to realize about this trying to solve mysteries is that they are oftentimes not so mysterious as we make them seem. Villains are not always inexplicable monsters as were Lord Henry Ashbee or Dr. Palmer the poisoner. Sometimes they are simply murderous husbands like Peter Lane who cannot stand losing control over their wives. And Barsad was no murderer, no terrible monster. He was but a confidence man with a strange gift who found himself beyond his depth.

When we arrived at Bow Street with our prisoner in hand, a strange crowd was waiting for us as if the end of the case had been signaled throughout the city by jungle drums. Collar and his man were there, checking up. Captain Hawkins and Broken Bert, with his obscene parrot perched rakishly on his shoulder, had ventured out to inquire into the progress of the case and had decided to wait. Those four worthies were eyeing each other warily when we drove up and escorted the bloody husband in.

Collar, predictably, needed to be told all, though no mention was ever made either of Angela Burdett-Coutts's stolen money or of her mysterious annulled husband, who, to my knowledge, was never mentioned again. Perhaps the one thing we Victorians had learned to do better than any of our forebears was to keep our important secrets secret. Collar also displayed little interest in Dickens and me once Field and Rogers had handed over the murderer to him all bagged and dressed like a Christmas turkey.

Field, probably just to get rid of the annoying little man, made it clear that Collar could claim all the credit for the solving of this particular case (or cases), and that worthy acquiesced graciously to Field's wishes.

"What a twit!" Field laughed as soon as Collar and his man had passed out of sight with their prisoner.

Field sent Rogers directly to Newgate to liberate Miss Ellen Ternan, and within the hour she had joined our jolly little circle at Bow Street. It was well after midnight, but the sunshine of Dickens's joy when they were reunited shone like midday. Miss Burdett-Coutts and my Meggy rushed to welcome her even as Marie de Brevecoeur looked on under the protective wing of Florence Nightingale.

All would turn out well for all of these women. Within a fortnight, Field would arrange to have Marie de Brevecoeur remanded to the custody of Angela Burdett-Coutts, who would promptly install her at Urania Cottage for a recuperative period of adjustment.

Things would never be the same for Dickens and his Ellen again. He could never again be her guardian and protector. Irish Meg and I knew that he was her lover, though his adoring public never would. And Irish Meg and I would never be the same again, either. The Women's Emancipation Society had taken care of that.

"Oh, Charles"—and Ellen Ternan looked into Dickens's eyes with a love and gratitude that seemed so genuine—"you have saved me once again."

"Saved 'er arse. Saved 'er arse," the obnoxious parrot felt impelled to comment.

Broken Bert, with startling swiftness and accuracy, knocked the offending parrot off his shoulder and halfway across the room.

Only momentarily distracted, we all turned back for Dickens's answer, for whatever news of the case he was surely going to impart.

But his Nellie was the only presence in his eyes. For a moment he looked a bit uncomfortable at her pronouncement. He hesitated, as if choosing his words with care.

"No, dearest Nellie," he finally answered. "You did nothing wrong. The truth saved you, not me or Wilkie or Field. We merely served to bring that truth out into the light."

As I think back upon it, that admission upon Dickens's part was somewhat of a Rubicon for him. It was the first time ever that he gave the lie to the Saint George, slayer of dragons, role that he so favored playing on the stage of his rather awkward relationship with his Nellie.

By this time, the bedraggled parrot had dragged himself back up onto his master's shoulder and regained his petulant voice. Despite his so recent chastisement, he could not refrain from commenting upon this happy domestic scene. "Frilly beggars and frothy 'ores. Frilly beggars and frothy 'ores," he crooned, capturing all of our attentions. "All's well that ends well. All's well that ends—" Broken Bert's sharp hand cut him off in midsoliloquy.

A NEW WOMAN

ॐ

(September 10, 1852—Morning)

Though the case was closed, and one of the shadows which hung over the difficult attraction of Dickens to his young actress love was lifted, the last blow was left to be struck. That, to my chagrin, was reserved for Irish Meg.

She insisted upon going to work, as a teller at Coutts Bank.

I insisted that I still had a great deal of secretarial work for her to do at home in our tidy little Soho domestic establishment, but she would have no more of that illusion. Miss Burdett-Coutts had offered her a job at the bank and it was all she could think about. She even dragged me out to help her buy what she called her "banker's duds." We, I should say "she" since all I did was pay, settled upon a grey silk lady's suit in two pieces: a rather tailored jacket (taking into consideration Irish Meg's generous form) to be worn with a high-necked white blouse; this wedded to a long skirt tapered down over her hips to the floor. I must admit that in it she greatly resembled the legions of "new women" who seemed to be asserting themselves more and more in London society every day. Nonetheless, it was difficult for me to see her in that way, since I was so attracted to what she was and to what she had once been.

"But I must be respectable now, Wilkie, now that I'm workin' in her bank," Meg laughed as she tried on her dress and modeled it for me in the seamstress's shop. "And in order to be respectable, you has to looks respectable."

She said that with a mischievous twinkle in her eye.

"Oh, Wilkie, I can't wait till tomorrow." She was so happy, so content with herself. "Oh, Wilkie"—and she kissed me on the ear—"you gave me this chance. Now it's like I'm finally free of the streets, no more a whore."

"You were never a whore to me," I protested. "I loved you from the first moment I saw you."

But it was a lie, and I knew it as soon as I said it (and perhaps she knew it as well). I was drawn to her precisely because she was a whore and the pleasures of her world excited me.

"You were drawn to me, all right," she laughed, "but not with the purest of intentions. Oh, I knows you loves me, Wilkie, and the best part is that we're friends, you and me."

I had no idea where this was going, as was so often the case when she ambushed me with her philosophy.

"It's different with this job though, Wilkie. It's my chance to be out on my own, to be real in the world and do respectable work for a change, but it's more than that, too. I loves you, Wilkie, but I'm not the same girl you fell in love with."

For an instant that vision of her, my fire woman, her sitting before the blazing hearth at Bow Street Station, the flames sending bright light burning through her rich red hair, flashed into my mind. I fell in love with her fire, and now I felt as if it was burning me up.

"These women have made me see meself in such a different light. That's why I'm goin' to work at the bank. It's the last step, don't you see?"

I must admit that I did not see at all why she had to leave our comfortable little domestic establishment, but I nodded my head up and down nonetheless.

"You saved me from the streets, Wilkie, and I shall always love you for that, but I have to do this, you see, I just have to."

240

"But I love you." It was the only feeble argument I could muster.

"Oh, I knows you do, Wilkie"—she kissed my pitiful mouth—"but I loves me, too, and this is somethin' I has to do for meself."

The tragedy was that I couldn't get excited at her prospects. All I could think about was how I was losing her, and how there was really nothing I could do about it.

The next morning, her first day of work at Coutts Bank, I counterfeited happiness and pride in her triumph. She kissed me fervently in the doorway. "I shall be home at six and tell you how it went," she assured me eagerly.

As she bounced out of my arms and tripped off down the street in her smart new suit, she seemed so alive. When she turned to wave, her face lit up in a smile so radiant that it brightened the length of that grimy Soho street. I knew that it was only a matter of time until I would be losing her. Her passion was palpable. I had never seen her so excited.